WHERE HAVE ALL
THE BIRDIES GONE?

WHERE HAVE ALL THE BIRDIES GONE?

Aaron and Charlotte Elkins

This first world edition published in Great Britain 2004 by
SEVERN HOUSE PUBLISHERS LTD of
9–15 High Street, Sutton, Surrey SM1 1DF.
This first world edition published in the USA 2004 by
SEVERN HOUSE PUBLISHERS INC of
595 Madison Avenue, New York, N.Y. 10022.

British Library Cataloguing in Publication Data

Elkins, Aaron J., 1935-
    Where have all the birdies gone?. - (Lee Ofsted mysteries)
    1.   Ofsted, Lee (Fictitious character) - Fiction
    2.   Women golfers - United States - Fiction
    3.   Detective and mystery stories
    I.   Title II. Elkins, Charlotte
    813.5'4 [F]

    ISBN 0-7278-6132-8

Typeset by Palimpsest Book Production Ltd.,
Polmont, Stirlingshire, Scotland.
Printed and bound in Great Britain by
MPG Books Ltd., Bodmin, Cornwall.

Acknowledgements

We would like to thank the many people who gave freely of their time, expertise, and support in helping us along the way:

Robert McLaughlin, former assistant manager, Pinehurst Resort and Country Club, answered our many questions about this grand old place and helped make our stay there as enjoyable as it was educational.

Lieutenant Jerry B. McDonald of the Pinehurst Police Department cordially filled us in on the ins and outs of local law enforcement in North Carolina.

At the Sunland Golf and Country Club, friend and golf pro Kelly O'Mera straightened us out on many golf-related issues and did (and continues to do) his best to make decent golfers of us. We would also like to express our appreciation to the men and women of Sunland who have been our playing partners and have graciously refrained from making rude remarks comparing our play to that of the professionals we write about.

One

'Two-time Masters champion,' the starter crooned into his microphone, his solemn tone reflecting the mighty words, 'two-time British Open champion, winner of forty-three tour events, leading PGL money-winner in 1988, 1990, and 1995, number nine on the all-time earnings list . . . Ladies and gentlemen, please welcome Roger Finley to the beautiful, highly acclaimed Pinnacle Course here at beautiful Troon North Golf Club in beautiful, sunny Scottsdale, Arizona. Mr Finley, you're up, sir.'

The audience surrounding the first tee broke into its loudest and most prolonged applause of the day, along with words of welcome from those close enough to be heard: 'Hiya, Roger!' 'Good luck, Roger!' 'Go get 'em, Rog!'

Roger Alonzo Finley, fidgety, anxious, and middle-aged, was one of the most loved athletes of his generation, in large part because he looked so charmingly out of place in the sumptuous and patrician country clubs that were the sites of much of the professional golf tour. Just as Arnold Palmer had been loved because he looked like an ex auto-mechanic (he wasn't) and Lee Trevino had been loved because he looked like some Latino kid who'd learned his golf at a municipal driving range (he had), Roger Finley was loved because he looked as if he should have been anxiously walking the floors of a department store with a boutonniere in his lapel, saying, 'May I help you, moddom?' In fact, he rarely made it out of his local I. Magnin's without being asked where the ladies' room was, or how one got to housewares.

Stepping through the opening in the ropes and on to the

1

well-trampled grass of the tee box, he acknowledged the fans making way on either side of him with a bright, nervous smile and a tip of his trademark straw boater. 'Excuse me. Thank you, I'm glad to be here. Hello, hello, hello, nice to see you, hello, thank you very much, I appreciate it, really happy to be here.' He shook hands with the starter. 'The course looks wonderful, just wonderful.'

'Thank you, Mr Finley, it's always an honor to have you here.'

The crowd hushed itself expectantly and settled down while Finley, characteristically biting his lower lip, studied the first fairway. Here at Troon North, each hole had its own name, and this one, seemingly straight but full of tricky, fool-the-eye deceptions, was aptly named 'Illusion'.With a sigh and a final friendly wave at the crowd, he lowered his chin and spoke to his caddie under his breath. 'I hate this goddamn place. I *hate* it.'

The caddie said nothing. Last year, when they'd played here in the same tournament, Roger couldn't say enough about what a masterpiece it was. But now that his game had started falling apart, Roger hated all golf courses.

'Well, we're here,' Roger said, 'so we might as well get it over with. I'll take the driver, Dylan.'

The caddie grasped the requested club, hesitated, and paused. 'Uh . . .'

Finley stiffened. 'You think not?'

'Well, it's only three hundred ninety-six yards, Rog. A three-wood would put you on the green in two, the same as a driver. And—' He hesitated. '—it's a lot safer. Why take the chance?'

Finley's face clouded. 'I see. And your advice is that, with the way I've been going lately, I'm better off playing it safe, is that the idea?'

Dylan flushed. Finley got more sensitive, more defensive, every day. 'No, sir, I only meant to say—'

Finley quickly put his hand on the young man's arm. 'That's all right, Dylan. I apologize, I'm not myself, I don't know what's the matter with me. As a matter of fact you're absolutely right. But today it's going to be different, I feel it. I think I finally have a handle on what I've been doing wrong, you'll see. I'm going to tee off with the driver to start with. If I can't handle that, I'll switch to something else later, all right?'

'Whatever you say.' Dylan pulled the driver out of the bag, whipped the head cover off, and handed it to his boss. 'Good luck, Rog. Break a leg.'

Finley tried to respond with a joke. 'As if I didn't have enough troubles.'

At least it'd give you an excuse, Dylan thought but didn't say.

Fluttery to the point of nausea, as always before the first drive of the day, Finley took two deep breaths, stepped up to the ball, focused, and swung. And with the first smooth, confident movement of the club backward, the fussy, nervous department-store floorwalker vanished, metamorphosing into a sure-handed, marvelously balanced, perfectly coordinated athlete with the easiest, smoothest swing in professional golf, a joy to the educated eye.

The familiar, power-laden, soft *clook* of metal club head against balata-covered ball was followed by the usual brainless yelp from the crowd, but Finley knew in his bones, even before the shock of contact, that he had mis-hit it, and in a couple of seconds the cheer became an embarrassed silence, then turned into a groan as the ball began to veer left, and then further left. A hook, a duck hook. The only question was whether it would end up in the far end of the fairway bunker or, God forbid, miss the lush grass altogether and disappear into the arid 'transition area' of rock-filled sand and scrubby desert vegetation; countryside more suited to the local javelina, bobcats, and coyotes than to humans in search of golf balls.

Finley himself didn't bother watching to see where it landed. Grimly, his lips compressed, he bent over to jerk his tee out of the ground, then slapped the club into Dylan's waiting hand the way a surgeon who's just taken out the wrong kidney gives a scalpel back to his nurse.

'Lord have mercy, here we go again,' he said as they started walking. 'I'm afraid it's going to be a long day, Dylan.'

The weekend had started off like just another Saturday morning, or rather what was probably just another Saturday morning for people with normal lives: lazy, meandering, eventless, wonderful. Lee and Graham had awakened at nine, picked up donuts and milk at a store a couple of blocks from Graham's condominium in Pacific Grove, then cut across the wooded grounds of the Asilomar Conference Center to the rocky, iceplant-bordered beach just as the morning mist began to unravel into ragged, sunlit tendrils. They had sat side-to-side in the damp sand to eat their breakfast, then wandered along the tide pools, looking at hermit crabs and sea anemones, talking without pattern or point, floating on the sounds and smells of the sea. A perfect morning.

And, for Lee Ofsted, an extraordinary one, the first Saturday in thirteen weeks that she hadn't been out on the golf course – a different course each week – straining to keep ahead of the competitors a stroke or two behind her, and struggling to catch up with the ones a stroke or two in front. Tense, draining work, but, for a pro golfer on the Women's Professional Golf League tour, she knew she had little to gripe about. The fact that she'd been playing twelve Saturdays in a row meant that she'd made the cut twelve Fridays in a row, which meant that she'd walked away with earnings twelve Sundays running when the purses were divvied up at the ends of the tournaments.

In Lee's fledgling career with the WPGL, now in its third year, nothing like that had ever happened before. It was true that in these twelve weeks she'd only once managed to place higher than twentieth – tying for thirteenth in light snow at the sparsely attended Kopje Carburetor Classic in Fairbanks; mostly she'd been down around thirtieth or fortieth. Still, it meant that for the last three months she'd been earning enough from golf to cover her expenses –

4

travel, caddie, food, lodging – and even a little to spare. For once in her twenty-four-year-old life, she was in the black. Even more important, she'd done it on her determination, her self-discipline, and her natural abilities with a set of golf clubs, holding her own among the best female golfers in the world. It was a marvelous feeling, and she could sense herself growing more confident and accomplished with every passing week.

And tireder, grubbier, and more all-around blah. Three solid months of motel-hopping was enough to do that to anybody, even someone on a roll. When she'd found herself bogeying four of the last five holes at the previous week's Greater Fresno International and thereby plummeting from eighteenth to fortieth, she'd realized it was time for a break, promptly withdrawing from this week's TipTop Timber Challenge in Coos Bay, Oregon.

Of course the fact that her fiancé, Graham Sheldon, lived in Pacific Grove, a mere hop, skip and jump from where she'd been in Fresno at the time, had something to do with it too. Also the fact that his being between consulting assignments would give them a whole, lovely, leisurely week to spend together. The nice, clean, coinless Maytag in his laundry room didn't hurt either.

Lovely and leisurely it had been. They had driven south along the coast to Morro Bay and north to Mendocino, they had dined on crab *à l'Américaine* at the Fairmont in San Francisco, and picnicked on sourdough bread, red wine, and hard salami on a rocky overlook above the breaking surf on the Big Sur. But mostly they had been resolutely lazy, sleeping late, wandering along the iceplant-bordered coastal paths closer to home, eating when they got hungry, and basking shamelessly in each other's nearness. When they had first met two years earlier, Graham had been a Carmel police lieutenant, but last year he had quit the force to open his own security consulting firm, Countermeasure Inc. A risky move, it had been wildly successful; now, at the age of twenty-nine, he had an international roster of clients, a staff of three, and a classy, well-appointed office on Calle

Principal in Monterey. Today, after breakfast on the beach, a morning spent browsing through the *New York Times*, and a mushroom omelet lunch that he'd cooked for her, he had driven to his office to tidy up some details that he'd been letting slide during her visit.

He hadn't been gone more than five minutes when her plan for a dozey, pleasantly unstimulating afternoon of finishing the *Times Magazine* and watching the third round of the PGL tournament from Troon North was emphatically stood on its head by what she would forever after think of as The Telephone Call.

'May I speak to Lee – let me see, what is it – Lee Ofsted, please?' The voice was vaguely familiar, but she couldn't quite place it. Familiar and distracted.

'Speaking,' she said.

'Oh, that's good. Finally. What a time I had tracking you down. We've stopped play on account of a thunderstorm warning down here, and I wanted to take the opportunity to—'

'Who is this, please?'

'Who—?' The question seemed to surprise him. 'Oh, I'm sorry, I thought I said . . . I thought you realized . . . it's . . . well, it's, ah, Roger Finley?'

Oh, sure, thought Lee. *Certainly*. Who else would be calling her but Roger Finley? It was just that for a moment she thought it might have been that darned Jack Nicklaus pestering her again. Or that exasperating Tiger Woods.

'Very funny, Uncle Ervin,' she said. 'So tell me, did Aunt Irene get that knee taken care of?'

Silence.

She was starting to get a funny feeling. 'Uncle Ervin? That *is* you, isn't it . . . ? Uncle Ervin?'

But even as she said it the sick, dropping sensation in her chest intensified. Good gosh, now that she listened to the voice in her mind again, it *did* sound like Finley. But . . . but why—?

'Believe me,' he said, 'I'm telling you the truth. I could

6

let you talk to one of the officials if you like. Er, no, what am I talking about, that won't work. I've run back to my suite at the Four Seasons to put my feet up and get some peace and quiet for a few minutes. You could call me here at the resort, though, if it would make you feel better. They'll tell you at the desk that it's me, all right.'

Omigosh. She groped behind her for a kitchen chair and sat heavily down. She'd met some of the gods of golf before, even Finley himself, not that he'd remember, but only to say hi in passing at one tournament or another. More often, it wasn't even hi, but only a shy nod, because you didn't want to risk disturbing their focus. Even so, it had always been a thrill. She'd rarely *spoken* to one, though, in the sense of having a conversation, and she'd certainly never gotten a telephone call from one of them.

'Oh,' she said, trying desperately not to sound like the adoring fan she was. 'Yes. I see. I'm – I'm sorry about the confusion, I just thought it was . . . I mean . . . um, how may I help you, Mr Finley?' Great, wonderful, now she sounded like the woman behind the bakery counter. The particularly rattle-brained woman behind the bakery counter.

'Well, as you know, I'm captaining our Stewart Cup team this year.'

'Yes, of course.'

Well, not exactly, but she knew that the honor went to people of Finley's stature, so the information wasn't surprising. The Stewart Cup tournament was one of golf's prime events. A biennial tradition going back to the late forties, it pitted the greatest American golfers, male and female, against their counterparts from Great Britain. Like the Ryder Cup, the Stewart Cup was about teamwork and national pride, and the competition for slots on the teams was fierce. Lee Ofsted, however, had never had reason to give it any thought. The slots were based on points, and the points were based on cumulative performance over the season. As she understood it, the top four female players and the top four male players made the American team, period. And Lee Ofsted was not among the top four, or the top ten, or, sad to say, the top forty. Her recent play, as solid as it had been, had moved her from seventy-ninth on the list to fifty-first; wonderful as far as she was concerned, but wildly out of the running for a spot on the Stewart team. As a result she was more concerned with making the cut in Boise the following week than she was about the Stewart Cup goings-on.

'And congratulations, Mr Finley,' she added quickly. 'I know you'll bring home the cup.'

'Thank you.' He paused. 'The fact is, I'm expecting you to help. That's why I'm calling. Better sit down now . . . you're going to be on the team, what do you think of that?'

Clunk. Her head was suddenly stuffed with cotton, her tongue glued to her palate.

'I . . . I'm afraid I don't . . . I mean . . .' *Uncle Ervin*, she thought, *if this* does *turn out to be you, I will personally kill you. With my bare hands.*

'You've got the women's Rocky slot,' he said cheerfully.

'Um . . . rocky slot?' she said.

'Yes, Rocky slot. You know.' He was, not that it was any wonder, starting to sound a little impatient. 'You've been chosen in the lottery to be on the team.'

'Oh, I see,' she said dully. What lottery, what in the world was he talking about? This was what came of concentrating too much on her own game and not following the news in her sport.

'The *Rocky* slot,' he said again, with added emphasis, as if that made it clearer. 'You know? As in the movie, where the journeyman fighter gets picked to fight the champ? One man and one woman on the team are picked by lottery; have been for the past four competitions. Er – you *are* aware of this, aren't you?'

'Of the lottery? Oh, of course, yes, the *lottery*. And I've been picked? I'm the one?'

She heard him laugh. 'Ah, comes the dawn. I thought you'd be excited.'

He sure had that right.

'A little nervous too, I'll bet?'

8

He was right about that too, except that 'scared out of her mind' would have been closer to the truth. No, it was more complicated than that. If someone had asked her just what it was she was feeling at this moment, she'd have had a hard time putting it into words. Panic, amazement, self-doubt, exhilaration, dread . . . What would she do if she mishit a crucial putt or her stroke went blooey under the pressure? It had happened to her more than once, and of course she had survived to play again, but blowing it in the ShopWell Supermarket Challenge, where you were playing for yourself and the money, wasn't the same thing as blowing it at the Stewart Cup, where you were out there for your team and your country. People like Roger Finley and Ginger Rolley would be depending on *her* ability and consistency, a terrifying thought. A single misplay, or stupid risk, or failure of nerve on her part could . . .

No, that was no way to think. This was an incredible opportunity to shine, to do something really special. She wouldn't have made it even this far as a professional golfer if there hadn't been that glowing, impossible-to-douse flame of optimism in the pit of her stomach. Who was to say she wouldn't be at the top of her game? She'd had great days before, why not now, in – wherever it was going to be held, with the whole world watching?

'I'll do my very best, Mr Finley,' she mumbled. 'I just hope I don't let you down.'

'First of all, make it Roger. Or Rog, if you like; we're teammates, after all. Second, take my word for it, you won't be any more nervous than the rest of us. I know you'll do a wonderful job, Lee. Oh, and as I'm sure you know, you'll be my partner for the team play; that's the tradition.'

'Oh, no!' she blurted, then winced.

'Flattery will get you nowhere, my dear.'

'Oh, I didn't mean it that way, Mr Finley—'

'Roger.'

'—Roger. It's just that – I mean, the idea of actually part-nering somebody like *you*—'

A bark of wry laughter interrupted her. 'My dear girl,

I'm anything but a bargain to play with right now. I've never been in a worse slump in my life. Let us hope I come out of it before the match. Otherwise you're going to have to carry me.'

She managed a weak laugh of her own. 'I don't think that's going to happen.'

'I wouldn't bet on that if I were you. Oops, I'd better go, I've just been paged. They're announcing the resumption of play. Any questions at this point?'

'No, I don't think so. I – I'm still having trouble believing this.'

'Well, let me assure you it's true. Goodbye for now, then. I'll be in touch with the details. My advice for the moment is to work on your short game – chips, lay-ups, pitch-and-runs. The greens will be killers.'

'I sure will, Mr – Roger. Thank you for the advice. I certainly will. And *thank* you for calling me! I'll do my very—'

But he was gone; she was babbling into a dead telephone. For a few moments she remained stone-still, trying to take it in. It was the most incredible thing that had ever happened to her. *I'd better sit down*, she thought numbly, then laughed out loud; she was already sitting down. That seemed to take the edge off her astonishment, and the fragments of thought whirling in her mind began to arrange themselves into something like coherent patterns. She'd told him she had no questions, but she had a million of them, buzzing around her head like mosquitoes. Where would they be playing, Great Britain or the United States? Which course? When was it going to be held? What was the format? Would she have to miss a regular WPGL tournament? Would her travel expenses be covered? Was there any compensation involved . . . ?

Irritably, she waved it all away. What difference did it make? Whatever the answers were, there was nothing that would make her miss a chance like this. She just prayed she didn't disgrace herself. The Stewart Cup matches were one of golf's premier events. The galleries would be huge from beginning to end, and they would televise every minute of it, clear across the globe. What if she got up there on the first tee, with several million people watching all over the world, and muffed it? Once, on the first hole of her second tournament, she had been so scared and tense that her swing had tightened up and she'd topped it like the worst kind of hacker, so that she'd had to watch in horror as it slowly, erratically trickled about five yards, not even making it out of the tee box.

'Give her a mulligan!' a man in the sparse gallery had yelled, to her intense embarrassment. 'Mulligan' was the term that weekend hackers used when they demanded a free shot if they mishit from the first tee, and they most definitely weren't part of the protocol of the WPGL. They didn't give them at the Stewart Cup either, so if she did the same thing—

No. Ridiculous, there she went again. Get a grip. She was a seasoned professional now, not a frightened-out-of-her-wits twenty-year-old. A fantastic opportunity had just fallen out of nowhere into her lap, and she meant to take advantage of it. She would get hold of the unflappable, dependable, unflaggingly loyal Lou Sapio, the best caddie she'd ever had (what did a few eccentricities matter?), and sign him up. She would work harder than ever. She would practice her chips and lay-ups until her hands blistered . . .

But not now, not today. Now was the time to soak in her unbelievable good fortune; to dream of glory, and sponsorships, and scoring the pressure-laden point that brought the Americans roaring back from defeat at the last minute.

And wait till Graham heard. He'd be as flabbergasted as she was; he'd want to drive into Carmel and celebrate, or maybe even San Francisco. But that wasn't what she wanted. Tomorrow morning she was going to be out on the range at daylight and that meant she had to make an early night of it. Besides, she wanted to celebrate quietly, just the two of them. And the best way she could think of to do that would be to surprise him with a celebratory dinner right there (although, truthfully, any meal she cooked for him was bound to be a surprise).

11

She picked up the telephone and called his office. 'Graham? I've just had a little good news.' Talk about understatement. 'Pick up a bottle of wine on your way back, will you? I'm cooking dinner.'

He gasped. Loudly. '*You're* cooking . . .?'

'Funny, funny. I've been threatening all along, and tonight's the night. I'll cook you a three-course meal, including my world-famous, number-one gourmet dish. So, say something.'

'I'm speechless; I never thought this would come to pass. Red or white?'

'Red, I guess. No, white. I don't know.'

'I'll play it safe and get a bottle of each. Should I bring anything else?'

'Just a loaf of sourdough. I think you have everything else here.'

'For a world-famous gourmet dish? That's hard to believe, but I'll take your word for it. Are you going to tell me what we're having? Or what your news is?'

'No and no. But it's pretty good.'

'Well, I'll get champagne then.'

'Absolutely, better yet.' If ever there was a night for champagne, this was it. 'And get ready to be surprised.'

She hung up giggling to herself. Surprised wasn't the word for it. And he was going to love Wanda's Casserole, the spectacular dish that she'd learned to make from a fellow tour rookie with whom she'd shared a motel room for a few tournaments. They'd cooked the whole thing in a Crock-Pot set up on the dresser back then, but Graham had some pretty sophisticated kitchen things that would let her do it properly. She laid out the required cooking utensils and found an apron in the cupboard. Her gourmet friend had taught her that this particular combination of ingredients tasted better if it was allowed to 'set' for a while in the refrigerator, so she might as well get started on the first step right now.

Now then: where did Graham keep the canned chili?

Two

'Now let's go to the ninth hole, where Roger Finley is teeing up,' the television announcer said. 'As always, the biggest gallery of the day has been following him right along, cheering him on, but in spite of that picture-book swing of his, things don't look good, do they, Mary Ann?'

'No, Skip,' said her co-anchor. 'As we all know only too well, he's been struggling for most of the season, but one thing you have to say about Roger Finley is that he's got plenty of heart; you can't ever count him out. For a great competitor like Roger to be fighting for nineteenth place must be a living hell, but he's taking it like a real pro.'

'You mean he's blaming it on his putter? Ha, ha, only kidding, Mary Ann. You're right, though. Roger's one of the game's great competitors.'

'And one of the sweetest little guys in sports, Skip. Everybody in Golfland has to be pulling for him to find his game again.'

Lee stopped in the middle of opening a jar of green olives and leaned both elbows on the counter, propping her chin so that her face was just a foot from the little television set sitting on a bread box up against the wall. She had seen Finley a hundred times before, but now it was different, now she was hungry to get a good look at the man who had just changed her life.

The four-inch black-and-white Sony was meant for catching the news or listening to a talk show while cooking, not for watching a golf tournament. Graham had a normal-sized one in the den, but she had to make do with the little one if she wanted to keep working. While she was straining to see Finley's face, his expression, his attitude as he went through his setup, she caught sight of a squat, round-shouldered, bow-legged figure in the background just this side of the ropes, hardly more than a tiny blur but instantly identifiable all the same – Lou Sapio, her caddie; she'd know that dour, monkey-faced little character anywhere.

Well, good for him! With Lee taking the week off, he'd told her he planned to head to Scottsdale to see if he could pick up a temporary bag at the men's tournament; someone whose regular caddie was sick, maybe. And although she'd had her doubts that he'd find one – Lou wasn't everyone's cup of tea – he'd obviously lucked out. He was caddying for Jack McGhee, a famously good-natured guy and a first-rate golfer to boot. Since McGhee was in the same threesome as Finley, it meant that he was at roughly the same place in the tournament standings. And inasmuch as caddies were paid a percentage of their players' earnings, that meant a good payday for Lou. Nineteenth might be living hell for Roger Finley, but it was the Promised Land for somebody who was used to caddying for Lee Ofsted.

That thought sent an uneasy tremor up her spine. What if McGhee recognized Lou as the gold mine he was and tried to spirit him away from her just when she most needed that sobering, steadying presence? No, she told herself firmly, that was not going to happen, no chance. And it wasn't just that Lou Sapio was old for a touring caddie – more than twice Lee's age – or that he didn't look like much, or that he had a rather vague and questionable past (and present, for that matter), or that he had more than his share of irritating idiosyncrasies. It was Lou himself and the way he felt about her. It had taken her a while to figure it out, but she understood now that he needed her as much as she needed him. She was more than a bag to Lou; she was, she'd come to understand, his mission. As far as he was concerned, he had discovered her and he intended to break her into the top twenty money-earners if it killed him, which at the rate she was going, it very well might. And the faith of that gnarled, chain-smoking, hard-headed, hard-working gnome of a man had come to mean a great deal to her in this most ego-deflating of sports.

No, he wouldn't desert her, but she'd put in a call to him before the day was out, just to be on the safe side.

She turned her attention back to Finley and his swing. It was picture-book, all right, a thing of beauty, as simple and free of quirks and excess motion as a swing could be. But it wasn't enough. She couldn't see the ball, but she could hear the anchors.

'Uh-oh, he's pulled it to the left this time,' Mary Ann Cooper said.

'And left isn't where he wants to be,' said Skip Cochrane. 'Not with that water running almost the full length of the fairway.'

There was silence, from the anchors and from the fans, for two or three seconds while the ball was in flight, and then Skip spoke again.

'Hoo, boy,'

By the time Finley reached the twelfth green, Lee still had the TV on, but she'd lost interest, or maybe lost heart. He was now five strokes over par, wallowing somewhere around twenty-fourth place – it would hardly be 'wallowing' for Lee, of course, but then Lee was Lee and Roger was Roger – and it was distressing to watch the poor guy. Every swing was the same: that effortless sweep of the club with its perfect tempo, that high, relaxed finish – followed a second later by a dejected slumping of the shoulders and a death-march trudge as he started after his ball. And his putting, usually a strong point of his game in its machinelike precision, was tentative and uncertain, even though he'd recently switched to one of the long-handled clubs that the older players seemed to like.

Well, every golfer went through bad snaps when nothing they tried would work. What most golfers didn't have were *good* snaps when everything they tried worked – and Roger Finley had had plenty of those and would no doubt enjoy plenty more. In any case, feel for him though she did, his present troubles couldn't touch the joy that was lighting every cell in her body.

Every time she replayed that telephone call in her head she

laughed – Uncle Ervin, indeed! There would be time enough later to get good and scared about what it would mean to play in the Stewart Cup, but for now all she wanted to do was to hug the knowledge to herself and revel in its warmth.

Humming happily if tunelessly, she stirred the Fritos carefully into the other ingredients: the canned chili, the stuffed green olives (the recipe called for black, but how much difference could it make?), and the SpaghettiOs, which were not to be found in Graham's cabinets, but which could fortunately be retrieved from her duffle bag, where she always kept a can or two of microwavable comfort food for emergencies. After that it was only a matter of sprinkling the grated Parmesan cheese (the recipe called for cheddar, but again . . .) over everything and popping it in—

Her head came up as she heard Skip Cochrane saying something about the Stewart Cup. She dropped the canister of cheese on the counter and ran into the den to turn on the full-size set.

'. . . don't really think his recent problems will affect his ability to captain the team,' Mary Ann Cooper was saying. 'Everybody has a lot of respect for Roger. Incidentally, they announced the Rocky-slot winners today. The male player's Jordie Webster, who you may remember as having scored a hole-in-one in the first round of the 1999 Western Open—'

'And then failed to make the cut,' Skip said.

'That's right. As you know, he's had his troubles, but this may be his chance to put them behind him. And the female winner—'

Lee held her breath, suddenly petrified. What if—?

'—is Lee Ofsted, the little-known twenty-five-year-old from Oregon now in her third year on the tour.'

Whew. She let the breath out and sagged back in her chair.

'Yes, Lee's a talented youngster who has all the tools, but hasn't quite put them together yet, although she's been having a banner year, having been in the money for something like ten tournaments in a row.'

'Twelve,' Lee told the television set happily. 'And I'm twenty-four. Get your facts straight.'

'Yes, and that's after a shortened second year as a result of an elbow injury at the Cottonwood Classic.'

'Which I believe she was leading at the time, which made it all the more of a tough break. Well, that's enough trivia for now; let's check in with Chick on the twelfth, where . . .'

Lee sat back and let the good feelings wash over her. As she saw it, this made it definite; they couldn't change their minds now. She was in! A contented smile spread across her face and stuck there. She didn't even mind being relegated to trivia. With the phenomenal good luck that had come her way, this was probably the last time that 'little-known' would be attached to her name. Of course, if she crashed and burned at the Stewart, which was hardly an impossibility, 'little-known' was going to sound like a compliment compared to what people would be calling her. But she wasn't about to let—

The telephone on the table beside her chirped. 'Nuts,' she said to herself as she reached for it, sure it was Graham calling to say he was going to be late.

'Nuts to you too. Lee, I can't believe it!'

'Peg?' The question was rhetorical. With a voice like a cheerful bugle even when she was speaking normally, Peg Fiske excited was impossible not to recognize.

She'd met Peg, an avid weekend golfer, a few years earlier, when she had been one of the amateurs in Lee's foursome at a pro-am tournament. Despite a vast distance in age, class, and income – Peg was forty-three, Lee would turn twenty-five in five months; Peg's mother and father had been a psychiatrist and a professor; Lee's father laid concrete and her mother was a housewife and part-time food-server in a school cafeteria; Peg was married to an engineer and ran her own $800,000-a-year management-consulting business out of Albuquerque; Lee's best year (last year) had netted her $9,500 after expenses – despite all this, the two of them had hit it off from the first and had quickly, surprisingly, become fast friends.

'Lee, how could you not tell me right away? I just saw it on TV! I almost had a heart attack!'

17

'I called you first thing,' Lee told her truthfully. 'Check your answering machine.'

'I'm not home, I'm in Denver on a job. I have to meet my clients for drinks in a little while, so I just wanted to kick off my shoes for a few minutes and relax in front of the TV. And the minute I turned it on ... well, why the heck didn't you call my pager or my cell phone if you didn't get me at home?'

Lee smiled. 'Peg, this isn't exactly an emergency.'

'Are you kidding? It's the most important thing that's ever happened to you. It *is* true, isn't it?'

'Uh-huh. I've been dying to tell you about it.' She kicked off her own shoes, tucked her legs up under her, and gave in to the urge. 'Well, we just finished lunch, and Graham had to go off to his office, and suddenly the phone rings, and it's this sort of nervous, mousey voice that sounds a little familiar. You won't believe what I said. I thought it—'

'Not now, hold the fort. I just wanted to make sure it was really true.'

'Oh,' Lee said. 'Sure. I just thought—'

'You don't have to sound so hangdog. Believe me, I want to hear every single detail, I just don't have time right now. I'm due at the Brown Palace in twenty minutes and before I take off I want to get started on making my reservations for the Stewart Cup. Do you realize how tough it's going to be for me to get a room anywhere near the course? The rest of the team members were announced two weeks ago, and their fans have had all this time to book rooms. It's not fair. Your fans—'

'What fans?' Lee said, trying to stem the flow. 'Aside from my family and Graham – no one could call any of them golf fans, and they probably won't be coming anyway – there's you. That's it. My one and only fan. Surely there ought to be *one* hotel room still left.'

'I am not your only fan. I am far from your only fan. What about that kid who wrote you that sweet letter with all those cute questions?'

'I don't think that counts. It was a class assignment; she

had to write a letter to an athlete. *She* probably got me in a lottery too.'

'Minor detail. Look, why am I chatting on like this when I have a gazillion things to do? Goodbye, I'll call you tomorrow for all the details. I have to—'

'Peg, wait! One quick question. Where's this thing going to be held?' She moved the receiver well away from her ear, and just in time.

'*What?* I don't believe it! Lee, you never cease to amaze me. How could you possibly not know where the Stewart Cup is being played? Where have you been, on Mars? How could *anyone*—?'

'I've been concentrating on my own game pretty hard,' Lee interrupted. 'And I didn't see how the Stewart Cup had anything remotely to do with me.'

'Well, you sure turned out to be wrong about that,' Peg said with a hearty, happy laugh that warmed Lee's heart. 'It's at Pinehurst.'

'Pinehurst?'

'Pinehurst, North Carolina? Pinehurst as in, "Pinehurst, the St Andrews of the New World"? You've heard of Pinehurst? You've heard of North Carolina?'

'Well, of course I've heard of it,' Lee said a bit snappily.

You couldn't be a golfer and not have heard of Pinehurst, a stately turn-of-the-century resort tucked away in the gentle hill country of North Carolina. Although not a stop on the regular tour, its celebrated Number Two Course (there were eight altogether) had hosted a score of golf's most prestigious championships, including the US Open, the PGA Championship, and the Ryder Cup. 'St Andrews of the New World' wasn't that far off the mark.

'And not only have I heard of it,' she went on, gathering strength, 'I've played there. In a tournament.'

'Did you, really? I didn't remember that.'

'Well, not exactly *in* a tournament,' Lee allowed. 'It was during my rookie year. I played in the Monday qualifying round . . . but I didn't make it. Those greens did me in.'

It was no wonder Finley had told her to sharpen up her

19

short game, Pinehurst was notorious for its 'domed' greens, a particularly devilish innovation of designer Donald Ross. The holes themselves – the cups – tended to be at the high points of the greens, so, wherever the ball landed, it had a maddening tendency to roll away from them and off to the edges, sometimes even into the adjacent sand traps.

'Close enough,' boomed Peg. 'You'll do great, Lee, you've come a long way since then. Do you realize who you're going to be playing with? I mean, not only Roger, but Dinny Goulapoulos, Dave Hazelton, Ginger—'

'Peg, stop! I'm scared enough as it is.'

'OK, sorry, kid, I was trying to cheer you up. Look, I'd better get out of here . . .' She paused. 'Ah, you do know *when* it is, I assume?'

'Um . . . in six weeks?'

'*Three* weeks,' Peg said with a despairing sigh. 'I mean, good gosh, Lee.'

Good gosh is right, a dazed Lee thought as she hung up. Three weeks – that changed it from the comfortably distant, hazy by-and-by to the hair-raising, terrifying, immediate future. Three weeks to get ready for those bloodcurdling greens, three weeks to get over the shock of being selected, three weeks to get herself psyched up to be on the same team as Roger Finley and . . . whoever else Peg said was on the team, three weeks—

No, this simply wouldn't do. She could start worrying tomorrow. Today was Celebration Day. Back into the kitchen she marched, but her mood had been undermined. Even Wanda's Casserole, that stalwart of her cooking repertoire, didn't look quite as wonderful as she remembered it, and Graham was a pretty sophisticated diner; he'd had meals in Paris, London, Madrid . . . Confidence flagging, qualms rising, she turned the oven on and slid in the casserole. Was this stuff really going to go with champagne (which, if she was going to be truthful, she didn't really like anyway)? *Fritos*, cheese, chili . . .

On second thought, maybe what she should have asked him to pick up was a six-pack of Bud.

Three

'Hey, I got an idea,' Lou Sapio said, squinting around the smoke from the half-inch-long, unfiltered cigarette stub wedged in one corner of his mouth. 'Maybe you ought to start sticking a sand rake in your bag and carrying it around with you, so you wouldn't always have to be looking for one.'

'I'll keep that in mind,' Dylan Blanchard said, smiling in spite of himself. 'Look at this sand wedge, will you? It looks as if it went through World War Two.'

They had come off the Troon North course twenty minutes earlier, and now, like most of the other caddies, they were cleaning their players' equipment in the caddie yard, a roped-off area between the bag room and the golf-cart garage.

'I mean, that guy of yours couldn't have found a fairway today if he had a compass,' Lou said. 'It got so I couldn't watch any more, it made my stomach hurt. So how'd you come out?

'Terrible, we wound up tied for twenty-seventh. What about you? How'd McGhee end up?'

'Us, we came out great!' Lou said enthusiastically, his monkeyish face split by a lipless grin. 'Thirtieth!'

Dylan had the impression Lou didn't see the humor in that. Well, thirtieth probably was pretty good for him; with today's purse it was worth almost $10,000 to the player, so his caddie would walk away with five per cent, $500; good money for a Lou Sapio. You had to hand it to the old guy, though, packing that heavy bag in this heat at his age. How old was he, fifty, fifty-two? What could he weigh, maybe a hundred and thirty pounds soaking wet? Of course, he

21

was built like a mini refrigerator truck, but it was still amazing. They didn't make them like him any more.

When Lou had started, back in the Dark Ages, he'd have fitted right in with the caddies of the time, many of them not much more than car-pooling hobos running from alimony payments or jail time, and picking up a few dollars here and there to keep body and soul together, with a little left over for a jug of cheap wine. But they were good at what they did, or at least a lot of them were; reservoirs of useful information about the game, the courses, the ins and outs of play. A person like Lou knew more yardages from more points on more fairways than Dylan and his cohorts would ever come close to knowing. But who cared? Nowadays every course on the tour had a detailed yardage book, to say nothing of the GPS devices that everybody had – illegal during tournaments of course, but not during practice, which was plenty good enough. And so it was with all the other things Lou knew. They were no longer required. He was a dinosaur, a dodo bird who was already extinct. He just didn't know it yet.

Well, so what, that was the way of the world. When golf had entered its big-money phase, the old-time caddies with their seat-of-the-pants knowledge and their school-of-hard-knocks expertise had begun being replaced by the young and the presentable, the enterprising up-and-comers who'd gone to college and played golf there, who shaved every day, who were psychologists, valets, public-relations agents, and travel assistants as well as caddies – in short, the Dylan Blanchards of this world. Like most of his cohorts, Dylan had negotiated an annual salary from his player, over and above tournament earnings. Lou, on the other hand, was like a lot of the other old-timers, preferring to sign on tournament by tournament, refusing to be 'tied down' week in, week out. As if he had all these other important engagements he had to allow for. It was laughable, really.

Dylan Blanchard had been at it for only three years, but he was willing to bet he'd earned more money already than Lou had made in his entire life. Of course, linking up with

Roger Finley after Roger's old caddie had to quit with a bad knee had had a lot to do with it, but even that had taken some pretty deft behind-the-scenes maneuvering. That was another difference between Dylan and Lou; Dylan didn't leave things to luck, he made them happen.

And unless he was having pipe dreams, he would soon be making something happen that would dwarf everything he'd ever—

'Hey, you done?' Lou asked, snapping the cover on his bag. 'What do you say we stow these and go get a beer?'

'Pardon?' Dylan surfaced. 'All right, why not? You want to go up to the clubhouse?'

'You mean here? The country club?' Lou was aghast. 'Are you kidding me?'

'Oh, I can get us in, no problem. I always go there when we're here.'

Lou slowly shook his head. 'Hey, you come with me, buddy. I'll show you where the real caddies do their drinking.'

The real caddies, it seemed, did their drinking in Turk's, a tacky roadside bar on the sandy, barren outreaches of Highway 87, some ten miles (and ten light-years) from the lush lawns of Scottsdale and Paradise Valley. It wasn't the kind of place Dylan would have chosen on his own but he was in high spirits, and besides, he'd been toying on and off with the idea of writing a book about the life of a caddie on tour, which had turned out to be even weirder than he'd expected. He wasn't going to be caddying that much longer, after all, and a book like that would be a natural to kick-start the writing career he had in mind. A dive like this, full of 'real' caddies – the kind from whom he usually kept his distance – could provide some good fodder. A book like that could use some comic relief.

Besides, it would do Lou good, give him some increased cachet with his fellows, to be seen palling around with one of the new breed – with Roger Finley's regular caddie, no less. It'd be good for the old guy's self-esteem too. And

Dylan didn't mind at all doing Lou a good turn. He was a funny old coot, nobody he'd ever want to spend any time with, of course, but nice enough at heart in his own way. Besides, he couldn't help what he was: a product of his generation and cultural mores, totally unable to keep up with the changing demands of a world he hadn't made.

He pulled open the rickety screen door and bowed. *'Après vous, mon ami.'*

Four

What the hell, Lou thought, it wasn't as if the kid could help being the way he was. It was how they got brought up these days, that was the problem – hearing right from the get-go that they were God's gift to the world. How could they turn out to be anything but conceited, over-stuffed twits? *Après vous, mon ami*, for Christ's sake. But underneath, he thought, there was something decent about Dylan. Three or four times during the round, he'd made Lou's job easier by replanting the flag stick even though it had been Lou's turn. Sure, he'd made kind of a show out of it (bright, polite, young college graduate assists decrepit, ignorant old fart), but still, his heart was in the right place. And as for the snotty manner, who could tell, maybe it'd pass when he got a little older and took a few knocks himself.

In the meantime, it wouldn't hurt the kid – maybe make him some friends on the tour, which Lou was pretty sure he could use – to be seen hanging around with an insider like Lou Sapio. People might start treating him like one of the crowd, which was probably the best thing that could happen to him for getting his head screwed on straight.

As soon as they walked in they were waved over to a table by two of the other caddies, Bear and Pokey, old-timers who'd been around as long as Lou had. What their last names were he didn't know, but they were both good guys. As he'd expected, they went out of their way to bring Dylan into the conversation, which, as usual, centered around the amazing string of unlucky breaks they'd had during the day's round. (Lou had yet to meet a caddie – or a golfer –

who believed he'd had an unusually lucky day.) Dylan pitched right in with a story about Finley's sand-trap woes, but he got off on the wrong foot, making himself look good while making Finley out to be a chump. You didn't do that to a guy who was making you more money every week than Pokey, Bear, and Lou put together; especially a guy as popular with the caddies and as all-around nice as Roger Finley. By the time he finished he was the only one laughing. Bear and Pokey were staring into their beers.

Lou could see that Dylan knew he'd hit an off-note but didn't have a clue as to what he'd done wrong. And when the overweight, middle-aged waitress showed up for their orders, he didn't waste any time making matters worse.

'How ya doin', Doris? I'll have what these guys are having,' Lou had said, pointing to a pair of boilermakers – shot-glasses of bourbon with twelve-ounce beer chasers – already on the table.

'Same?' she asked Dylan. She was wearing crepe-soled, lace-up shoes and she looked as if she'd been on duty a long time, and as if her feet hurt and she wanted to go home to her kids.

'No,' Dylan said, 'I think what I'd like is a Boodles martini, straight up. And just a breath of vermouth.'

Lou, Bear, and Pokey exchanged glances. Lou shrugged, as if to say: Hey, don't blame me, I was just doing the kid a favor bringing him here.

Doris took a while to reply. 'I don't think we got Boodles, mister.'

'Tanqueray?'

'Uhh . . .'

'Beefeater?'

'I'll see. You want an olive or a twist?'

Dylan snorted. 'An olive, of course.'

He shook his head as she lumbered away toward the bar. 'As far as I'm concerned, if it doesn't have an olive you can't call it a martini.'

'Course not,' Bear said soberly. 'Anybody knows that. A martini got to have an olive.'

'So true,' said a straight-faced Pokey. 'Also a breath of vermouth.'

From there things kept going downhill, with Dylan ostentatiously picking up the check ('This one's on me too, sports') round after round; not a good way for a twenty-something to get on the good side of men twice his age, though nobody turned him down. By the time Lou had finished his second boilermaker – his limit, as he had long ago learned the sad, hard way – and Dylan had had his fourth martini, Lou knew it was time to get him out of there. It had been a mistake to bring him in the first place and it wasn't going to get any better. He'd drained the first couple in a hurry, two gulps apiece, the way they did in old movies, and had grown noisier, sloppier, and redder-faced with each one. Pokey and Bear, ordinarily cheerful, had slowly turned sulky and argumentative.

Lou set his empty shot-glass on the table with a bang. 'I think we should go get something to eat,' he declared, but the others were deep in a technical discussion of Roger Finley's difficulties. Pokey and Bear, up to their eyeballs in whiskey and beer thrust on them by Dylan, were showing off in their own way, telling him exactly what Finley's problems were.

According to Pokey, it was his backswing that was at the root of his troubles, anybody could see that; he was dropping the club down and back at the top of the backswing and hitting with a closed club face, which was starting the ball to the right and then bending it back around to the left. A simple hook. All he had to do was fix that backswing, that would take care of it.

Bear thought differently. 'I been watching him, you know? And I see that he starts the downswing all right, but then, just before he hits it, he rolls that right shoulder over. So what happens is, the left hand pulls in, see, so the ball gets dragged to the left, only, sometimes he leaves his clubface open, and then it goes right. That's all it is. He has to keep that shoulder from rolling over too early.'

'You think so?' said Dylan with an odd expression on

his face. 'Well, I'll certainly tell Rog what you think. I'm sure he'll be tremendously grateful for your help.'

Bear's slablike face darkened. 'Listen, you little—'

'Sometimes,' Lou cut in, 'it doesn't have anything to do with a guy's swing. It's just a question of your luck going south for a while, that's all. You just have a slump, like a baseball player. You're better off not messing with your swing. You just ride it out until you come out the other end.'

Dylan laughed meanly. 'Is that right? Well, I'm sorry to tell you this, but you're wrong . . . and you're wrong, and you're wrong. I happen to know exactly what Rog's problem is, and it has nothing to do with his shoulders, or his back-swing – or his luck either.' He took a third gulp of his current martini, draining it, and pulled the olive off the toothpick with his teeth, squishing it wetly around his mouth and grinning at them before he gulped it down.

'OK, I'm game,' Bear said. 'What does it have to do with?'

'That,' an increasingly bleary-eyed Dylan said, 'is for me to know and you to wonder, heh, heh.'

He was thoroughly, visibly plastered now, which offended Lou's sense of decorum; a caddie could get as snockered as he wanted in private, but not in public, not in a golf town, not during a tournament – it reflected badly on his player. He clapped Dylan on the shoulder. 'Come on, kid, pick yourself up. Let's go get ourselves a couple of T-bones.'

Angrily, Dylan brushed the hand away and glared at the three of them. 'You think I don't know whum . . . what I'm talking about? Hell, I know exac . . . exactly what I'm talking about. I know *exactly* wuss wrong with Roger's game, and I know exac . . . exactly who's responsible.' He nodded to himself. 'Zackly.'

'What the hell is that supposed to mean?' Pokey said.

Dylan smiled cunningly at them. 'An' . . . wuss more, I know . . . I know *why*.' He tried to fold his arms but gave up when he got tangled up in the process. 'Heh.'

'So what are you telling us about it for anyway?' Bear asked reasonably. 'Why not tell Finley?'

'Finley?' Dylan's eyelids began to close. His head wobbled.

'Enough already,' Lou said, standing up. 'Can't you see the kid's—?'

'No, I want to know,' Bear said. 'Come on, Dylan. The less money Finley earns, the less money you earn. So why let him keep screwing up if you're so sure you could cure him? Tell me that.'

Dylan jerked himself awake. 'Because, my frine fendered – my . . . my fine-feddered friend, caddies' wages're peanuss compared to what I goddin mind. There's real money to be made here if I jus' . . . if I . . .' Again his eyes slowly drifted closed and this time his head began to fall forward as well, but now he had engaged Bear's interest.

'What do you mean, money?' he said, roughly shaking Dylan. 'Hey, wake up, what the hell are you talking about?'

'Hey, will you lay off the kid already?' Lou said. 'He's just making the stuff up, you know that.'

'Well, now,' Dylan mumbled through a yawn. 'Well, now, as to that,' he said, then burped softly, said, 'Excuse me,' very distinctly, and promptly fell face-down on the table, snoring away even before his head hit it.

Five

With the champagne bottle prudently pointed away from them and a kitchen towel draped loosely around its neck, Graham gently twisted, paused, twisted the other way, and out came the plug with a soft pop and a wisp of vapor. He filled the two long-stemmed glasses on the driftwood coffee table, handed one to Lee, and lifted his own.

'Here's to the newest member of the American team at this year's international competition for the Stewart Cup.' He clinked his glass against hers, drank, and then said, 'It sounds impressive, but what am I toasting, exactly?'

'It is impressive, Graham,' Lee said happily. She'd recovered her spirits even before he'd shown up, and now with him there beside her and the first mouthful of champagne tickling her nose she couldn't remember why she'd been in any kind of a funk at all. And Wanda's Casserole, awaiting them in the oven, had turned out beautifully, with a lovely golden-brown crust. 'Aside from the Ryder Cup and the Curtis Cup, it's the most important, prestigious – you have heard of the Ryder Cup, haven't you?'

'Uhhh . . .'

'The Curtis Cup?'

'Mmmm . . .'

'Graham, how can you possibly call yourself a golf fan?'

'When did I ever call myself a golf fan? I'm a Lee Ofsted fan. The golf part is a necessary evil that came with the package.'

She laughed but he was telling the unvarnished truth. As he'd once put it, he'd prefer watching guppies spawn in a fish tank to watching a round of professional golf. And yet, with almost no grasp or appreciation of the game, he'd followed her career eagerly, offering support, motivation, and encouragement as needed. And often enough, after a tough match, a shoulder to cry on (or gripe on, as the case might be). Most of the time, with their careers keeping them a continent apart and sometimes more, it had been a long-distance shoulder, but that hadn't made it any less important.

'OK,' she said, 'let me explain. The Ryder Cup is the granddaddy of them all, going back to the 1920s, I think. I guess you could call the Curtis Cup the grandmother—'

He held up his hand like a cop stopping traffic. 'Stop. Don't clutter my mind with all this family history, I can only handle so much. I just want to hear about the Stewart Cup.'

'My absolute favorite subject,' Lee said happily, sipping champagne. (Delicious, charming stuff; what had made her think she didn't like it?) 'Graham, it's hard to put into words how excited I am about being a part of this.'

While he loaded a cracker with salmon-cream-cheese dip that he'd bought at a deli on the way home and leaned his tall frame back into a black leather armchair, she tried to explain what was so important about it: it drew from the cream of the crop of American and British pros; it was the only major team tournament that had both male and female players; it was about national pride – there was no purse involved – and about playing under pressure, and coming through for your team and your country; it was the object of fierce rivalry for slots on the teams—

'No wonder you're excited,' Graham said when she stopped to draw a breath. 'Listen—' he hesitated. 'When you say there's no purse, you mean there's no prize money, right?'

'That's right,' Lee said, stiffening a little. She knew where this was going.

'But you're still going to have expenses, a lot of them. You have to get there, you have to pay your caddie, you're going to need some decent clothes—'

'Graham, forget it.'

He leaned earnestly forward. 'Lee, I just don't understand you. I want to help. It would give me pleasure. If you like, just consider it a loan. You can pay it back when you win a major. It'll all be community property anyway, once we get married. I don't see—'

'Graham,' she said more firmly, 'can we just forget it? Thank you with all my heart, I really appreciate it. But can we just forget it?'

It was hard to explain – she'd tried before but failed – how important it was to her to make it on her own. If she succeeded – when she succeeded – it was going to be as a result of her own skill and effort, and, if necessary, luck. But it had to be her own luck. Peg had wanted to lend her money more than once too, and Lee had just as adamantly turned it down. (Did other golfers have this problem of having too many generous, rich friends?) When she'd first begun she'd accepted a life-saving loan from her golf coach, but that was the last time, and it had weighed her down until she'd finally been able to finish paying it back last year.

'Right.' Graham raised his hands in surrender, although it was clear he didn't really understand and never would. 'So. The team members get picked how again?'

'By merit. Statistically. The top money-earners on the men's and women's tours.'

'Well, then,' Graham said, clearing his throat, 'no offense, ma'am, but I can't help wondering . . .'

Lee grimaced. 'In my case it was luck. They have what they call a 'Rocky' slot – one for a man, one for a woman. Those two are chosen by lottery. I'm this year's female Rocky . . . Rockette, I guess,' she added with a wry smile.

'Well, what are you suddenly looking so down-in-the-mouth about? This is a wonderful break for you, isn't it?'

'Sure it is, Graham, and I can hardly believe my luck. It's just that – well, whatever tournaments I've been in before, I got there by merit too, I earned my right to play. This just feels different; it could just as well have been anybody. And the responsibility is awesome. I mean, I'm representing the United States! What if I shank? What if—'

He leaned across the table and put a large, warm hand around her wrist. His fingertips were pleasantly cool. 'Lee, you'll bear up to the responsibility just fine. Look, it's not as if they just picked you off the streets, you know. You're a card-carrying member of the WPGL; that makes you one of the two hundred best women golfers in the world, right?'

'Fifty-first, actually, if you want to be precise. As of this weekend's results.'

'There you are, then. Fifty-first. In the whole world. That's pretty select company, my friend. Does the fifty-first best golfer in the world go around shanking? Certainly not, the idea is ridiculous. What's shanking, by the way?'

'I love you,' she said, laughing, and squeezed his hand. 'Thanks, Graham, I know you're right, but I'm going to be playing with the best of the best. Roger Finley will be my partner; he'll be depending on me. I guess that's what's got the butterflies fluttering around inside.'

'Those aren't butterflies, those are hunger-rumblings. You haven't eaten in six hours. Which brings me to that . . . um . . . interesting smell coming from the kitchen. You really made dinner?'

'You don't have to sound so amazed. I have a lot of talents you don't know about.' She stood up, pulled him out of his chair, and stood on tiptoe to kiss him lightly on the lips. 'Come and see. It may look a little strange, but wait till you taste it.'

He followed her doubtfully into the kitchen, his forehead wrinkled. 'That smell – it seems to be coming from the oven.'

'Well, of course it's coming from the oven. Now how about giving me a hand?'

With Graham holding the plates, she pulled the lid from the steaming casserole and ladled out two sizeable helpings. Only after they'd carried them to the alcove, laid out the salads, opened a bottle of red wine, and sat down at the table did Graham speak.

'Um, what is it?'

'It's called Wanda's Casserole.'

He peered gravely at his mounded plate. 'Is it some sort of nachos?'

'In a way, yes, but different. Better. Go ahead, dig in, you'll like it.'

But he just sat there staring at it.

'Graham, aren't you even going to taste it? I practically lived on this my first year on tour.'

'What's in it?'

'Lots of things. Can of chili, can of SpaghettiOs, can of olives—'

'Excuse me?' he said with a peculiar expression. 'I thought you said SpaghettiOs.'

Lee's confidence began to ebb once more. 'Well, what's wrong with SpaghettiOs?' she said testily. 'Besides, after it all cooks together, you can't really tell what's in there. Anyway, you mix it all up – well, you add a bag of Fritos first, then you sprinkle some cheese—'

'Lee, this Wanda – would I be correct in assuming this is not a professional chef?'

'No, she was a college roommate of my friend Helga. I keep meaning to get her address and drop her a line to tell her how much it meant to us.'

He used his fork to gingerly poke at his food. 'Don't bother. I think we can safely assume she's dead.'

'Graham—' And suddenly, unexpectedly, the tears were there, right behind her eyes, trying to force themselves out. She covered her eyes. 'I don't know why I'm – why I'm so—'

Graham quickly set down his fork and came around the table, kneeling beside her chair and taking both her hands. 'Lee, I'm sorry,' he said miserably. 'I'm just kidding, I had no idea . . .'

'Oh, it's not that important. I don't know why I'm reacting this way. It's been a heck of a day, and I guess my emotions have gotten kind of tangled up.' She managed a pale smile. 'I guess Wanda's Casserole is pretty awful, now that I think about it.'

He let go of her hands, gently drew her face down to his, and softly kissed her. Then again, meltingly. 'I love you, you know that,' he said with his wonderfully clear blue eyes full on hers.

'I know.'

'And I'd do anything for you, make any kind of sacrifice . . . well, almost any kind.'

'You're not even going to taste it, are you?' But now she could feel the laughter tickling the back of her throat.

Solemnly, he shook his head. 'But you know what I'll do to make up for it? Get ready for this now. . . . you know, of course, that the PGL and the WPGL are clients of mine?'

'Yes,' she muttered. 'Not that you ever show up around a golf course.'

When he'd told her, months before, that the men's and women's tour organizations had both engaged the services of Countermeasure Inc., she'd been delighted, naively assuming it meant that he would be right there at the tournaments with her, running security operations, but it wasn't that way at all.

'I'm a consultant,' he'd explained to her. 'I don't actually work.'

Instead, his responsibilities ran to behind-the-scenes activities, mostly at league headquarters in Florida and California: training the security staff, supervising character checks on job applicants, and advising the brass on 'comprehensive strategies and contingency plans' and other mysterious matters.

'Well, maybe I ought to spend some time at one. You know, according to my contract, I'm supposed to be at a minimum of two tournaments a year and more or less observe and be generally available, so I know what it's like in the trenches. Which makes sense.'

'No, I didn't know. How come you haven't shown up?'

'Because I've been procrastinating,' he said candidly. 'Hoping against hope that I could get out of it before the season's over. Who knows, there might be a strike, the tour schedule might get canceled, an asteroid might hit the Earth, you never know.'

She couldn't honestly say his attitude surprised her. Even for her, Graham had never been able to force himself to watch golf for more than a day at a time, and even that much had obviously taken some impressive intestinal fortitude.

'However,' he said, raising his hand, 'the fact is that I've been meeting with league management on preparations for the Stewart Cup, on and off, for the past four months.'

'What?' She stared at him. 'I thought you didn't even know what it was.'

'Well, I don't, or rather I didn't; I do now. But I don't have to know what it is in order to help get the security arrangements up to snuff. All I have to know is that it's a golf tournament, and where and when it's going to be held, and how many people are expected, and a few other details. And on those scores, I've been out to Pinehurst twice in the last few weeks.'

'So you even knew it was in Pinehurst. I'm flabbergasted. Why didn't you ever—'

'Let me finish, will you? I'm trying to give you some big news here. Strictly speaking, the Stewart Cup thing isn't one of the regular tour events, but I'd be surprised if they wouldn't let me stretch a point and partially fulfill my contractual obligations at Pinehurst. I could spend my spare time cheering you on from the sidelines. And your spare time occupying you otherwise.'

'Graham, do you mean that?' Having him there with her would make all the difference in the world, something he apparently realized. 'Is that really a promise?'

'Absolutely. Didn't I tell you I'd do just about anything to convince you of the depth of my affection? But as for Wanda's Casserole—' He threw it a glance and shuddered. 'I'm sorry, I'm just not that brave.'

Now they were both laughing. He stood up and pulled her to her feet, and they kissed once more, Lee hugging him hard. 'Thank you, thank you, thank you—'

'I'll help you get rid of the stuff,' he said, still holding her. 'Let me go out to the garage and get my blowtorch. Maybe it'll burn.'

'Not on your life. I'll put it in the freezer. I can have it some time when you're not around. But what do you want to do about tonight?'

'I'll call Gourmet to Go and get us a prime-rib dinner from Simpson's with all the trimmings. We can finish the champagne while we're waiting. How's that sound?'

'Well, it's not Wanda's Casserole,' she said gravely, 'but I guess it'll have to do.'

36

Six

This was the life. Beyond any conceivable, imaginable doubt, this was the life.

She was sitting in a fragrant, buttery-soft, cocoa-colored swivel-chair, swinging gently back and forth, comfortable and utterly relaxed, waiting for the first strategy session to begin. Around her the other team members, slow in taking their seats (she'd arrived fifteen minutes early, fearful of being the last one there), were joshing and chatting. They were in the stately Centennial Boardroom of the Pinehurst Golf and Country Club, there were two pewter pitchers of rich, wonderful coffee in the center of the gleaming oval table, there were cups and saucers in front of them, and all was right with the world.

'How're you this morning, Lee?' the great Ginger Rolley said, sliding into the chair beside her.

And, 'Fine, Ginger, how are you?' Lee had replied, as if it were the most natural thing in the world. Ginger Rolley, for gosh sakes!

It had begun yesterday, surely the most glorious day of her fledgling career. The American and British teams had arrived – by sleek, chartered jets – within minutes of each other at North Carolina's Moore County Airport. A hundred or so enthusiastic but polite fans had been on hand to welcome them, and Lee, striding through the waiting room with some of the greatest golfers in the world, had found it easy to imagine she was one of them, there because she deserved it. People had clapped as the players walked by. 'Good luck, Lee,' they had called; and, 'Go get 'em, Lee,' and, 'You can do it, Lee.'

37

It had been a far, far cry from the other time she'd played Pinehurst, when she'd arrived in a beat-up 1978 Chevy Nova with four other equally strapped rookies. The only local resident who had had anything to say to them had been a woman from whom they'd asked directions to the Motel 6.

Hustled into spotless white vans by plus-four-clad attendants, the team members were driven to the resort to freshen up and change clothes in their rooms, and then taken to the ballroom for the welcoming ceremonies and the traditional group pictures. She'd shaken hands and exchanged pleasantries with the mayor, the governor, and a flirty congressman, none of whose names or faces registered through the daze in which she was ever so gently floating, about eight inches off the floor. Then back to her room, unresisting and slightly goofy with sheer pleasure, to rest, and to change again for the opening dinner.

And never had changing for dinner been such a treat. Ordinarily when she was on the tour, her non-golf wardrobe consisted of sweatshirts, jeans, and a single, all-purpose, mix-and-match outfit – simple skirt, a couple of blouses, low-heeled shoes, decent, tailored jacket from Macy's – for those rare occasions when it was necessary to be seen in public off the golf course. But now, this . . . !

The day after Roger's telephone call a form had arrived on Graham's fax machine, on which she was to note down all her clothing measurements, including some she hadn't even known existed. Then, a week before she'd left, she'd gotten three big UPS packages in which were a new Stewart-Cup-logoed travel bag and suitcase packed with two beautifully tailored dress suits, one with pants and one with a skirt; three silk blouses; two pairs of wonderful, soft, leather dress shoes; a couple of casual sweaters in a handsome charcoal gray; and a drop-dead-gorgeous black evening dress (a little low in the front and frilly in the back for her taste, but who was complaining?)

When she had described the incredible haul to Peg on the telephone, Peg had laughed and said: 'What were they

38

afraid of, that you might show up in an old sweatshirt or something?'

Lee had gently coughed and made no comment.

The golfing side of things hadn't been neglected either. There were six golf shirts (thereby doubling her existing supply), six golf sweaters, two sweater vests, three pairs of golf shoes, a dozen golf gloves, three logoed sun visors, a windbreaker, and two warm-up suits, all of them in the pale-green, black, and white that were the American team's colors. And of course a magnificent, matching golf bag with black lettering that her eyes couldn't help wandering to any time she was in range of it.

Lee Ofsted
United States
Stewart Cup

This was glory indeed! And to top it off, along with the gear and clothes had come a new leather purse inside of which were five neat, slim, beautiful booklets of ten $100 traveler's checks each, which she was instructed to sign at a local bank – *five thousand dollars* – and a letter from the committee graciously explaining that the money was for 'any expenses that may arise in connection with your stay at Pinehurst'. What those might be was hard to imagine, since the committee was even putting up the caddies and paying their wages. It wasn't for food or lodging, certainly. The team had been given eight luxurious rooms – one entire wing – on the fourth floor of Pinehurst's rambling and historic Carolina Hotel – the 'Queen of the South', the elegant old resort that had started it all and was still its focal point – and had an open account in the Carolina Dining Room, of which she'd made good use this morning, with a wonderful, stomach-comforting breakfast of pit-smoked ham, eggs, and biscuits with thick, white, Southern-style sausage gravy.

And, oh, yes, one more thing. There had also been a note from a nearby car dealership, welcoming the team to North

39

Carolina and explaining that a telephone call to Larsen Motors would result in the prompt delivery of a complimentary, white Cadillac Seville for each member's personal use during the length of his or her stay.

Whew. Getting used to being back on the tour as number fifty-one on the money list was going to take some doing.

Need it or not, the pleasure of having a reserve of $5,000 to handle anything that might come along was a rare and delicious feeling. If the idea was to lower the players' stress, the committee knew what it was doing, because, if her stress level was any lower, she'd be asleep. Partly that was because of the unaccustomedly heavy breakfast, but mostly it was because she'd been up long beyond her usual bedtime the night before. Dinner in the crystal-chandeliered ballroom had been followed by speeches, presentations, and another hour of team photos. After that, there had been dancing and schmoozing until one.

Unfortunately, Graham, who'd arrived in Pinehurst the day before, had been busy with security matters (or maybe fortunately, because dancing was one of the few things he wasn't good at, and although she'd once or twice been able to talk him into it, he generally made it pretty clear that it wasn't his idea of a good time). Instead, she had danced with several of the men from the British and American teams, two CEOs of something or other, Senator Somebody, and, if she got it right, a former secretary of the treasury, none of whom seemed to feel in the least that her dress was cut too low. She'd been tongue-tied and dazed throughout, but she'd felt like a queen and she'd been treated like a star.

And Peg, who had arrived early and bought an expensive patron's badge for the tournament, one that got her into even the private functions, had been there to see it all, and to share it with her. Twice during the evening, when Lee couldn't stand it any more, they'd sneaked outside on to the terrace to giggle and chatter like a couple of high-school girls who'd managed to doll themselves up and crash the grown-up party of the year without being found out.

The only fly in the ointment was that there had been no chance for private time with Graham. But that, she was certain, would soon be taken care of, even though Graham wasn't in the main building, but in one of the fancy condominium four-plexes, where Peg had also gotten herself a suite.

'Lordy, what time did you get to bed?' Ginger asked now, reaching for a pitcher with a groan.

'Not till one,' Lee said.

'Early,' Ginger said, pouring coffee. 'Why didn't I have that much sense?'

Like most of the others, Ginger had consumed quite a bit of champagne last night – even Lee had had three glasses, matching her all-time record – and she was showing the effects now. A warm, amicable woman in her mid-forties, Ginger was one of the older players in the WPGL (she had debuted when Lee was a year old), an established star who could belt the ball 270 yards, right up there with the men, and twenty yards more than the furthest Lee could expect on her best day. Hippy and muscular, with a penchant for boxy Bermudas that didn't do anything for her bowling-ball calves, she had turned out to be wonderfully down-to-earth, approachable, and ready to laugh. She reminded Lee of her mother, in fact; something she nearly blurted out to Ginger after the second glass of champagne, before coming to her senses in the nick of time.

And now here was this terrific, famous lady greeting her like an old pal, choosing to sit in the seat right next to her, and actually pouring coffee in her cup.

Roger rapped on the table to get everyone's attention. 'Well, it's eight ten,' he said with a fine edge of impatience, 'which happens to be ten minutes after our agreed-upon starting time. I suggest we begin. I want to establish at the start that I don't intend to make a practice of waiting for latecomers. If the early birds have to wait for the latecomers to arrive, then they have to sit around twiddling their thumbs, don't they, while the latecomers are rewarded by having the meeting begin as soon as they arrive. That is not the tone we are going to set.'

41

'Well, well, he's a little testy this morning, isn't he?' Ginger whispered to Lee. 'But what's he lecturing us for? We're the ones who are here.'

It was true that Roger was sounding a bit prissy. It didn't seem like a very good way to begin, but Lee knew what was bothering him and she knew that everyone else did too. There were eight players on the American team: four men, including Roger, and four women. But present at this meeting – described as 'mandatory' in a letter from Roger last week – were only six people – three men and three women.

The missing female was Toni Blake-Kelly, but she wasn't the source of his annoyance; she'd made an apologetic telephone call yesterday to explain that her plane had been unable to take off from Boston because of fog, and she expected to arrive a little later this morning, in time for their practice round. But Jordie Webster was another story. Jordie was Lee's counterpart, the no-name golfer in the male Rocky slot. No, 'no-name' was wrong; Jordie had a reputation, all right, but not the kind anybody wanted. Twenty-eight years old, beautiful of face and form, the blond, blue-eyed Jordie had burst on the golf scene like a comet three years ago, the same year that Lee had started. A hole-in-one in his first tournament, three top-ten finishes in his first six tries, and a big win in his seventh. The new Tiger Woods, everyone said. He was idolized.

But then people got to know him. The handsome, gifted Jordie, it turned out, was a pill – whether because it had all come to him too easily, or it was simply his nature, nobody could be certain. But he cussed out marshals, argued with fans, missed tee times, dropped out of matches if he fell too far behind to suit himself, and got plastered and unruly in country-club bars. He was loose-lipped, swaggering, immature, and all-around unpleasant, one of the tour's big-time boozers; the sort of person who made you turn around and go the other way when you saw him coming. And as the gloss had worn off, his game had suffered, so much so that he'd dropped out in the middle of the season

42

last year amid rumors of a stay at a rehab center and had had to return to qualifying school this year to get back on the tour, which he'd managed to do with a stunning if brief return to his old form.

Since then he'd been playing at about Lee's level – far below what you'd expect with the God-given talent he had (Lee would have killed for his low, screaming, incredibly beautiful draw), but well enough to stay in the big time.

Anyone would have realized (anyone with any brains), Lee thought, that being picked for the Stewart was a fantastic chance for him, an opportunity to mend his reputation, to contribute something positive, to get back into the good graces of fans and fellow golfers; a shortcut back to glory.

So what does he do last night, the idiot? He publicly contradicts Roger, takes a poke at a photographer, gets sloppy-drunk, and becomes generally obnoxious, with the result that Jordie Webster – not the Stewart Cup – was in the golf headlines in this morning's sports pages. ('Webster at It Again', 'Possible Assault Charge against Stewart Cup Golfer', '"He Hit Me!" Says Photog. "Bulls—t!" Says Jordie'.)

And then this morning he fails to make it to the very first strategy session. No wonder that Roger, usually so charming despite being rather tightly wound, was sounding annoyed. But at last things were getting underway. He was passing out oversized loose-leaf binders with thick, soft, leather covers.

'My-oh-my, Roger, what do we have here?' Dave Hazelton hefted his notebook and puffed out his cheeks for dramatic effect. 'Don't we get a cart or something to roll these things around in? It'd take us all four days just to read the thing, and I seem to recall we got ourselves a little tournament to play.'

More tenseness in the air. Hazelton was trying to be funny, but there was a strain in his voice that even his soft Tennessee accent couldn't hide. A tall, cadaverously thin, self-taught golfer with a horsey, blotchy face and a hangdog expression, he had barely missed out to Finley for the captaincy

43

of the team, and although he managed to resist griping to the press about it in so many words, it was no secret around the circuit that he was of the opinion that Roger, in the spirit of team play, should have voluntarily relinquished the post when he'd started to slump so badly – relinquished it and left it to the obvious next in line – namely, David Francis Hazelton. Personally, Lee was thankful he hadn't.

Ordinarily, she would have been happily oblivious to these sub-surface goings-on, but in this case she'd had Peg to fill her in, and Peg was the nearest thing there was to a walking encyclopedia of golf gossip. Once, exasperated by hearing too much of it at one time, Lee had called her exactly that to her face, and a delighted Peg had taken it as a compliment.

Roger didn't reply to Dave except with a taut, glassy smile. Whew, everybody had warned her about the tension associated with international cup competition, but Lee had thought they were talking about golf. At this rate, by the time they got around to actually playing, they'd be at each others' jugulars.

Visibly collecting himself, Roger tried another smile, more successfully this time, returned to his place at the head of the table, and cleared his throat. Here, in street clothes, wearing reading glasses low on his nose, and without the trademark straw hat, he was an even less formi-dable-looking man than Lee had realized; nobody's idea of a superb athlete, but then that was a big part of Roger's considerable popularity. 'Now, these manuals may look a little forbidding—'

'A little!' hooted Dave. 'As in "the Pacific Ocean may look a little large"?'

Lee had the impression that he knew he'd started off on the wrong foot and was trying to make amends, but if that was supposed to be a joke it was pretty flabby stuff, lead balloon number two. This was a man, Lee thought, who'd be better off if he stuck to his golf. Lighthearted banter wasn't his strong suit.

Roger ignored him and spoke with quiet dignity. 'Ladies

and gentlemen, I'd like to say something. Now, you're all here for one reason and one reason only: you're the finest golfers in the United States—'

Well, all but one, Lee thought humbly, but it was nice of him not to call attention to it.

'—and you don't need me to teach you the game, that's not my job. But what I can do is make life easier for you by seeing to it that all the bases are covered and nothing's left to chance, and there aren't any screw-ups, pardon my French, that throw us out of kilter. I've been on three cup teams before – I know some of you have had that honor too, and you know from experience how much the little things can affect your play. So, you'll find everything you need to know here: daily schedules, including dining and public functions, which outfits we'll be wearing each day so that we look like a team, an annotated set of the tournament rules, the match schedule itself, and . . . well, I guess that's about it. A few other details.'

He waited while those around the table leafed through the notebooks, rather tentatively.

'Uh-oh, Rog, we've got ourselves a problem here. Big-time.' The speaker, sitting directly across from Lee, was the dark, sinewy Dinny Goulapoulos (her real first name, she claimed, was something that no non-Greek could pronounce).

'And what is that, Dinny?' Roger asked politely.

She rapped her open notebook with the flat of her hand. 'I don't see any bathroom breaks for the next four days. Now, I don't know about you, but . . .'

Lee laughed with the rest of them but stopped short when she realized that Roger hadn't thought this was funny either. Was it just the anxiety that went along with heading the team, or could it be that he was always this sensitive, that the amusingly self-effacing, ever-so-slightly overwhelmed man of the television interviews was a fabrication? But even if that was so, she felt a twinge of disloyalty to him for laughing. She owed Roger; he was her partner, after all, and although he hadn't had anything to do with choosing

45

her, it was he himself who'd delivered the momentous news, personally and gracefully.

She was beginning to have an inkling of just how hard his job was going to be. Golf wasn't a natural team game – just the opposite, in fact. It was as individual and self-focused as a game could be: you versus the ball, not you versus your opponents. It wasn't like other sports. Your teammates couldn't help you by blocking for you or bunting you along the base paths, and your opponents couldn't hurt you by making diving catches of your shots, or trying to block them, or throwing golf balls at you. You were on your own; you stood or fell on your own merits.

That was the way Lee liked it, of course, and she had little doubt that every other pro golfer felt the same way. They were individualists with their own ways of doing things, their own practice methods, their own views on tactics and strategy. They didn't appreciate being told how to play golf, and molding them into a unified, cohesive group with a common, overarching goal was going to take some doing.

Which, thank God, was Roger Finley's responsibility, not hers.

And he did seem to be doing his best. 'Well, you know me, Dinny,' he said pleasantly, trying now to get into the spirit of things. 'They don't call me Mr Micro-Manage for nothing. I'll tell you what. I'll look over the schedule again, and maybe we can fit one in some time late Friday, or Saturday morning at the latest.'

Everybody had been looking for an opportunity to chuckle at something Roger said, and that was what they did. The mood lightened perceptibly.

Dougal Sheppard, sitting next to Roger, raised his hand.

'I have a serious point to make,' he said, gravely stroking his sand-colored, soup-strainer mustache. 'I'm looking at page thirty-one, bottom paragraph, line two: "Team members are expected to get a full eight hours' sleep each night; this requires an informal curfew of ten thirty p.m. Please see me if you anticipate requiring an exception."

46

Now, I think you ought to take into consideration the fact that sleep needs vary from individual to individual. Speaking for myself, I've determined, using empirical methods, that my motor coordination is at its best with seven to seven-and-a-half hours, and it may be that others also differ from the norm you've set, even though it's admittedly the general norm. In addition, I think there's something to be said for keeping to the same daily habits that one is used to at home. The more familiar the routine, the fewer the sources of stress.' He closed the notebook and looked earnestly at Roger. 'I would appreciate your response.'

This was pure Dougal: sensible, serious, analytical . . . and long-winded. Dougal was probably the most joyless golfer – at least the most joyless good golfer – Lee had ever known, attacking the game as if it were a problem in calculus. That said, he somehow managed to be quite likable, with a sober, earnest sincerity that frequently made her cover a smile. He had been born of Scottish parents in Canada, and that faint, rolling burr didn't hurt either.

She found herself smiling now, and also agreeing with him. Keeping to her regular habits as much as possible was something Lee too had found beneficial, not that Roger's ten thirty 'curfew' would present much of a problem to her. For Lee, life in the fast lane meant staying up past nine thirty, by which time she was usually snuggled up in bed with a book. With her internal alarm clock waking her up at six, that gave her a little over eight hours, her ideal sleep time – empirically determined, of course.

'I think you've raised a good point,' Roger said, pleased to have someone take his manual seriously at last. He had visibly relaxed. 'I hope we'd all agree that we can't have people gallivanting around at three o'clock in the morning – we depend on each other and we all owe it to the rest to be at our sharpest – but maybe I have been a little too rigid, at that.'

With his fingers on the temples of his reading glasses, he gave them a little shake to adjust them on his nose, a motion Lee was already finding familiar. 'Well, look, we

47

still have some time before the shuttle bus picks us up for our practice round. Maybe we ought to open the subject for discussion. Tell me, how do the rest of you feel?'

'Ten thirty will suit me fine,' Lee said, looking for something to contribute to the session. 'If I keep to my daily habits, by ten thirty I'll have been in bed for an hour, at least.'

'Fine, fine,' Roger said absently. 'Anybody else?'

She had a hunch that he didn't particularly care how she or any of the rest of them felt about it. Unless she was mistaken, he had pegged himself accurately as 'Mr Micro-Manage'. But it seemed to her that he was doing the smart thing; picking something relatively unimportant, something that he was willing to give ground on, and letting Dougal and the others have their say and maybe even get their way. 'Participative decision-making,' Peg called it, and it was supposed to make for a happy crew.

Well, Lee was already happy; besides, given her normal bedtime, it wasn't a topic that held much interest for her, and while they discussed it (talked it to death, in her private opinion) she browsed through the notebook, stopping at the page with the schedule for tomorrow, day one of the tournament. The morning format was alternate-stroke, in which two-member teams played with a single ball, alternating shots until the ball was in the cup. Finley and she would lead off as the first team, and she would be teeing off on odd-numbered holes.

She had moved on to the next page before it struck her, and struck her hard, that 'one' was an odd number. Lee Ofsted would be the very first golfer to tee up in the Stewart Cup tournament.

Sheesh.

Seven

Roger's laid-back mood lasted all of twenty minutes. It had begun to frazzle slightly when Jordie Webster strolled into the strategy session an hour late ('Gee, weren't we supposed to start at nine? I was sure this started at nine. Dinny, didn't you think this started at nine?') and then immediately began griping – wittily, he thought – about the thickness and specificity of the manual. ('Jeez, Roger, "All previous day's clothing to be turned in for laundering/cleaning no later than eight thirty a.m." What if it's not dirty yet?')

Still, Roger had managed to handle it magnanimously, with no more than a barely noticeable tic under his left eye. And a few minutes later, when Toni Blake-Kelly finally limped in with a twisted ankle suffered while running for her flight ('Don't worry, I'll be fine by tomorrow. Probably. I think.'), a few more chinks in the Finley façade had started to show through.

But it wasn't until the shuttle had delivered them to the players' entrance of the clubhouse, a palatial, white-pillared shrine that made it clear (if one had managed to miss the point before) that golf was the hallowed be-all and end-all of life at Pinehurst, that he had really come unglued. Waiting for the team on the clubhouse steps were the caddies, an even more varied group than usual because most of them weren't professional caddies at all, but brothers, or sisters, or sons of the golfers, a common arrangement at the more glamorous international competitions, where the players wanted their relatives to share in the glory. The problem was, there were eight golfers on the shuttle van, but only

49

seven caddies on the steps. And the one who was missing was Dylan Blanchard, Roger's caddie.

'Where is he?' Roger was softly moaning – well, whining – now. 'How could he do this to me?' He looked utterly helpless, as unlike the sterling captain of America's Best as anyone could possibly be. 'I have to be able to count on him, Lee.'

'Oh, he's probably just taking care of something for you,' Lee said soothingly. 'You know, those last-minute details.'

'What last-minute details? Everything's taken care of, there aren't any last-minute details.'

'Roger, you know how reliable Dylan is, he's bound to be here any minute,' Lee told him with airy confidence. She didn't have a clue as to how reliable Dylan Blanchard was or wasn't, but she was on pins and needles herself and she desperately wanted him to relax so that he could calm her down. Really, it hardly seemed fair that Finley, with four major championships and forty-three tour victories under his belt, needed Lee, at her very first major event, to do the feather-smoothing.

But it was either her or Dave Hazelton, and Dave wasn't being much help. As for the others, they had gone happily into the clubhouse with their relatives-cum-caddies. This was not the usual tour practice, inasmuch as regular tour caddies weren't allowed inside the players' clubhouse. But here the amateur, non-card-carrying caddies were welcomed. Lee's caddie, the inimitable Lou Sapio, had watched with undisguised contempt as they had trooped inside. Only Lee and Dave had remained outside with their regular tour caddies, along with the seething Roger.

'I'm telling you, it's the last straw,' Roger said bitterly. 'I won't tolerate it.'

'Lighten up, Rog,' Dave put in. 'Give him a break, he just slept in, that's all. The kid's jet-lagged, like the rest of us.'

'Sure,' Roger shot back, 'but the rest of us are here, aren't we? Anyway, how much jet lag do you get on a trip from New Jersey to North Carolina?' He jerked his head. 'Damn it, this is just awful.'

He was making Lee jumpier by the second. She was starting to wonder if he wasn't going to make nut cases out of them all by the time this was over.

'Well, where is he then?' Dave said unhelpfully. 'You tell me.'

Roger scowled. 'That's what—'

'Lou,' said Lee pleasantly, 'would you have any idea where Dylan might be?'

Lou shrugged. 'I don't know, I haven't seen him since last night.' He thrust the logoed duffle bag holding her glove, golf shoes, and other necessities at her. 'Let's go, let's go. We gotta warm up. We can't go out there cold.'

We. That was a good sign. When Lou was at his most upbeat and supportive (in his own way, of course), it was always we, never you. Again, she thanked her lucky stars for having him with her.

'Maybe Dylan's had himself an accident,' Dave said cheerfully. 'For all we know, he could be lying in some ditch with a broken neck.'

'That's right,' said his caddie, the aptly nicknamed Too-Tall Jack. 'Or got run over by a truck.'

Roger blanched. 'That's ridiculous. You don't really think—?'

'Hey, you never know,' Too-Tall Jack said. 'I once knew this guy – he was a caddie – who grabbed a nap right in front of one of them big, heavy rollers they use to flatten the greens. When it was parked, you know? And the driver climbs in without seeing him, and starts the thing up. Drove right over him and never knew it.'

Roger looked genuinely appalled. 'Maybe ... maybe I ought to ask the security people to look for him.'

'This guy,' said Too-Tall Jack, 'was squashed so flat—'

'That's a good idea, Roger,' Lee said hurriedly. 'I'll bet anything they find him safely in his room, dozing. In the meantime, why don't you arrange for one of the regular Pinehurst caddies to start?'

'But ... but Dylan has my clubs, my shoes, everything.'

'They'll still be in the bag room if Dylan hasn't picked

'em up yet,' Lou offered. 'I'll make sure your guy gets them if you want.'

'But Dylan has my yardage book. I can't . . . this is . . .'

Lee came close to laughing. In a way it did her good to see that superstars could get just as flustered as anybody else. 'Roger, we're talking about caddies who work Pinehurst twice a day, five days a week. They've been doing it for twenty years. They don't need yardage books.'

'Oh. Yes, of course, that's a point. Yes, I'll do that, I'll do that now. Obviously, it'll have to do for the practice round.' He wandered disconsolately off in search of a marshal.

'Don't worry,' Lee called after him, 'you'll have him long before tomorrow.'

'So, what about this guy you were talking about, Jack?' Lou asked after a moment. 'What'd he look like? After, I mean.'

'I was trying to say,' replied Too-Tall Jack, stretching his enormous arms out wide. 'He was spread out from—'

Lee snatched up her bag. 'Lou, I'll see you on the range in ten minutes.' She fled to the women's locker room.

Eight

'Holy Moses, what a night that was,' Henry Sanchez said, wearily wiping down the tables. 'I'll never understand how they can drink that much and still manage to haul those bags around the next day. How can they smoke that much? How can they talk that much?'

Merle Gibbons sighed in agreement as she dumped metal ashtrays, one after another, into the garbage pail she'd set on the bar. 'Oh, they're always pretty chipper the first night of a tournament, you know that. It won't be so bad tonight, not after they've gotten up at dawn and carried all day.'

It was a little past ten a.m., an hour before Duffer's opened for the day. The bar, in Pinehurst Village only a block from the resort grounds, was the hangout favored by the caddies in the evenings. Merle and Henry, longtime waitress and bartender, were cleaning up after the previous night's jollities. Ordinarily, they would have done that when the bar closed down at two in the morning, but they'd been so bushed they'd decided to quit and return early the next day.

Henry made a face as he wiped off the last of the six round tables. 'I have to get us some new wash rags. These are getting pretty rank.'

'Get me a new pair of knees while you're at it,' Merle said, tying a twist around the garbage-pail liner. 'Well, I'll drop this in the dumpster, and then I'm going to get me a bowl of soup at Grounds and Pounds. Be back in half an hour. Want me to bring you anything?'

'No, I brought a sandwich. See you later.'

'Damn,' he said as the back door slammed behind her.

53

He'd noticed that a bulb was burned out in the revolving Budweiser lamp and he was pretty sure there weren't any spares in—

'Henry! Henry!' The cries were accompanied by a furious rattling at the back door. 'Henry, let me in!'

'It's open, Merle,' he called. 'Just come in, will you?'

But she just kept shaking the handle, and with some irritation he walked to the door to open it. 'For God's sake, Merle—'

When he saw her face he was struck mute. She looked five years older than she had two minutes earlier, as if she'd stepped into some fantastic heavy-gravity dimension when she'd walked out the door, and the G-forces had dragged down all the planes of her face. She was still holding the garbage bag, although she didn't seem to be aware of it, and under the bright makeup her face was gray.

'Merle, what is it? What's the matter?'

'Henry, there's somebody dead out there,' she said in a near-monotone. 'One of the caddies. By the dumpster. You better call the police.'

'Oh, hell, he's probably still sleeping it off. Let me go and—'

She clutched his arm so hard and so suddenly that he gasped. 'No, he's not drunk, his head is all—' Her voice rose, trembling, as she spoke. 'Henry, I didn't even see him, I tripped over his arm – I stepped on his fingers!'

She shuddered violently, along the whole length of her wiry body, and for the first time in fourteen years of working together, night in, night out, he put his arms around her. 'Hey, Merle, easy, easy. I'll call the police now,' he said. 'Here, you sit down.'

'It's the smart-aleck one,' she said vacantly as he went to the telephone. 'The Boodles kid.'

Nine

Ordinarily, five minutes of stretching and two or three dozen practice hits, beginning with her wedges and working up to the driver, were enough to loosen her up and calm her pre-tournament nerves to manageable proportions. Not today, even though it was only a practice round. Roger's attack of nerves had rattled her more than she'd let on, and a not-so-small part of her was hoping he wouldn't be able to find a caddie and would call the whole thing off.

Walking from the driving range to the practice putting green, trailed by Lou (who was looking his usual crabby, unflappable self, God bless him), her stomach felt hollow, despite the monster breakfast of only a few hours before, and her knees were distressingly unsteady. Roger was already at the green, bent over a seven-footer, his straw hat tipped back. A few yards away his Pinehurst-supplied caddie, a gray-haired black man named Gabe, who was probably even older than Lou and not much bigger, seemed about as thrilled to be participating in the Stewart Cup as he would have been to be working the Semi-Annual Over-Seventy Senior Ladies' Best-Ball Tournament at the local country club.

A good thing too, she thought. His calming influence seemed to have settled Roger all the way down to his normal level of fidgetiness, even though Dylan had yet to be heard from. Roger sank the curving putt successfully and straightened up with a satisfied nod.

'Rog?' Lee said, trying to sound nonchalant. 'I've been thinking – you know, about me taking the odd holes . . . I just wondered if it might be better—'

He was quick to understand. 'Worried about teeing off first? Don't. You'll be fine; it'll be good for you. Just whack that first ball the way you always do and you'll be over the hump. You'll forget all about nerves.'

'Well, but how about just for today?' she pleaded. 'If you go up there first it'll give me a chance to sort of—'

'To sort of tie yourself in knots about tomorrow, when it really counts. Now you listen to me, my girl.' He smiled encouragingly at her. 'Do you think I'd have put you up there first if I didn't think you were the right one for it? Believe me, you'll do fine. I know you're not so sure about that, but I am, and I'm the captain, aren't I, so what I say must be right . . . right? Now get in your putting practice. The last of the Brits have already teed off, and they'll be calling us in a few minutes.'

Well now, that was better. That was the kind of thing she needed from Roger, and she felt her tension begin to ease as she lined up a string of balls for her pre-play putting routine.

But twenty minutes later the call for the Americans to report to the first tee came over the loudspeakers and her heart promptly started whumping so hard she was sure the people in the front ranks of the gallery could hear it. It was a big, excited crowd, bigger than she'd ever seen come out for a practice round before, and it took a couple of marshals to clear the players' way to the tee box. When someone grasped her forearm she jumped three inches into the air.

'Yeek!'

Peg sprang almost as high. 'Don't do that! Good gosh, Lee, what's the matter with you?'

Lee emitted a weak laugh. 'Whoo. I guess I have a slight case of nerves.'

'If that's a slight case of nerves, let's hope you never have a major one. Relax, will you? Of course you're a little nervous right now. By tomorrow you'll be fine.'

'Assuming I live through today.'

'Lee?' an impatient Roger called from the tee box. 'You're up, let's get it rolling.'

'Oh, God,' she mumbled, turning from Peg. 'What ever made me think I wanted to do this?'

The women's tee box was set eighteen yards ahead of the men's, but it seemed more like 1800 as Lee plodded grimly to it, feeling as if she was in one of those awful dreams where you're trying to walk through a landscape of glue. There was polite applause and a steady clicking and whirring of cameras. Terrific, she thought, everyone can get me collapsing in living color.

Lou placed something white in the palm of her hand when she got there. She stared blankly at it.

'It's a tee,' he said after a moment. 'You stick it in the ground.'

'I know that,' Lee said. 'Gee whiz, Lou.'

'The pointy end goes in.'

It came as such a surprise – Lou was a lot of things, but being intentionally funny wasn't usually one of them – that it actually made her laugh as she bent to insert it in the turf, and when she straightened up she found that her muscles, or at least her stomach muscles, had pretty much unclenched. Without waiting to be asked, Lou handed her the driver.

'Quiet, please,' said the starter. 'Up first, Lee Ofsted, Portland, Oregon. No picture-taking, please.'

Nice and simple. A brief smattering of applause followed, and then a relative hush. This wasn't so bad, she thought. If she worked at it, she could make herself pretend it was just the Greater Fresno Open.

Well, maybe not the Greater Fresno Open, but nothing to lose her head over either. As she took her stance over the ball and looked out over the fairway, her mind was clear and focused enough to fully appreciate for the first time why Roger had decided she should be first off the tee. The first hole here at Pinehurst was fairly simple and straight-forward. Designer Donald Ross had held the delightful belief (if only every designer held it!) that the opening hole shouldn't be so difficult that it would get the golfer off to a frustrating start that might ruin the rest of the round. A par-four, it was 378 yards to the green from the women's tee, but would have been 396 yards for Roger, hitting from the men's. And while Lee was a long hitter for a woman – not in Ginger's league, but pretty good – Roger was only an average-distance-hitter for a man; his great strengths lay in his short game. So, a good tee shot from Lee – say 240 yards and straight down the middle – would leave the ball less than 140 yards from the green. Roger, taking the next shot, would have an easy eight-iron to the green; with a little luck he could target-shoot it to within a one-putt distance from the cup. Then – with just a little more luck – Lee could putt it in. An easy birdie; one under par.

At least that was the idea.

She took her usual slow, deep breath, briefly waggled her wrists, and tried to make her mind go blank, letting her instincts and her training take over. The club went back and around, curling her body into its familiar, supple coil. Then it unwound: hips first, then shoulders, then wrists, building to a centrifugal force that whipped the club head back down and through the ball at something close to 120 miles an hour. It was a good shot, she knew it from the feel. She looked up to see the ball arcing high against the soft blue Carolina sky – God what a sight – soaring on, and on, long, straight as an arrow, and perfect. Two hundred and forty-five yards, maybe more. As good a tee shot as she could make.

Laughing, she looked exultantly back at Roger.

'Not bad,' he said.

Ten

'Well, I appreciate your coming in, Mr Sheldon,' Chief Oates said, dipping his chin into his collar to muffle a yawn. He was doing his best to be polite, but he was obviously impatient to get back to the folders on his desk. 'I'm not really sure how I can help you, though.'

'Oh, I don't need any help, Chief, at least not yet,' Graham said. 'This is just a courtesy call. I thought I ought to introduce myself before the tournament starts, so you know who to blame if things get too crazy around here.'

The chief laughed good-naturedly. A folksy, lanky, leathery man in chinos, with a face as creased and pock-eted as his scuffed boots, he seemed like a nice enough guy. He just had other things on his mind. 'We're used to golf tournaments at Pinehurst, Mr Sheldon. We've got them down to a system, and I don't expect the Stewart Cup to be any crazier than most.' He unpropped his crossed ankles from the opened lower drawer of his desk and prepared to stand up. 'Well, thanks for—'

'I hope you're right, Chief. When I was on the force in Carmel, we had one or two tournaments at Pebble Beach that I wouldn't want to live through again.'

Oates had been halfway out of his chair, with his hand extended, but now he promptly sat down again. 'You were a police officer?' For the first time, his interest was now fully focused on Graham and not on his desk.

Graham smiled at the change in the atmosphere. In the eyes of a working policeman, as he well knew, the gap between a glorified rent-a-cop (his current status) and an

59

actual brother police officer was gigantic, and it was nice to have gotten himself on the other side of it.

'For six years. Mostly as a detective.'

'In Carmel?'

'For two years. Before that, Oakland, mostly in Homicide.'

'Oakland!' Oates blew out his breath with a whoosh. 'I bet you got into some pretty heavy stuff in Oakland.'

'Twenty-eight homicides in three years. Twenty of them closed.'

'Whoa.' They were friends now. 'At least you never got bored.'

'No, but I damn near got killed. I found out I prefer being bored. No one's pulled a knife on me all year, not even once. I'll leave the heavy stuff to you, Chief.'

'Name's Nate, Graham. Hell, if we get one homicide in two years around here, that's a lot, and it's always just a couple of drunks in a bar. The last time—' The phone on his desk buzzed. 'Scuse me.' He punched a button and picked up the receiver.

'What is it, Sal?' His face first dropped in surprise, then settled into a frown. 'You gotta be kidding,' he murmured, and then: 'No, Sal, I know you're not kidding. It was just a figure of speech.'

Slowly he lowered the receiver to its cradle. 'I'll be damned.'

'Problem?' Graham asked.

'Yeah, I'd say I have a problem. So do you.'

'Me? Why, what's happened?'

'Well, it looks like one of the caddies – one of you people's caddies – went out and got himself killed. So, we've got ourselves a homicide after all. You want in on this, Graham, or you want to leave it to us?'

'Of course I want in on it.' Graham was surprised at the surge of adrenaline that he could practically feel flow up his spine. Until this moment it was something he hadn't realized he'd missed.

'I thought you preferred being bored.'

'So did I. I guess I was wrong.'

'Let's get going, then.'

In the police parking lot, Oates stopped to fit his Stetson just right before swinging himself into the driver's seat of the patrol car. 'Hey, Graham?'

Graham paused with his fingers on the door handle. 'Nate?'

Oates tipped the hat to the angle he wanted and grinned. 'Welcome back to the big time, buddy.'

The village of Pinehurst, North Carolina, population 8,212, prides itself, and rightfully so, on its clean, friendly, small-town charm. The turn-of-the-century cottages on its tree-shaded streets are spotless and well taken care of, and the compact business district – boutiques, restaurants, and 'collectibles' – is as neat and pretty as an architect's model set up on a table. Thus, the two blue-and-whites pulled up helter-skelter in front of Duffer's Sports Bar on Barrett Road, a block north of Boutique Row and only a few hundred yards from the stately grounds of the Pinehurst Resort Hotel, looked out of place, a vulgar intrusion from a coarser, later time.

Oates added his own blue-and-white to the jumble out front, then strode through the dim bar with Graham. A gray-faced, middle-aged woman in a waitress's outfit sat at a table, staring numbly at a black-and-white wall-photograph of a smiling Bobby Jones on the first tee of Pinehurst Number Two. An open but untouched bottle of Evian and an empty glass were in front of her. Oates stopped.

'You all right, Merle?'

She looked at him gratefully. 'I'll be OK, Chief.'

'You're the one who found him?'

She closed her eyes. 'Yes.'

'Stick around. I'll need to talk to you a little later.'

He squeezed her shoulder, poured water from the bottle into the glass and slid it toward her. 'Drink.' Obediently she sipped about a teaspoonful, then went back to staring at the picture.

61

Graham followed Oates out to the back, where, in the rank smell of rotting vegetables from the nearby restaurant dumpsters, the brisk business of crime-scene investigation and evidence-collection was underway. Three men and a woman, two of the men in uniform, were scuttling about, absorbed in their tasks. One of the men, in polo shirt and jeans, was slowly panning the area with a video recorder balanced on his shoulder, the woman was sketching in a large pad, one of the plastic-gloved cops was on one knee, using a ballpoint pen to poke little bits of who-knew-what into small plastic containers, and the other uniform, also kneeling, was dusting a beer can with bright yellow finger-print powder.

'Figure the killer stopped for a beer, Davey?' Oates asked.

The policeman went on working. 'You just never know, do you, Chief?'

'You got that right, my friend.'

With all the activity going on, the body that was the reason for it seemed strangely neglected. It was on the far side of the nearest dumpster, up against the brick wall at the rear of the bar, blocked from view except for its right hand, which stuck out into the alley proper, its fingers loosely curled. Graham understood well enough why nobody was paying attention to it; they were waiting for the medical examiner before touching it, as good police procedure dictated. Also as good procedure dictated, they had outlined the corpse with chalk, preparatory to moving it once the doc had arrived and had his look. Oates, he thought with approval, might be a laid-back sort of guy, but he ran a knowledgeable, efficient outfit.

'Oh, hi, Doc,' he heard Oates say beside him, and turned to see the chief addressing a pale-skinned, gray-mustached African-American, portly and cheerful-looking, and the first man he'd seen since he'd come to Pinehurst who was wearing a suit and tie. 'Ed Tuck, this is Graham Sheldon, tournament security. He'll be working with us.'

'Howdy-do, Mr Sheldon. I'll just have a look, if you'll step out of the way, Nate.'

'Sure, help yourself, Doc, and thanks.'

'My pleasure. We live to serve.'

Toting a metal attaché case, he headed for the body, humming a tune that it took Graham a moment to place: 'Whistle While You Work'. Now there was another question he'd often wondered about. Why did medical examiners tend to be such happy people? You'd think that dealing with death day in and day out, and often wretchedly ugly death at that, they wouldn't be so damn jolly. How come cops, who dealt with the same kinds of situations, were anything but jolly, by and large? What did medical examiners know that cops didn't? Maybe it was just that the coroners and MEs only dealt with the dead ones. Maybe it was the live ones who turned you old before your time.

'Now, Fred,' Oates said, addressing a depressingly young, fresh-faced cop who until then had been standing quietly nearby, obviously waiting to make his report to Oates, 'what exactly do we have here?'

'Sir—' the officer began crisply, then stopped and glanced doubtfully at Graham.

'It's OK, Fred,' Oates said soothingly, 'he's with me. You've talked with Merle, have you?'

'Yes, sir, Merle, and Henry too – the bartender. And I removed the deceased's wallet for identification purposes, making sure not to disturb the remains or the surrounding area in any way . . .' He paused, waiting for Oates's approval.

'Good, good,' Nate said.

'The deceased appears to be Dylan Blanchard, of Tucson, aged twenty-five. Cause of death appears to be a massive head wound resulting from blunt-force trauma. Merle believes he may be in town caddying for one of the Stewart Cup competitors.'

'If he is, I'll find out for whom,' Graham said, drawing another suspicious look from Fred.

'This is Graham Sheldon, Fred,' Oates said with a sigh. 'He's in charge of tournament security. Going to be working on this with us.'

'Mm,' said Fred.

'He's ex-Oakland, California PD. Homicide.'

Fred's military demeanor cracked long enough for him to relax and let a brief, sunny smile shine through. 'Hey, pleased to meet you.' He cleared his throat and Officer By-the-Book took over again. 'According to Merle and Henry, who were interviewed separately to avoid influencing each other . . .'

This time his pause was met only by an impatient movement of the fingers from Nate: Come on, come on.

'. . . he had four Boodles martinis to drink – they know, because nobody else was ordering Boodles – and he'd become argumentative and contentious. He remained until nine or nine-thirty, at which time he—'

'Who with?' Oates asked.

'Sir?'

'Argumentative and contentious with who?'

'With the others at his table. There were two men, also caddies, according to Merle.'

'Locals?'

'No, sir, she never saw them before. But they were talking about caddying.'

'Assuming they're with the Stewart Cup players,' Graham put in, 'they shouldn't be too hard to locate. There are only eight of them all together.'

'Mm, that's good,' Nate said. 'Was Merle able to hear what they were arguing about?'

'She says no, sir, except that it was golf.'

'OK. So what did Blanchard do at "nine or nine-thirty"?'

'That's what Merle said, sir,' Fred said a little defensively. 'I was unable to pin her down any more—'

'That's OK, Fred. Is that when he left?'

'Yes, sir, with the others.'

'Out the back door?'

'He—' The officer flushed. 'I don't know, sir. I didn't think to ask. I thought . . . I mean—'

'It's all right, Fred. We can find out easy enough. Do you know if they were still arguing when they left?'

'Yes, sir.'

'Yes, sir, you know, or yes, sir, they were arguing?'

'The, er, latter.'

'Friendly argument or real fierce argument?'

'I asked her that, sir,' Fred said eagerly. 'She said they got pretty loud, but it didn't sound that serious to her – nothing anyone would kill somebody over.'

She'd be surprised, Graham thought.

'You'd be surprised,' Nate said.

'OK, so let me summarize,' Nate said. He drummed his fingers on the side of the nearby dumpster. 'From the looks of it, we probably don't have anything premeditated here. They all got drunk enough, and hot enough under the collar to finish their argument outside, and one or more of them bashed his head in and took off and left him here for dead. Which he probably was.'

'Yes, sir, exactly.'

Nate turned to Dr Tuck, who had quietly come up to them and had been listening. 'Does this sound right to you, Doc?'

The ME chuckled. 'Well, I'll go so far as to say you're right about his being dead. I'm ready to stake my reputation, such as it is, on that.'

Graham smiled, but Nate didn't find it funny. 'OK, and what am I not right about?'

'Nate, Nate, don't get touchy on me. C'mere, let me show you some things.'

With Nate, Graham followed Dr Tuck around the dumpster and back to the body. It was mostly on its back and sprawled as only the dead can sprawl – like some weird scarecrow whose joints weren't quite right – in a niche between the dumpster and the outer wall of a brick fireplace; a man of about twenty-five, his eyes half open, lightly built and on the short side. (Why, Graham wondered, were caddies so often little guys? In a typical round of golf they had to lug an awkwardly shaped thirty-pound bag on their backs for nearly four hilly miles, setting it down and picking it up seventy times or more. You'd think they'd tend to be big, husky gorillas, but no.) Graham remembered seeing

65

this one the day before; he was caddying for one of the Americans.

'Yeah, he's one of the tournament caddies, all right.'

The three men looked down at the dead man for a minute. 'Massive head wound resulting from blunt-force trauma,' Nate said grimly. 'I'd say that was about right.'

Even through the tarry black varnish of dried blood that matted Dylan Blanchard's hair, the deep, straight-line cleft high on the left side of his head was clearly visible.

'Looks like he was hit with a pipe, or a piece of rebar, or something like that,' Nate said. 'You can find all kinds of junk in an alley like this.'

'The killer must have been right-handed,' Graham said. 'Wound's on the left.'

'That's assuming he was hit from in front,' Tuck pointed out.

'True,' Graham said.

'But that isn't what I wanted to show you,' Tuck said, kneeling beside the body. 'Now, this is the position he was found in. I haven't turned him over.' He pointed to the dead man's face. 'See that?'

Graham and Nate got down on their haunches beside the ME and took a closer look at the blotched, plum-colored skin of the left cheek and forehead. The right side wasn't discolored, if you didn't count the normal gray waxiness of death. Both men nodded, but Graham let the chief speak first. As welcoming as Nate had been, this was his turf, and Graham had no intention of upstaging him.

'*Livor mortis*,' Nate said after just a moment's hesitation.

'*Livor mortis*,' agreed Tuck, looking up. 'You see what it means?'

'He's been moved,' Nate said. No hesitation this time. 'He wasn't killed here.'

Graham was pleased. It was a relief to know that Nate, despite his lack of experience with homicide, wasn't a babe-in-the-woods. *Livor mortis*, more commonly called lividity, referred to the settling and pooling of the blood. This was something that didn't happen in life because the heart kept it pumping through the body, but with the heart stopped, gravity took over. The blood settled in its vessels. Down. And given an hour or two, that's where it stayed, even if the dead person was later moved or turned over. Thus, the purple discoloration indicated that Dylan had lain on the left side of his face somewhere for an hour or more, before being dumped in the alley on his back.

The presumption that he had been murdered by a fellow caddie on the way out of the bar was now history. He'd been killed somewhere else, brought back here, and left, very likely for the express purpose of misleading the police.

Nate and Graham got to their feet. 'OK, Ed, looks like we need ourselves another theory. Can you say anything about how long he's been dead?'

Tuck was still on his knees. He reached forward, grasped Dylan's wrist, and tried, without a great deal of pressure, to unbend his elbow. It held stiff. 'Rigor mortis has set in pretty thoroughly and isn't yet showing any signs of dissipating,' he said. 'It was pretty chilly last night. Depending on how much time he's been outdoors and how much time indoors, that'd mean he's been dead, oh . . . say somewhere between six or eight hours and twenty-four hours.' He pressed a finger against the purplish skin of Dylan's left cheek, then lifted it. 'No blanching,' he murmured. 'Yes, six to twenty-four, that would be my estimate.'

'Except, of course,' Graham said, 'that he was seen alive about nine thirty last night, so that would mean . . .'

Tuck nodded along with him. 'Correct. We make that somewhere between six and thirteen hours. I'll have plenty more to say about that after we get him to the lab.' He got to his feet with a grunt and brushed off his knees. 'Any objection if I do that now? The sooner the sooner.'

'He's all yours,' Nate said.

'Sir?' Officer Fred was beside them. 'Merle says she remembers something about the men that were with the deceased. She says—'

'I'll talk to her,' Nate said, loping back to the bar on his long legs, with Graham striding along beside him.

Merle was sitting where they'd left her. The glass of water that Nate had poured was still full. As far as Graham could see, she hadn't moved an inch.

'It just came back to me, Chief. I don't know why I didn't remember before.'

'That's OK, Merle,' Nate said, pulling out a chair, turning it around, and straddling it. Graham remained standing. 'What do you remember?'

'Well, the two fellas that were with him? I remember that they struck me as kind of Mutt and Jeff. The one was ten feet tall – well, maybe six-six or six-seven. The other one was a weird little guy, all wrinkly, like a funny little monkey.'

'Lou Sapio,' Graham murmured under his breath.

Eleven

By the ninth-hole turnaround, practice-round play had backed up. Some of the delay had come as a result of the hoary tradition of allowing spectators to approach the players for autographs between holes, a perk that would not be available during tournament play, when security would be tighter.

Mostly, however, it was those infamous domed greens that were to blame. On the 166-yard par-three ninth, Lee and Roger had just watched Dave Hazelton drive straight from the tee on to the green (against Roger's express earlier counseling) to within three yards of the hole, only to see his ball roll slowly down the far side of the green and disappear into the nearby foliage. It took him two strokes to get back on the green, and then his first putt came within two inches of the hole, paused as if to tease him, and then, slowly at first, but picking up speed, it rolled twenty-five feet down the other side of the green, by which time Dave was talking to himself. In the end he four-putted, giving him seven strokes, an appalling quadruple-bogey.

At least Roger got a kind of grim satisfaction out of it. 'Maybe now he'll think I just might know what I'm talking about,' he said to Lee. He tried to catch Dave's eye to signal his displeasure, but Dave wasn't having any of it. Red-faced and tight-lipped, and even more cadaverous than usual, he was single-mindedly staring at his shoelaces as if it was all their fault.

As for Roger and Lee, they had started off wonderfully, playing the first two holes at one under par, but then Roger's game had headed south. His distance wasn't a problem, but his ball seemed to find every hot spot on the course: trees, rough, and sand. Fortunately, there weren't any water hazards for him to hit into. In any case, since she had the alternate shots, it was Lee who had to do all the scrambling; the difficult task of pitching, or chipping, or sand-blasting the ball out of trouble and back into a decent position on the fairway . . . so Roger could plunk it into the next bunker.

But this particular cloud had a silver lining. When it got through to her that she was spending more time worrying about Roger Finley's game than her own, the absurdity of the situation made her smile and went a long way toward steadying her nerves. She thought it best, however, not to mention this happy consequence to him.

His problems were a real puzzle. Stance, swing, and follow-through were as elegant, effortless, and impeccable as ever, but the ball didn't seem to know it. It wasn't that he was outrageously wild, spraying shots over into the next fairway. His game, she guessed, was something like fifteen or twenty per cent off, but the botches and mis-hits were consistent; perhaps once in ten tries would he hit what Lee would call a Roger-Finley-class shot. And in a game as finely honed as Roger's, that threw him completely off his stride. It was enough to make for extremely heavy going, and though neither of them had talked about it, they both knew the outlook for tomorrow was getting bleaker by the minute. Whatever it was that was dogging him, it wasn't going to be cured overnight.

With a twenty-minute delay ahead, Roger went off to grab a hot dog, while Lee decided to stay there. For one thing, she'd have a chance to watch some of the British team tee off, giving her a first look at some of the competition. For another, she wanted to play safe with her stomach, which was iron-coated (in Graham's words) under normal circumstances, but a tad sensitive when she was on edge. However, she needed some sustenance, so she'd had Lou pick up one of the energy bars available for the players at a table set up for them as they left the ninth. He was sitting off to the side on the end of her bag, within the roped-off area out of the reach of the spectators. When she joined him, he tossed her the foil-wrapped bar.

'Did you get one for yourself?' She perched beside him, on the supported top end of the bag.

'Yeah, would I pass up a chance to eat pink glue?'

'It's good for you, Lou. Low-carb, high protein, no trans-fatty acids.'

'Pink glue,' he muttered.

She opened the bar and took a bite. 'You do have a point, though.'

Nearby, one of the marshals held up a 'Quiet' sign. The happy chatter of the crowd behind the ropes died down, while one of the Brits, looking smashing in plus fours and argyle socks, teed off.

The tenth was the longest hole on the course, a 578-yard par-four. Some of the big hitters could reach the green in two if they could start with a long draw that landed the ball well left of center. Lee held her breath as the player swung. The shot was gorgeous. Even now, after seeing so many thousands of balls take to the air, she was moved by the beauty of a soaring, well-struck shot against the blue sky.

Lee groaned. 'He hits further than Jordie Webster, and he sure has more control.'

'Big deal,' Lou said. 'Drive for show, putt for dough. Hey, the way we've been playing today, we could clean their clocks.' He sniffed, and the lines on his seamed face settled in more deeply. 'If we had a halfway decent partner, that is.'

Lee brightened. 'We' again. Lou wasn't much of a talker, so she usually relied on his choice of pronouns for feed-back on how well he thought she was doing.

Munching thoughtfully, she said, 'Finley's in a slump, all right. What's your take on his game?' It struck her that she probably should have asked him a long time ago. Lou was a sharp observer when he wanted to be. More than that, he had caddied for Roger's partner at Troon North, giving

71

him an entire tournament to watch him. 'What's he doing wrong?'

'What do I know?' he said. 'I was watching my guy.' Then he looked sideways at her. 'If you hear his caddie tell it, he knows, but he's not telling.'

'What? Dylan said that? When?'

'Back in Scottsdale. He wouldn't shut up.' He half-closed his eyes and twisted his mouth, imitating a drunk. 'I know zackly whum talkin' abou', I know zackly whuss wrong, I know zackly who's 'sponsible, 'n I know zackly why. Hic.' He shook his head disgustedly. 'And then last night at Duffer's he starts in all over again.'

'But what a strange thing for him to say. What do you think he meant? And why in the world wouldn't he tell Roger, if he thought he knew something that could help?'

Lou shrugged, looking as if he already regretted having said anything. Whatever else you could say about him, Lou Sapio was as close-mouthed as they came. 'Aw, the guy was just blowing hot air, just showing off. He gets a few drinks in him and he gets stupid. I don't think he's used to drinking. I'm probably a bad influence on him.'

'Still,' Lee mused, 'it's a strange thing to say.'

'Never mind Dylan,' Lou said. 'And stop worrying about Finley. You can't analyze this stuff. Finley just lost it; it happens. One year they're hot, then, just like that, they're ice-cold. Then, if they're lucky, it comes back. You just have to play through it.' He stood up and stretched. 'We better loosen up. Here comes Finley, and we're up next.'

As the round progressed, Lee had trouble getting her concentration back. Although Lou was a bottomless font of golf-related wisdom, he could be miles off the mark at times, and she was pretty sure this was one of those times. Sure, some golfers did lose their games 'just like that', and for no identifiable reason, but Roger Finley wasn't one of them.

Professional golfers, in her experience, fell into two general classes, not quite all-inclusive, but pretty nearly so. She thought of them as the mechanics and the magicians.

The mechanics concentrated on perfecting the technicalities of the swing: analyzing its every micro-motion, tearing it apart, putting it back together, and then practicing thousands of hours until every aspect of it was engraved in muscle memory and their timing was not merely split-second but split-millisecond. They were as close to perfectly ordered machines as human beings could be. And Roger Finley was the current standard-bearer.

Lee herself was a magician, or at least an apprentice magician. Like Sam Snead or Babe Didrikson Zaharias (but not, alas, in their league), she had come to the game as a natural. Possibly more gifted to begin with, the magicians played intuitively. Plenty of time on the range, yes, but the last thing in the world they wanted to do was to pick apart their swings to see how they worked. To Lee, her golf swing was everything; it was like a gift hen that could lay years of golden eggs for her, and she had no intention of cutting it open to see how it did it.

Consequently, Lee and the other magicians were more laid-back about their games, trusting more to their natural rhythms and timing. But because natural rhythms tended to ebb and flow, it was the magicians whose games tended to fall apart – and come back together – overnight. When mechanics like Finley had trouble with their timing, or their rhythm, or their tempo, they just got their coach, went to the video analyzer, and analyzed the heck out of it until they got it back, or until age, or infirmity, or loss of the necessary drive made it impossible. But they didn't wallow for months among the also-rans, as Finley had.

So what was his problem? And what, she asked herself for the twentieth time, had his caddie meant? 'He knows, but he's not telling,' she repeated to herself. OK, forget that peculiar *he's not telling* part. But what about the rest of it? What could he know? She knew a little about Dylan Blanchard by reputation: efficient, hard-working, self-serving, ambitious, shifty. Some golfers loved him, some wouldn't touch him. But she had never heard anyone say he had any great knowledge of the principles of the golf swing. So what could he know that could possibly have escaped Finley?

Equipment.

She didn't think of it until the twelfth hole, as she walked with Finley toward the hardpan and wire-grass rough that ran along the right side of the fairway, where Roger's tee shot now lay. But when it finally struck her it stopped her in her tracks. Equipment! The slightest change in club-head alignment, in loft angle, in – in anything, and a super-honed mechanic like Finley would be thrown off. Just a matter of a few degrees or a few millimeters, but the result would be like throwing off the components of a finely machined piston engine by a few degrees or a few millimeters: it would still sound good, it would still look good . . . it just wouldn't be good.

Finley stopped when she did, and looked at her. 'What?'

This wasn't the right time or place, but she couldn't help blurting it out anyway. 'Roger, have you made any changes in your clubs these last few months?'

He peered owlishly at her. 'What in the world are you talking about?'

'Have you been using new clubs?'

'No, these are—'

'Have you had them regripped, have you had them repaired, have you—?'

'Lee, as much as I'm enjoying this conversation, do you suppose we might continue with the round? It's been slow enough as it is.'

He started walking and she hurried to catch up. 'Roger, has it occurred to you that what's wrong with your game is that something might be wrong with your clubs?'

'With my clubs?' he said blankly.

'You know . . .' She searched for an example. 'Maybe you got them regripped and they put on the wrong size. That would change your wrist action—'

He stopped again, considering.

'Something like that happened to me once,' she prattled. 'I suddenly developed this horrendous slice that I couldn't

74

do anything about. Then I realized it wasn't me, it was my—'

He began walking again, a little irritated now. 'Impossible. I have my own home workshop. I get the components from my sponsor, but then I put them together myself.'

'Well, couldn't the supplier have accidentally mislabeled the boxes?' She forced a laugh. 'Who knows, maybe a machine went screwy, and it stamped the wrong numbers on the irons? You know, a "seven" on the eight, an "eight" on the nine . . . ?' She was feeling dumber by the second.

He stared at her as if there was only one thing screwy in sight and he was looking right at it. 'What? You think I can't tell the difference between an eight-iron and a nine-iron without looking at the numbers? Please, I have enough problems without inventing any new ones. What an idea. Jeez.'

'But—' She was on the verge of telling him to talk to his caddie, of telling him what Lou had told her about Dylan, but she had a nervous-making sense of having over-stepped her bounds. By a mile.

'Sorry, Rog. Just trying to be helpful.'

'Lee, sweetheart, you'll be a *big* help if you can get us back out on to the fairway.' He summoned the ghost of a smile. 'One more time,' he added with a sigh.

Twelve

With Roger's old form making sporadic reappearances and Lee continuing her steady game, the back nine went more smoothly than the front, allowing them to finish with a not-too-embarrassing but hardly distinguished three over par. She'd gotten over the worst of her nerves by the thirteenth or so, but the tremendous pressure on her to do well, the unaccustomed, unrelenting presence of cameramen, and the equally unaccustomed jostling of the crowds, always edging closer, closer, closer, sometimes literally brushing her aside, for the glory of basking in the magic glow of Roger Finley, had utterly drained her.

Usually, when coming off the eighteenth green, Lee's mind and energy were fixed on one overarching goal: generally a cheeseburger and shake, occasionally a pizza. Today she longed for nothing more than a nap in the cool, blessed solitude of her room. She understood now why Roger had added an hour's 'quiet time' to the daily schedule following each day's post-play press conference, and she was grateful to him for it. Unfortunately for today's quiet time, however, they were already running late. Still, with a little luck she'd be able to grab a twenty-minute snooze before meeting Peg, whom she was treating to afternoon tea. She thought briefly of calling her and canceling, but she just couldn't do that to her old friend. Peg was a deep-dyed romantic at heart, and she'd been talking about the posh, celebrated daily tea on the colonnaded veranda since she'd arrived.

Even getting to the press tent was a new experience. Sure, she'd occasionally scored high enough, or done something sensational enough (or dumb enough) to warrant an invita-

76

tion from the media, but this was the first time she'd needed a team of marshals to form a running wedge to facilitate their movement through the crowd, as if they were on their way to speak to a joint session of Congress and not to a distinctly scruffy bunch of golf reporters sprawled every which way on folding chairs in a tent. The crowds were there for Roger, of course, but that didn't make it any easier on Lee.

Inasmuch as today's score wasn't official, she expected to walk right by the scoring tent, where their scorecards would be signed and turned in in the days to come, but the lead marshal held open the door flap and motioned them in. Inside were not the usual tournament officials, but four or five men, including two policemen, milling around, talking to each other. One of them, she was happy to see, was Graham, who broke off his conversation to come and meet her. Meanwhile, Roger was taken in hand by one of the others and led off to a small grouping of chairs and tables.

'Lee!' Graham's transparently pleased smile was like balm to her soul. How utterly marvelous to see this wonderful man's face light up at the sight of her. She still didn't understand why or how it had happened – what it was he saw in her – but she wasn't about to try to talk him out of it. 'How'd it go out there?'

'Fine,' she said. When Graham asked questions like that, he really didn't want to hear about the golf. And even if she told him, he wouldn't understand two thirds of it. 'I'm glad to see you. I didn't expect to, until tonight. We've hardly had two minutes together.'

'I know, I—' His enthusiastic smile faded. What she thought of as his cop's face replaced it. 'We've got a problem, Lee. You know Dylan Blanchard?'

'Sure, he's Roger's caddie.' Roger's no-show caddie. She hesitated. 'What did he do?'

'He *was* Roger's caddie.'

It took a second to sink in. 'He's . . . he's not . . . ?'

He nodded. 'Dead, yes.'

Inexplicably, the first thing that jumped into her tired

77

mind was Too-Tall Jack's story of the caddie who took a nap in front of a heavy roller. She blanched. 'An accident?'

'I wish it was. No, somebody clobbered him and dumped him in an alley behind a bar, in the village.'

She was irrationally relieved. Clobbered, shot, stabbed, poisoned . . . anything sounded better than being flattened. How strangely the mind worked. But a moment later, the full weight of what he'd said landed on her. 'Somebody murdered him?'

Understanding that Roger was being told the same thing, she looked back over her shoulder toward the tables. Roger was sitting with a weathered, lanky man in chinos, who reminded her of an old cowpuncher. The cowpuncher was doing all the talking. Roger sat staring at him, occasionally giving his head a half-shake, as if he couldn't quite take in – or didn't want to take in – what was being said.

'How terrible,' Lee said to Graham. 'Do you know who did it?'

'Not yet,' he said, and filled her in on what they did know, as well as the fact that he was working on the case with Police Chief Oates, the man in chinos.

'So, you're going to be working on a murder,' she mused. 'That wasn't what you bargained for when you signed on with the tour.'

'No,' he said, surprising her with a smile, 'and of course I'm sorry there was a murder; I wish there hadn't been. On the other hand, as long as there was one, I'm kind of glad it happened on my watch. Security logistics can be on the dull side.'

She smiled back at him. 'You'll always be a cop, won't you?'

'Fraid so.' He put out a hand and gently tapped the engagement ring on her finger, which she'd discovered by almost choking on it in a cardboard cup of caffé latte at a ferry terminal one memorable day in Rhode Island; an absurdly romantic memory that could still make her laugh. 'Want to re-think this?' he asked. 'It's still not too late to change your mind.'

'Not a chance, pal. You're in this up to your ears. There

is no exit-strategy option.' They looked fondly at each other for a few seconds, and Lee said, 'I'd better go over and talk to Roger. He looks like he's in shock.'

'Sure, go ahead. Oh, and where can I find Lou?'

'He'll be in the bag room. It's in the basement of the clubhouse. Why?'

'We'll want to talk to him. He was with Dylan at the bar last night.'

'You don't think that Lou had anything to do with—'

'No, of course not. But he was one of the last people to see him alive. I'd like to know what they talked about.'

'I can tell you that,' she said, 'or at least some of it. Dylan was talking about . . .' She paused, thinking. 'Graham, this might have something to do with the murder!' she said excitedly. 'Dylan claimed he knew what was wrong with Roger's golf game but was keeping it to himself!'

'Uh-huh,' Graham said blandly, waiting for more.

'Well, couldn't that be why he was killed?'

He peered at her, looked away, and peered at her again. 'Why?'

'Well, because . . . because he might have . . .' She faltered a second time and ran dry. 'OK, I don't know, exactly, but don't you think there could be a connection?'

'Possible. I'll work on it,' he said with about as much conviction as if she'd told him there might be a connection to the man in the moon. 'I'd better go get Lou now.'

He started off, then turned back to her. 'We're going to have some time together tonight, aren't we?'

'Absolutely. You're my escort for the entire evening: reception, dinner, and gala.'

He rolled his eyes. 'You superstars sure lead a heck of a life. I don't think I've ever been to a gala.'

'I think it's just another word for party.'

'Ah, thank you for explaining that. But what I meant was, are we going to have some time together alone any time soon?'

She smiled at him. 'I'd like to see you try and get out of it.'

Chief Oates had gone on to talk with somebody else, leaving Roger alone at the table, slumped on a folding chair and looking utterly stricken. He turned dully as Lee came up. 'Did you hear?' he whispered.

She nodded and sat down beside him. 'It's awful.'

'They . . . they bashed in his head. Why would anyone do something like that?'

There wasn't much she could say to that, so she did her best to convey silent commiseration.

'What am I going to do, Lee? Without Dylan . . .' With a shrug and a shake of his head, he let the sentence die away.

Why, he was like a child, she thought. With this happening on top of everything else, all his props had been knocked from under him.

'Now listen, Rog,' she said soothingly. 'The caddie you had today—'

He nodded. 'Gabe, yes.'

'Well, he was pretty good, wasn't he?'

'Yes, sure, but he doesn't know my game, he doesn't understand the problems I've been having.'

'He knew the terrain, didn't he? He didn't give you any bad advice, did he? He never handed you the wrong club, did he?'

'Well, no, but the thing is—'

'All right, he's not Dylan, he doesn't know your every whim, but we have to make the best of a bad situation, don't we? Sign him up before he gets away. This is an important tournament. We're playing for the United States. We have to do the best we – what?'

He had been looking at her with a quizzical smile as she spoke. 'Do you remember,' he asked, 'that the first time I spoke with you on the phone, I told you that you might wind up having to carry me?'

She nodded.

'Well, this wasn't quite what I had in mind, but it seems to me that's just what you're doing.'

She felt herself flush. Had she gone too far? 'Golly, Rog, I'm only—'

'And doing a darn good job of it too,' he said. He seemed much more in control of himself now, more centered, more like the old Roger. He stood up and looked earnestly down at her. 'Lee, thank God I have you on the team.'

Now it was his turn to look flustered and embarrassed and he turned quickly away. 'I'd better go find Gabe.'

She sat watching him go. Life was sure strange, she thought. If someone had told her a month ago that she'd be sitting in Pinehurst giving moral support to her playing partner (who just happened to be Roger Finley) after the murder of his caddie . . .

Graham came back into the tent with Lou and walked him over to Chief Oates. Lou had a look in his eyes that Lee didn't like: glowering, recalcitrant, balky. She was close enough to hear their conversation.

Oates: 'You're Louis Sapio?'

Lou: 'If that's what it says on my card.'

Oates: 'You caddy for Lee Ofsted?'

Lou: 'That's what they tell me.'

Graham: 'He caddies for Lee Ofsted.'

Oates: 'You were with Dylan Blanchard at Duffer's last night?'

Lou: Shrug.

Lee rolled her eyes. Lou could be the most infuriating person in the world. He wasn't answering because he didn't like being ordered around, he didn't particularly care for the police, and he was constitutionally just plain pigheaded when he got it into his mind to be. But couldn't he see how it was making him look?

Oates: 'Who else was with you?'

Lou: Silence.

Oates: 'Jack Odiorne? The one they call Too-Tall Jack?'

Lou: 'If you say so.'

Oates: 'What did you talk about?'

Lou: 'Private conversation. Personal stuff.'

Graham: 'Lou, just answer the questions, will you? Somebody's been murdered. We have to ask all these questions, you can see that.'

81

Lou: Shrug. 'I didn't kill him.'

Oates: 'Well, I tell you what, Mr Sapio. If you'd rather talk down at the station, I'll be happy to accommodate you.'

Lou: 'Whatever.'

Lou! Lee shrieked inwardly. What is the *matter* with you? She jumped up and went to the three men as Oates began to signal to an officer to cart Lou off. 'Chief, I'm Lee Ofsted, maybe I can help. Can I talk to him for a minute?'

Seen from up close, Chief Oates didn't seem quite so hard. He had a folksy, friendly gleam to his eyes and even a look of amusement playing at the corners of his mouth. He'd seen Lou Sapios before. 'Be my guest,' he said.

She dragged her caddie off to the side. 'Lou, what are you doing? Are you out of your mind?'

He stared obstinately at the grass floor of the tent, his chin practically on his chest. 'What do they want from me? I don't know nothing.'

'I know that. But you have to answer his questions.'

'I don't like his attitude.'

No, but he just loves yours, she thought. 'Lou. Now listen. Look at me.'

His head came slowly up.

'I need you,' she said. 'I can't have you in trouble with the police. You're my anchor out there. You keep me sane. Please just answer their questions. For my sake. I need you.' She had no trouble making it sound convincing; every word was heartfelt.

Lou's mulish expression showed signs of breaking down into something closer to sheepish. His narrow shoulders went up, then down. Lee could see that he was touched by what she'd said.

'OK, Lee,' he growled, looking away.

'Thank you,' she said. Thankyouthankyouthankyouthank-you.

The press conference, which she'd expected to take ten or fifteen minutes – it was a practice round, after all, totally non-competitive – ate up an hour, with all eight Americans sitting up front answering questions, or, in Dougal's case, giving lectures on golf theory and practice. If Roger hadn't been in a monosyllabic sulk, it would have taken even longer, but in any case the idea of a nap was now history. Not only that, but she was ten minutes late for the tea with Peg.

Slipping on her sunglasses against the outside glare, she managed to be the first of the team members out of the tent and to snag one of the few marshals still around for a quick cart ride to the hotel.

'OK if I let you off here, Miss Ofsted?' he asked a couple of minutes later. 'I have to hustle back to Number Three.'

'Sure, thanks for the lift.'

He had dropped her off at the head of the circular driveway that led to the columned port cochère, so that when she turned toward the Carolina Hotel she found herself looking at the grand old building across a wide expanse of mani-cured lawn bordered by majestic trees. It was, she realized, the first time she'd really looked at the place. Last night and this morning she'd been too excited and preoccupied to take it in. And when she'd played here a couple of years ago, she'd never come within sight of the resort itself. The Motel 6 she'd stayed in with the other 'rabbits' was way out on Airport Road, and after she'd failed to make the Monday cut she'd slunk out of town to the next tourna-ment, sharing a car with three other losers, and in no mood to take in the local sights.

Looking at the lovingly maintained white Victorian façade – it had gone up in 1901 – and the grand, glowing copper cupola of the main building now, she was struck afresh by the remarkableness of just where she was, of the hallowed ground on which she stood as an invited, full-fledged partici-pant in one of the sport's premier events.

Pinehurst.

The 'Temple of American Golf', it liked to call itself, and it could make a pretty good case for it. Just about every serious golfer who'd ever picked up a club had played here and walked the Carolina's halls, from the legendary pros (like Harry Vardon, Ben Hogan, and Babe Didrikson

Zaharias), to golfing presidents and generals (Gerald Ford, Dwight Eisenhower), to Golden-Era Hollywood stars (Bing Crosby, Douglas Fairbanks), to ordinary – but well-heeled – weekend duffers who considered Pinehurst a pilgrimage destination.

A few weeks ago she hadn't known all this. She knew it now because she had spent most of an evening gobbling up the handsome *History of Pinehurst* volume that had come in one of the UPS packages, along with the outfits. The funny thing about this 'Temple of Golf', she had learned, was that when the resort had been laid out in the late nineteenth century, golf had been an afterthought, and even then it had come about more or less by accident. Pinehurst had been built as a winter resort for wealthy northerners. The early visitors – the Rockefellers, the Morgans – had come to ride and to play tennis and croquet, and even to attend the new shooting school run by Annie Oakley herself.

The remoteness of the site in the sparsely populated pine hills of North Carolina had required the creation of a dairy farm to provide milk and cream to the hotel's guests and to the residents of the little village that was springing up nearby. This was at about the time that golf was beginning to catch on in America, and a few years after the establishment of Pinehurst, harassed dairy workers started complaining that some of the guests were frightening the cows (not good for milk production) by tramping through the dairy's pasture – the only sizeable open space in 5,000 acres of pine trees – in order to follow a little ball around and whack it with a stick.

With visions of barren milkers and soured cream, a little land was cleared in self-defense and a primitive nine holes were laid out. The 'course' caught on beyond anyone's expectations, and within twenty years there were four full eighteen-hole courses, all acknowledged as classics. Pinehurst's reputation as a modern golf Mecca had never been in doubt since, not that the old pre-golf, antebellum traditions of the croquet days weren't still gracefully maintained. People drank mint juleps. Elaborate afternoon teas were served on spotless white linen on the porticoed veranda, among potted palms and hanging flower baskets.

One of which she was now on her way to sample. It was, as a matter of fact, the first afternoon tea she'd ever gone to and she was aware of a ripple of self-doubt as she climbed the wide, green-carpeted steps. Antebellum culinary traditions were not Lee's forte and she knew it. She was more at home with a cheeseburger and fries than she was with a petit four, whatever a petit four was (or were). When she spotted Peg at a choice corner table, her trepidation increased. Not only was she seated with a dandyish man in a Navy blazer and dark tie, but Peg herself was sporting an elegant, wide-brimmed straw hat decorated with roses, and wearing a flattering, very un-Peg-like, softly draped summer dress. She looked as if she'd been born to afternoon teas, which in a way she had.

Looking anxiously down at her own sweaty golf shirt and grass-stained slacks, Lee was on the verge of dashing up to her room, late as she was, and changing into one of her new dresses – until she got hold of herself and remembered what this tea for Peg was all about. Peg Fiske was the ultimate golf fan – golf nut was closer to it – and with her money and prestige she could have been hobnobbing with the top stars on the tour, but instead she gave her wholehearted psychological support to Lee's not-quite-star-quality career. And if Lee had let her, it would have been financial support too. Peg wasn't going to feel any differently about her if her clothes were a little grungy.

Besides, Lee was a star today, even if by the luck of the draw. The waiter who led her to the table beamed with pleasure at being of service, and other diners on the veranda nudged each other as she passed, and threw her waves and thumbs-up signs. A couple of people even clapped, which made her feel silly. Would any of them have recognized her if she wasn't in her Stewart team outfit? She doubted it extremely. Still, she basked in the glow of their admiration, returning the smiles as she passed and hoping they'd still be smiling at her a few days from now.

'Here's my girl!' Peg said as airily as her foghorn voice

85

would allow. The man she was with jumped cheerfully to his feet, buttoning his jacket and extending his hand. She saw now that he was twinkle-eyed and ruddy-faced, an outdoorsy kind of man, like Hollywood's idea of a country squire. Lee didn't know much about clothes, men's or women's, but she could tell his blazer hadn't come off the shelf at Sears.

'Lee, this is Burton Fischer, as I'm sure you know.'

'Mr Fischer – of course!' Lee said enthusiastically, extending her hand. 'I'm so pleased to meet you.'

He laughed delightedly. 'Not nearly as pleased as I am to meet you! And call me Burt.'

When he grabbed her hand and pumped it, his palm was as hard and callused as her father's after twenty years of laying cement. 'I have to run off now, ladies – busy, busy, busy – but as I was telling the lovely Mrs Fiske, I hope you can join me in the lounge for one of their mint juleps – have you tried them? They're marvelous, the best on the planet. Say forty-five minutes from now? That should give you time to fully enjoy the wonderful tea they offer here. I wish I could stay myself, but opportunity calls – no rest for the wicked—' He gave her a lively smile. 'And I hope, when we're done talking, you'll find that opportunity has knocked for you as well.'

'Whew,' she said when Fischer had scurried off out of hearing, 'that man is a talker. I think he got that all out on one breath. Who is he, anyway? Does he work for the resort?'

'Of course not, are you joking? He's one of the big tournament sponsors; he has his own hospitality tent here, he—' Peg stared at her. 'Are you honestly telling me you don't know who Burt Fischer is?'

'Yes.'

'You never heard of him? The name is completely unfamiliar?'

Lee thought for a moment. 'I think so.'

'Then what was all that flibberty-gibberty "Mr Fischer . . . of course! I'm so pleased to meet you!"? You were practically batting your eyelashes at him.'

'I do not bat my eyelashes,' Lee said primly. 'And the reason that I sounded as if I knew who he was is that you made it sound as if I ought to know, so I thought I better not take a chance on offending him.'

Peg threw back her head to let loose one of her belly laughs, bringing startled looks from the people at nearby tables. 'Lee, it astonishes me to say it, but I think you're beginning to figure out how to get along in this world. If this keeps up, I think you may actually be dry behind the ears before too much longer.'

'If that's supposed to be a compliment—'

'What about Comet Golf? Does the name ring a bell? Have you ever heard of the Comet Sweetspot irons, the first truly new golf club since the invention of the cavity-back club head?'

'Well, of course I have. I'm not completely—'

'And who do you suppose is the ex-Georgia-Tech physics professor who came up with the concept in his garage, who now owns the company, and who is respected by one and all as one of today's great geniuses of golf-club design?'

'Um . . . gee, I can't . . .'

'Guess. I'll give you a hint. His initials are BF. Does that help at all?'

Lee was laughing by now. 'It wouldn't happen to be Burt Fischer, by any chance?'

'It would, indeed. And now he wants—' She frowned. 'What made you think he worked for the resort?'

'Well, the way he talked about it – the "marvelous" mint juleps, the "wonderful" teas.'

'Oh, that's just his manner. The man does tend toward hyperbole. I've known him for years. But what did you think he was talking about with that bit about opportunity knocking?'

'I had no idea. I thought maybe he was going to offer me an assistant-pro job here.' She grimaced. 'If I mess up badly enough in the tournament, I might be ready to take it.'

'First, you are not going to mess up in the tournament.

Second, he has something a lot better than an assistant-club-pro's job up his sleeve. Lee—' She leaned earnestly forward and lowered her voice. '—you know what he was asking me before you got here? He wanted to know if you had an endorsement contract. He asked if I thought you'd be interested in endorsing the Lady Sweetspots, a new line he's developing. That's what he wants to talk about.' She sat back, aglow with excitement. 'What do you think about that?'

'What I think,' Lee said smiling, 'is that it's absolutely terrific to have a friend who can be made so obviously happy about a good turn coming my way. Thank you for that, Peg.'

Lee had never seen Peg blush before, but she saw it now. Peg pretended to fuss with her hat. 'I was just—' For once she seemed at a loss for words, but the arrival of their waiter saved her. He removed Peg's teapot and set out fresh ones for both of them, and then, from his cart, loaded a three-tiered silver tray with a beautifully arranged array of tiny sandwiches, scones, and pastries that Lee couldn't name.

'Which ones are the petits fours?' she asked to give the still-blushing Peg something neutral to talk about.

'These.' She pointed at a group of tiny square cakes iced with marzipan and decorated with delicate designs in chocolate piping. 'And those are napoleons, and those are – well, I guess those are caviar canapés, and those are cucumber and cheese, and those . . .'

Lee suddenly realized that her hunger was no longer in abeyance. She snapped up two shrimp and two cucumber and cheese canapés in quick order, doing her best not to wolf them down in single gulps, and followed with a swallow of tea.

'Well, if he offers you a contract, are you going to accept?' Peg asked. 'And make sure you try one of those little Swedish Dream Cookies – sinful little things that melt in your mouth, filled with pecans and coconut.'

Lee complied with the second request first. 'That depends on how much he offers,' she said, chewing happily. 'It would have to be, oh, at least, oh . . . well, at least in the low three figures, although if he throws in a set of clubs I might settle for the upper two figures.'

They both burst out laughing at that, and Lee was still chuckling when it hit her that Dylan's death had completely fled from her mind. She put down the cream puff that had been about to go the route of the canapés and briefly filled Peg in on his demise.

Peg's response was anything but sympathetic. 'What? Of all the miserable timing! Here we are at the world's most important tournament—'

Lee smiled. Peg, loyal as ever, had just dismissed the Ryder Cup, the Masters, the US Open, the British Open, and the PGA Championship in a single breath.

'—and this idiotic young man goes out and gets himself killed?'

'Well, it's not exactly as if it was his fault,' Lee said. 'Somebody killed him.'

'He was murdered?' With a salmon-and-cream-cheese canapé poised three inches from her lips, Peg stared open-mouthed at her. 'Wow. Do they know who did it?'

Lee shook her head. 'Here's what I know.' She told Peg what Lou had related to her about Dylan, and about her suggestion that Dylan's supposed knowledge might have been related to his death.

'Possible,' Peg said with about as much enthusiasm as Graham had mustered at the idea. Then, thinking that she might have hurt Lee's feelings, she added, 'I mean, it's certainly something to think about, something to take into consideration, something—'

'OK, OK,' Lee said. 'So it's a lousy idea.' She lathered whipped cream and strawberry jam on a scone.

Peg laughed. 'Let's just say you've had better ones. Look, let's forget about poor Dylan. There's nothing we can do about him, anyway. Come on, let's finish up this "absolutely superb" repast – which it is – and go see how many millions Burt Fischer wants to offer you.'

Lee smiled as well as she could with a mouth filled with scone. 'I'm for that!'

Thirteen

The Pinehurst Resort was about golf, and the Ryder Cup Lounge was its beating heart. Every great golfer of the twentieth century had eaten or drunk there, and the hunter-green walls and softly lit glass cases were filled with mementos – photos, clubs, even bags – some from the 1999 US Open, but most from the great Ryder Cup tournament held there in 1951. Topics of conversation other than golf were permitted but not openly encouraged.

'You can practically smell a hundred years of history here,' a thrilled Lee said at the entry, then wrinkled her nose. 'Unfortunately, you can smell a hundred years of cigars too.'

'Well, you know golfers,' Peg said. 'They love their stogies. At least the ones in here are expensive.' She pointed to a humidor near the bar. 'Those are Davidoffs,' she said respectfully.

'That doesn't make them smell any better,' Lee muttered.

Peg scoffed. 'Don't be ridiculous. Expensive is always better than cheap.'

Most of the tables were occupied, but there were clearly two focuses of interest. In a niche near the bar, under one of the Victorian wall lamps, three tables had been placed together and at them sat Roger Finley and the whole American team other than Lee. (Roger had suggested they all go for a snack and a reprise of play after the practice round, but by then Lee had already made her appointment with Peg.) Their plates had been cleared but they were deep in earnest, quiet conversation – all except for the thick-bodied, well-dressed, middle-aged, carefully made-up woman beside Roger, who was doing her best to look fascinated but was failing miserably. That was Marie Finley, Roger's wife, whom Lee had met for the first time the previous evening. None of the other spouses or friends were there, but then Lee had already heard a snide sports reporter refer to Marie as 'the Velcro Wife' because of her propensity for sticking close to her famous husband at tournaments, never letting him out of her sight if she could possibly help it.

Lee could tell from their gestures that the subject, naturally enough, was golf. The people at nearby tables were obviously delighted to be in the same room with them but were too discreet to eavesdrop in any direct sense. However, there was little talk going on at them, and everybody's head seemed to tilt just slightly in the players' direction. If they'd been dogs, Lee thought with a smile, their ears would have been standing up and facing that way.

The other center of attention was at the bar itself, where Burton Fischer, propped on a stool with his back to the bar and his elbows leaning on it, was happily holding forth to half-a-dozen rapt men on the much-overlooked importance of 'variable inertia-determined shaft flex' to the average weekend golfer.

'What's variable inertia-determined shaft flex?' Peg asked Lee as they approached.

'Beats me,' Lee said. 'I don't know, and I don't want to know.'

'Well, boys, thanks for letting me harangue you, but my lovely companions have arrived now,' he said grandly when he caught sight of the two of them. 'Now, you stop by our hospitality tent any time. Walt Ebell is the best fitter in the business and can answer any questions you have. He knows more about golf equipment than I do.' The twinkly smile popped forth. 'Well, almost. Oh, and if you happen to decide to go for a set of Sweetspots – a decision that, speaking entirely objectively, I heartily endorse; you'll never regret it – you tell Walt I sent you myself. That'll be good for a fifteen per cent discount.'

'It's a little crowded in here,' he said as his listeners left,

91

murmuring their appreciation. 'What do you say we just sit at the bar? We can kind of sit at the corner here,' he said, waving them to the stools beside him with Lee between them. He signaled the bartender, got his attention, said, 'Dolph? Any time,' and looked from one of them to the other. 'Well, well.' He rat-a-tatted his hands on the bar for no reason that Lee could see, other than that he was a man who didn't like sitting still. Lee noticed now that he was wearing the kind of shirt that had a white collar and a blue body, with a little pin that ran through the collar points to keep his tie in place. And he was wearing cufflinks shaped like woods; three-woods, she thought. All very old-fashioned and yet stylish.

'Did you see those poor fellas? I just spent twenty minutes trying to explain to them that custom-fitting clubs is more important to the everyday duffer than it is to the pros. Am I right about that, Lee?'

'Well—'

'Sure I'm right. A player like you, expertly fitted clubs will fine-tune your game, take two strokes, maybe three strokes off. But you know as well as I do that you can grab any old used five-iron right out of a bin at Goodwill and belt the ball a mile. And belt it straight, too. Am I right?'

'Well—'

'But a weekend golfer, hell's bells, good, properly fitted clubs can turn them from absolute hackers who never know where the ball is going into damn decent golfers, pardon my French. Oh, I got 'em convinced, all right, they all believe it now, but it won't last, you can take my word on that.'

'I'm not so sure,' said Peg. 'I got the impression they were on their way en masse to talk to your man Walt right now.'

'Yes, but when they think about how much a new, properly fitted set of clubs costs, they'll think again. For half the price of a set of Sweetspot woods and irons – even with that fifteen per cent discount, which doesn't leave me a whole lot of profit, I might add – they'll remember that they can buy twenty gimcrack straps, and pulleys, and braces, and torture devices, each of which is guaranteed to solve all their difficulties. Not that any of them have ever worked for them before. But they never learn, the poor boobs. When, if they just got the right club with the right fit – the right fit for them – they'd be so far ahead . . .' He shook his head and let the sentence fade away.

Lee couldn't help glancing with some amusement at Peg, who had a garage filled with every golf gadget known to man. It was a never-ending source of amazement that a hardheaded, down-to-earth, eminently sensible business-woman like Peg could be so judgment-impaired when it came to golf. Fischer had hit her problem right on the head. Like the other 'poor boobs' he'd mentioned, she seemed truly to believe that there had to be some untried device out there, if only she could find it – some contraption that kept your hips from turning in advance of your shoulders (or vice-versa), or a golf club that made rude noises or collapsed into pieces if you swung on the wrong plane – that would turn her from the thirty-eight handicapper she was to a smooth-swinging scratch player.

The eternal search for The Secret, Lee thought. Only there wasn't any magic bullet. Just hard work, dedication, instruction, hours upon hours out on the range, decent clubs, and – if you were going to make it to the big time, a healthy serving of natural, God-given talent.

Peg, with her lips pursed, and determinedly avoiding Lee's look, replied somewhat coolly to Fischer's monologue. 'I suppose so.'

Fischer took no offense. 'I know so,' was his hearty response. 'Ah, here we are. Thank you, Dolph!'

They watched as the bartender, in bow tie and floral vest, set down three tall, frosted glasses of amber-colored liquor and shaved ice garnished with heavenly smelling mint leaves. Fischer rubbed his hands together – his palms made a clean, rustly sound – and lifted his glass.

'To success, ladies.'

'To success,' they echoed. The julep looked so much like iced, minted tea that Lee gulped rather than sipped and immediately realized that it packed quite a wallop. One of these, followed by anything alcoholic at the upcoming cock-tail party, and she'd be in no condition to walk tomorrow, let alone play.

'And, I hope,' Fischer continued, looking meaningfully at Lee, 'to the beginning of a happy and fruitful associa-tion.' He put down his drink, cleared his throat, and put on what he apparently considered his serious business face. 'I watched you quite carefully out on the course today, Lee – I may call you Lee? – and let me tell you, I was impressed. More than impressed. I don't know why you haven't already signed on the bottom line with some lucky equipment maker. How do I know you haven't? Because I've looked into it.'

'Well, actually—'

'Actually, I believe I do know why. It's because you have enough integrity – and how I wish I could say the same thing about all your colleagues – to refuse to endorse a product that you wouldn't willingly use yourself and honestly, sincerely recommend to others. Am I right or am I right?'

'Yes, well, I suppose—'

'And I'm not going to be modest, Lee. People have called me a lot of things, but "modest" isn't one of them.'

'I'll vouch for that,' Peg said.

He frowned at that, but only slightly, set his glass on the bar – how in the world had he managed to drink almost all of it while talking non-stop? She couldn't remember seeing him lift it to his lips. 'I think I have that product for you, Lee. In fact I know I do. What do you say?' He leaned forward, eyes dancing. 'Think we can do ourselves a deal? Who's your agent?'

'I – I hardly know what to say,' Lee said. She was thor-oughly flustered. The relentless barrage of words, the excite-ment at her first serious endorsement offer (and how much was he going to offer?), the alcohol rattling around her brain, the impossible-to-put-down thought that she, Lee Ofsted, was sitting in the Ryder Cup Lounge as a member of America's Stewart Cup team, talking to a famous equipment-maker about . . . about . . .

'I'm flattered,' she blurted, 'and I'm really interested in talking about this, but . . .'

Peg, who had been wearing a happy, tranquil smile throughout Fischer's speechifying, choked on her julep and stared at her. But? *But???*

'. . . but not now, not till after the tournament. If I play well and you're still interested in talking, I'll be glad to put you in touch with my agent.'

Now it was her turn to avoid Peg's eye. For it never ceased to amaze Peg that Lee had yet to take on a sports agent. Lee herself had to admit that she was being stubborn and perhaps silly about it, but she was determined to make some real success of her own before she hired some hotshot to go around trying to make deals for her. Anyway, if she did play well here at Pinehurst, she wasn't going to have any trouble landing an agent to talk to Burt Fischer.

Fischer looked at her with warm approval and lifted his glass to her. 'Well said, young woman. There's that integrity shining through again. All right, I'll take you at your word, but I don't have the least doubt that you'll do very well indeed.' He clinked glasses with them both. Lee took a gingerly sip and set her glass down on the bar.

Fischer, having emptied his glass, signaled for another, inquiring with his eyes if the women wanted theirs refreshed. Both said no.

Peg took a long swallow, and when she put down her glass, Lee noted a familiar, avid gleam in her eye: the old hacker-searching-for-the-holy-grail look. 'Burt, I don't doubt what you say about fitting, but I've been fitted by my local pro—'

'With Comet Sweetspots?'

'Ah . . . no. With Callaways.'

He sniffed. 'Well, Callaways aren't too bad,' he allowed.

'And I can't honestly say that the personal fitting helped my game that much.'

'Well, I wouldn't want to say anything against your pro, but I can't help but wonder what kind of technology he had . . .' And he was off and running on computer chips that could compute swing speed down to the yard, on 'harmonic loft adjustments' and – of course – on the incomparable importance of 'variable inertia-determined shaft flex'.

Peg was fascinated, but Lee's thoughts were wandering; so much so that she asked out loud the question that had been at the back of her mind since her conversation with Roger on the twelfth fairway. 'Burt, I know you said that proper fitting isn't that critical to a pro's game—'

'I didn't say that, not by any means. I said it was good for a few strokes. Are you going to sit there and tell me you wouldn't sell your soul for the advantage of two strokes on any given Sunday?'

'I just might,' she said, smiling. 'Make me an offer. But let me ask you this: do you think that misfitting could have a greater effect? Could poorly fitted clubs, or the wrong clubs in general, ruin a professional golfer's game?'

He cocked his head and grinned at her. He had now finished half his second julep and Lee wondered if he wasn't a little tipsy. 'You wouldn't be thinking, by any chance, about a man who shall remain nameless, but who happens to be the captain of the American team?'

Lee was startled. She hadn't realized that she was being that obvious. 'No, no, of course not, I was just – well, I was merely asking a hypothetical – I was just—'

At which point, Roger and the team – Ginger, Jordie, Dave Hazelton, Dinny, Dougal, and Toni – came past the bar on their way out. Marie, as usual, was holding tight to Roger's arm. 'Well, did you get her signed up?' a smiling Roger asked Burt, with a convivial wink at Lee.

'No, she's playing hard to get.' Burt smiled crookedly up at Roger; yes, he was a little tipsy, all right. 'However, this young woman thinks she knows exactly what it is that's been giving you trouble.'

Lee did her best to disappear into her stool. 'I didn't really—'

'She thinks you need a good fitting, preferably with a set of Comet Sweetspots. Speaking with total objectivity, I couldn't agree more.'

The others stiffened, but when Roger laughed and said,

'You know, she just might be right,' they relaxed and laughed too. Lee smiled up at Roger and tried to indicate with a set of facial contortions that Burt, of course, was only kidding; she had never said any such thing.

Roger understood and made a small motion with his free hand (the one not pinned down by Marie) dismissing the matter entirely and going on to something else. 'Lee, we're due in front of the conference center in five minutes for another group photo, and we go straight from there to the Golf League reception in our honor, and then straight from there to dinner. Now, it's all casual dress, but all the same – no offense, sweetie – you might want to think about changing . . .' He finished with another one of his self-explanatory gestures at her rumpled, sweat-stained outfit.

Lee looked down at herself. 'Oh, my God!' she exclaimed, jumping up. 'Five minutes?'

But it was twenty minutes before she showed up for the picture-taking, and understandably enough, people were looking a little impatient. Roger visibly restrained himself from saying anything, but he was obviously miffed, looking pointedly at his wristwatch as she arrived.

'I'm sorry, everybody,' she blurted. 'I got all the way up to my room and I couldn't find my key, so I went back down to the lounge, because I thought I must have left it on the bar, but I hadn't, so I knew I must have left it in the room when I left earlier, so I had to go back down to the desk and get a duplicate, and that took . . .'

She caught a friendly warning, made with the eyes and a minuscule tilt of the head, from Ginger Rolley. Enough already. *You're not making things any better.*

Lee made herself stop prattling. 'Well, anyway, here I am.'

With a pained, fixed smile on his face, Roger waited until she'd run out of steam. 'Then perhaps we might get on with it now? Lee, you'll stand there . . . ah, no, not next to me, if you don't mind, but over by Toni.'

Fourteen

'Well, hello, there!' Lee called over the racket and over the heads of the dozen chatting people between her and the toothy woman waving so congenially at her. 'So nice to see you too!'

Whoever you are.

She strode purposefully through the milling crowd, smiling but making regretful faces and shaking her head 'no' at invitations to join various groups of players, fans, officials, and VIPs, all prattling away at a headache-inducing decibel level that followed from too much excitement, too much booze, and too many people interrupting other people with their own reminiscences of past tournaments. The lively four-piece band ('Arlo and His Jazzamaniacs'), which – unfortunately – seemed to be having too good a time to require rest breaks, wasn't helping her head either.

If this was life among the superstars, she thought, it was no bed of roses. All those toasts (most of which she'd wisely faked), all those rich hors d'oeuvres (most of which she'd unwisely accepted), all that talking – shouting, really – to people she didn't know while keeping a smile plastered on her face. And this was after the lavish party the night before! Was it like this for Roger and Ginger and the rest everywhere they went? How in the world could they do it after an exhausting round of golf? How could they do it and then go out and play another high-caliber round the next day?

Yet from what she could see, everybody else was having a good time, just getting into second gear, while Lee was thoroughly washed out; done for the day and ready to call it quits. After she'd had some quality time with Graham, that is. And it was Graham she was now searching for, with a glass of stale champagne in one hand and a liquefying mini-éclair in the other so that the army of circulating waiters wouldn't thrust anything else on her.

She'd barely had a chance to spend any time in his company, other than at dinner, when they'd made sure they were seated together, but even then, the man on her left, a bigwig in the state legislature, had monopolized her. He'd been pleasant enough, but he'd never given her an opening to turn toward Graham without being openly rude. Before and after dinner, whenever they'd managed to find a corner to themselves, either someone else would come barging over, or she'd be dragged off to talk to somebody she just had to meet. She'd catch glimpses of him in the crowd, sometimes seemingly talking to himself – which meant he was speaking into his collar-mounted microphone – or just standing there with a slightly unfocused look on his face – which meant he was listening to something through the earpiece – but mostly circulating, or exchanging brief pleasantries with the guests, or chatting with one of the four members of his security detail who were on assignment there.

He'd introduced her to a couple of them; ex-cops who reminded her of him – not in looks, because how many men were as attractive as her blue-eyed, square-jawed Graham? – but in their bearing: straightforward, self-contained, quietly authoritative, cordial but with something steely just under the surface. Straight shooters. Possibly it was a manner people in law enforcement developed, or maybe it was the set of traits that drew them to the field in the first place. Every once in a while, Graham got a little too masterful to suit her – well, he was a man, he couldn't help it – and Lee wasn't slow in telling him where to get off. But other times, when her spirits were down or she'd been through an unsettling experience, as this tournament already was and would undoubtedly continue to be, it was lovely to let herself feel like a helpless, swoony female with this big, strong, commanding presence there to protect and take care of her. It was nothing she'd ever admit to him, of course, or to Peg, or to anyone else – it wasn't very often that she admitted it to herself – but there it was all the same, and at bottom she was very glad to have it there.

He spotted her before she saw him, from twenty feet away, and, with a tilt of his head, a lift of his sandy eyebrows, and a smile, he suggested exactly what she had been about to suggest to him: how about stepping out for some fresh air . . . and some peace and quiet?

She was where she'd wanted to be all evening, wrapped in his arms, the soft nub of his camel's hair jacket against her cheek, the clean, cedary smell of his cologne in her nostrils, and her own arms wrapped tightly around his waist, under the jacket. They were at the farthest reach of the huge lawn that fronted the hotel, deep in the shadows of the tall pine trees and hollies that bordered it. Above them, branches showed deep black against the lighter black of the starlit sky. The only hints of humankind were the blessedly distant sounds of Arlo and His Jazzamaniacs and the occasional isolated waft of laughter carried to them on the breeze.

He tipped her head up, kissed her softly on the lips once, twice, three times, then nuzzled her ear and buried his face in her hair. They both sighed aloud at the same time.

'That's better,' he said. 'I needed that.' One more squeeze, and he let her go. 'Come on, I'll walk you back. You have to be up early.'

They walked hand-in-hand, slowly to make it last, and after a few steps she said casually, 'You know, I'd sure get a better night's sleep and do better tomorrow if I had some nice, strong shoulder to rest my head on. It would be a service to your country.'

'Come on, now, don't tempt me,' he said, laughing that lovely, easy laugh of his. 'I'd have to fire myself for fraternizing with the clientele.'

He said it jokingly but Graham was, if anything, even more old-fashioned than she was – even a bit of a prude sometimes (in an endearing way, of course) – and to his mind, brazenly sharing a room when either of them was working was unprofessional. Lee, also sensitive about her professional behavior, generally found it easy to agree with him. And so, at Pinehurst, Graham had a suite in one of the hotel villas, not far from Peg's, while Lee's room was in the main building, where the top floor was reserved for the players and their families.

'Graham, I'm just talking about a little friendly cuddling, that's all. No hanky-panky. I'm too beat anyway.'

'Yeah, and where have I heard that before? Not that I don't share a certain amount of the blame.'

She sighed again. 'Just my luck to be engaged to the only male in America whose sex ethics are straight out of the 1950s. All I can say is, you're lucky you're good-looking. Well, fairly good-looking.'

'It's not a question of sex ethics,' he said, 'it's a question of work ethics. An entirely different thing.' He stopped walking. 'And I can prove it. What do you say we go over to my room, away from things? I've got what has to be the most comfortable bed in the world. You'd be asleep in no time. I believe I could stretch my ethical standards that far.' He held up his hand as if he were being sworn in in court. 'No hanky-panky.'

'That sounds wonderful, but I would be asleep the minute my head hit the pillow, and Our Leader has instituted a ten thirty curfew. We'd have to set an alarm for an hour from now to get me back in time, and that would probably mess up my sleep rhythms, whatever's left of them, which wouldn't do me any good tomorrow.'

'OK,' he said. 'Okayokayokay.' He draped his arm lightly over her shoulder. 'Come on, Cinderella, I'll walk you back to the hotel before you turn into a pumpkin.'

'That's the coach. But my clothes will probably self-destruct and turn back into my usual rags at ten thirty promptly.'

She thought it would make him smile, but he only said, 'Whatever,' with the gentlest of sighs. After a few steps in silence, he began: 'You know, Lee . . .' but let the rest of the sentence hang between them, unsaid. 'Never mind.'

It was moments like this that made her nervous. She knew exactly what he'd been about to say: You know, if we were married, we wouldn't have to keep up this stupid charade.

We could just be together whenever we wanted. Or words to that effect.

She knew because he'd said it to her before, and each time she'd put him off with excuses: Yes, she wanted to be married to him too, but there was just too much going on in her life right now. The tour consumed all her excess energy, physical and mental; the playing, the practice, the planning, the strategy, the grinding travel, the unrelenting pressure. Yes, she could think of nothing more wonderful than being his wife, but she was simply at a point in her career that demanded almost all her concentration. Yes, she longed to lead a life that was truly part of his, but just not now, not yet. Once she established herself a little more, once she felt like a permanent fixture on the tour instead of having to fight her way through Monday qualifying every week, once etc., etc.

The funny thing was, it was all true, every bit of it. But that sigh of his and the self-contained silence that followed it had scared her. She sensed that they were approaching fish-or-cut-bait time. At some point he was going to get tired of waiting for her, and he was too attractive a catch to be out there forever. The fact that he was waiting, that he was even interested in her in the first place, was a continuing source of amazement. But pretty soon now, he was going to force the issue. Of course, when he did, she would . . . well, what? It was impossible to imagine not having him in her life. But it was just as impossible to imagine letting anything get in the way of the goal she'd been pursuing with such fervor for over three years now.

Impossible to get married, impossible to let him go. Great.

Why couldn't they just go on the way they were – for a while anyway? Sure, it wasn't always easy, sure, there were times when they were both miserable, but what about the wonderful times, the times when—

'Goodnight,' he said, startling her.

Without her being aware of it, they had walked up the veranda steps, through the lobby, and to the elevators. She touched his sleeve and peered into his eyes. 'Graham, I—'

'I know,' he said. 'Don't worry about it. Sleep tight.' He kissed her lightly on the cheek. 'See you at breakfast.'

Fifteen

It was a hawklike bird, with a strange golden head and outspread wings of azure blue, that floated down in the dark, silently lit on the ledge outside her window, folded its wings around itself, and stood peering in at her, willing her to awaken before the Danger came. And although she struggled to respond, to drag herself up from the black depths of sleep, on she slept, and on and on. The great bird, seeking to awaken her but voiceless, tapped once upon her window with its golden beak.

Clack.

Lee's eyes shot open.

A dream? Of course, a dream. But so real. She had clearly seen the ribbing etched on each metallic feather, as on a bronze statue, she had seen the scaly, gleaming surface of its taloned feet, she had heard that muted, doomful clack with exquisite clarity.

It wasn't the kind of dream she usually had, so bizarre, so fraught with menace and ambiguity. All that strange food, all this unaccustomed excitement. She was relieved to be awake, but her heart was pounding, and the oversized T-shirt (Graham's) that she slept in was damp with sweat. The hair at her temples was pasted to her skin.

'Ho, boy,' she murmured, waving a hand in front of her face for the breeze and looking at her clock. Only nine twenty-five p.m. As impossible as it seemed, she'd been asleep less than ten minutes. The dream, already splintering into shards and falling away from her, had seemed to go on for hours. Anyway, it was over now. Too warm to sleep comfortably but too lazy to get out of bed and turn on the

103

air conditioner, she threw back the covers, forced her taut shoulder muscles to relax, and lay back with her eyes closed. What a curious dream it had been. Now she wished she could remember it, but she was drifting off again, floating tranquilly and gratefully into slumber, and the chances were that by morning she wouldn't even—

Clack.

She was sitting upright, her breath held, her ears straining to hear, before she realized she was awake. That had been real, not some imagined thing out of a dream. There was somebody in the room with her.

'Who's there?'

No answer, no further sound. And yet she sensed, deep in her core, that someone was nearby; someone breathing softly through his mouth, working to keep every muscle still.

'I know you're there. If I were you, I'd turn around and walk out right now. I'm warning you.'

Had that really been her own voice, so calm and self-confident? She felt anything but calm and self-confident. And what exactly was she warning him she'd do? Her arms and legs felt like spaghetti that had been on the stove too long.

She narrowed her eyes, trying to penetrate the darkness, cursing her earlier decision to close the drapes to shut out the light coming in from the rooms in the opposite wing of the hotel. She could see nothing . . . only a single, pale sliver of reflected light that fell from a hairline opening in the drapes on to the polished surface of the table in front of the windows. There were four wing chairs around the table, she knew, but she could see none of them. Just blackness, thick and impenetrable, with perhaps a ghost of a form visible here and there – the commode on the wall opposite the foot of the bed, the sofa and lamp table along the wall near the door, the opening to the bathroom, where a bit of luminescence filtered through the frosted glass. Her vision, it seemed to her, was improving. She could see more than she could a few seconds ago.

But she couldn't see *him.*

Quietly, she reached toward one of the lamps that she knew were on the tables on either side of the bed. 'All right, you asked for it, creep,' she said, running her fingers down the shade and feeling for the pull-chain. Where, she wondered, was all this gutsiness coming from? It wasn't only her arms and legs that felt like overcooked pasta; her whole body was like one big, wet cannellone.

Fortunately, her mind wasn't as soggy as her muscles, so that, just before tugging on the chain, she pulled herself to a stop. Wasn't she better off without lights? She'd been in the dark, asleep, for a while. He, whoever it was, must have just come in from the lighted hallway. Surely her eyes were better-adapted than his. She drew her hand back from the lamp and felt around on the table, searching for a weapon.

Nothing. The only thing she could think of was the five-iron that she kept with her for mirror practice, but that was on the other side of the room near the mirror, a universe away.

'I'm warning you. I . . . I have a gun . . . I'll use it . . .'

And she saw him. Not near the door, where she'd expected him to be, but on the other side of the room, near the commode, directly across from her. She saw hunched shoulders, a crouched body. He was moving slowly toward her, close to the floor, smoothly and noiselessly, seemingly on his hands and knees. She leapt quickly out of the bed, on the side farthest from him. Whatever happened she wanted to be on her feet, not lying there helplessly, with no possibility of leverage. When she did, he stopped, waiting.

Quickly, she compared the distance she had to cover to reach the door, and the distance he had to cover to reach her. About fifteen feet between her and the door and maybe ten feet between him and her. If they both broke at the same time, the odds were with him. She needed an advantage. A dim gleam from the lampshade caught her eye. The lamp, urn-shaped and made of heavy glass – that could be a weapon too. Her hand closed around its narrow neck.

She jerked it, pulling its plug out of the socket, and flung it at his head, or where she hoped his head was, and ran for the door, almost in the same motion. As she turned, she caught an indistinct glimpse of an arm coming up in self-defense and heard the lamp thump against him – something soft, not his head, unfortunately – and then, even before it hit the carpeted floor, he had launched himself after her. She heard his footsteps, heard him bump the corner of the bed, stumble, run again. He was practically on top of her, but she was only a few feet from the door. Her hand groped toward the knob—

I should scream! she thought suddenly. What's the matter with me? I should have screamed long ago! Running the last two steps, she opened her mouth, sucked in a breath – and he was on her from behind, throwing something – a towel? A blanket? – over her head and shoulders. The impact flung her against the wall and knocked the breath out of her, along with the too-late scream, and then his arm clamped around her head, pressing the towel tightly against her nose and mouth, so that screaming suddenly became the lesser of her worries. Breathing was the problem now. She twisted her head to one side, gasping, her mouth clogged with fabric, trying to find a little air, a little space.

'What do you . . . want?' she panted. 'What are you—?' But that was all she could get out.

He didn't answer. Grunting with exertion, he dragged her away from the wall, his arm still cutting off her air.

Why, he's trying to kill me, she thought dazedly. This is no thief, no sexual predator. He wants me dead. She managed to pull in a breath between the folds of fabric, and with it came a surge of strength. She struggled, flinging her arms out and her elbows back, trying to thump him in the ribs. She was strong for a woman, and she'd had some self-defense training in the Army; if she could hit him she could hurt him.

She managed to break his grasp around her midsection, but the towel – no, it had to be a blanket, it was too big for a towel – reached all the way down to her waist, so that her flailing arms were smothered. As she tried to twist around to face him – she could kick him if she were facing him – he grabbed her hard by the wrist and brutally forced her left arm up and back behind her in a way that human arms were never meant to go. And held it there. Her scream of pain was stifled by the blanket, but she did manage to pull a little away from him, choking and clawing at the blanket. She stumbled over something – the ottoman by one of the wing chairs? – and instinctively put her arm – her uninjured arm – out to brace herself and keep from falling. She knew that if she fell, it was all over. Her hand found a tabletop. She pushed herself upright and back into balance, and as she did, she realized that her fingers had closed on one of the heavy, cut-glass ashtrays that had been set out in the room.

Without conscious thought she hurled it into his face, into where his face ought to be, with all her strength. She knew instantly that she'd missed him. Oh, God, what would . . . ? An earsplitting clatter of crashing, breaking glass startled her into stillness; her attacker as well. But after the first stunned moment of paralysis she heard him move quickly toward her. Still clutching desperately at the blanket, trying to find a handhold to get it off her, she braced herself for whatever was coming.

Nothing came. She heard the door pulled open and saw light through the blanket, and then, as it swung closed on its own, she heard his footsteps rapidly receding down the hallway; not at a run, but at a rapid walk that would draw little attention to him.

It was over. Thank God.

Drained of what little strength she had left, she sank to the floor in a heap, momentarily too weak to get the blanket off her head. The ashtray must have flown into the big mirror over the divan. The noise, and it had been a heck of a noise, had frightened him off. But what had the whole thing been about? What was it that had just happened to her?

She finally pulled the blanket off and flung it aside. It turned out to be the thick hotel-issued terry-cloth robe, which she'd left over the back of a chair when she'd gone to bed. She made herself take a couple of deep breaths to slow down her racing heart and started to push herself up to turn on the lights. It was only as she did, that the twinge at her shoulder made her remember her arm, and at once she was seized with a different kind of panic. Her arm! He'd almost ripped it out of its socket, or so it had seemed to her. She was fairly sure it wasn't broken, but had he torn a tendon? Pulled a ligament from its mooring? Anything like that, and the tournament – this great tournament, this marvelous, once-in-a-lifetime opportunity – was over for her. Her very career might be over.

She collapsed again to the floor. Her head bent, her breathing shallow with concern, she gingerly fingered her shoulder and slowly, gently, began to rotate her arm.

That was the way the two young men from hotel security, responding to the noise in Room 442, found her a minute later: sitting on the floor in the dark, head bent, eyes closed.

'Miss?' one of them said worriedly when he'd flicked on the light. 'Are you . . . are you . . . ?'

The face she turned up to them was tear-streaked but beaming. 'I think my arm's all right,' she said.

Sixteen

'Finally,' Peg sighed. 'At long last, a little peace and quiet.' She firmly closed the door behind the team physician and the two officers from the Pinehurst Police Department, then leaned her weight against it as if to prevent their trying to get back in.

'Two *hours*,' she grumbled. 'Except for the doctor, I really can't see what couldn't wait till tomorrow morning.'

'Tomorrow morning I have a golf tournament,' Lee said quietly. Now wearing one of the green, black, and white team warm-up suits, she was huddled in a corner of the sofa, holding an ice pack to her shoulder, her bare feet tucked up under her.

'Tomorrow afternoon, then. Oh, don't mind me, I'm just grousing. Anyway, they're gone now. You can relax.' Her voice softened. 'How're you holding up, kid?'

'I'm fine,' Lee said.

'You don't look fine.' She returned to the armchair she'd been in.

'I'm fine, considering.' Unconsciously, she rubbed the ice pack against her shoulder. 'I was scared, though.' She gave Peg a wan smile. 'Thanks for taking care of getting me into another room. I sure didn't want to stay in that one any more.' She felt a shiver creep from her neck down to the bottom of her spine.

When Graham had learned what had happened, one of the first things he'd done was to have Peg located at the party downstairs. Since then, she'd been with Lee every minute, except for the time she'd taken to oversee the process of having Lee's things moved into the room the two of them

109

now sat in; the one remaining unoccupied room on the floor, six doors down from her original one and on the other side of the corridor. The move had eased Lee's mind considerably, as had the new presence of a twenty-four-hour guard that hotel security would now have right there in the hallway for the remainder of the tournament – in addition to the one who was already stationed in the lobby to prevent non-guests or unwanted visitors from getting up to the fourth floor. It had been Graham who'd seen to that.

'You're welcome,' Peg said. 'I know I wouldn't have—'

There was a double tap at the door. Peg growled warningly. 'Oh, this is too much!' Fire in her eyes, she stalked to the door and flung it open, patently ready to do battle. And Peg Fiske ready to do battle was a formidable sight, even in a blue polka-dot party frock and stockinged feet.

The visitor blinked and took a step back. 'Uh . . . isn't this Room . . . uh—'

Peg's ferocious glare changed to a welcoming smile. 'Now *you* I'm glad to see. Will you put it on the coffee table there?'

The room-service waiter entered, carefully giving Peg a wide berth, and put down the tray of hot chocolate and assorted biscuits where directed.

'Now,' said Peg when he'd gone, 'this is exactly what you need. A soothing cup of hot chocolate and you'll be ready to get a good night's sleep, or at least what's left of it.'

Lee shook her head. 'No, I'm afraid I'm finished sleeping for tonight. I'm too shaky to even think about it. All I can think about is . . .' Another shudder crawled down her spine.

'Maybe you should have taken Dr Matthews' advice and had a sleeping pill. He left a couple if you want one.' She poured two steaming, fragrant mugs of chocolate from the insulated carafe and set one of them on the end table next to Lee.

'No, thanks. It's already midnight. I'd have no chance of playing decently tomorrow with a sedative hangover. As it is . . .' Her voice trailed off again. It had been doing that a lot during the last few hours, she realized. At the obvious concern on Peg's face, she continued. 'But my arm's OK,' she said, mentally crossing her fingers. 'That's what's important. The ice is helping a lot. There'll be a heck of a bruise, but no real harm done. That's what Dr Matthews said, and I think he's right. I *hope* he's right.

'Knock on wood,' Peg said and did so on the coffee table. 'Lee, do you want to talk about it any more?'

'No,' Lee said, and then a moment later: 'Yes.'

She lifted the mug and took a sip, thankful for the instant surge in strength and spirits that the caffeine and sugar provided. As usual, Peg had been right. Another, longer swallow and she put the mug down.

'Peg,' she said, 'I know nobody believes me, but he was trying to kill me. He was.'

Peg sighed again. 'Lee, you've been all through that with Graham and the officers, and—'

'And they don't believe it. I know. But they weren't there. He had that bathrobe over my head, he was trying to cut off my air—'

'Why? Give me one good reason.'

Lee shook her head. 'I don't have one.'

'OK, give me one not-so-good reason.'

'One not-so-good reason?' Lee shrugged. 'OK, remember what I was saying before? About how maybe Dylan's murder had something to do with what he knew about Roger's problems? Well, maybe somebody wanted to kill me because of what *I* knew about Roger's problems, what about that?'

'But what *do* you know about Roger's problems?'

'Nothing, but that doesn't mean somebody didn't *think* I did. I'm his partner, aren't I? Look, maybe somebody is ... maybe somebody is sabotaging Roger's game—'

'Sabotaging? How do you sabotage somebody's golf game?'

'By messing with his equipment, for one thing. Maybe Dylan figured out who it was, and that's what got him killed. And maybe this person thinks I know too, and he wanted to make sure I didn't tell Roger either.'

111

Peg heard her out and held her tongue for a moment while she weighed the idea – and found it wanting. 'I have to tell you, I agree with those two policemen. The man was a thief, or more likely a souvenir-hunter trying to pick up some stupid memento from the team. He didn't know you were there. You surprised him and he panicked, that's all. Isn't that the simplest explanation?'

'Oh? And how did he get by the security guy downstairs?'

'Who knows? Maybe he had an accomplice to distract the guard. Maybe he waited till the guard took a bathroom break. How hard could it have been?'

'Right. So, he gets by Graham's hand-picked man just like that, and he makes it up to this floor, and then, with some of the most famous names in golf staying up here, he picks *my* room for his treasured souvenir? Please.'

Peg smiled. 'Well, I admit that's a pretty powerful point, but he probably didn't know it was your room. Chances are, he just knew that all the team members were staying up here.'

'So, it was just an accident that he picked my room to rob?'

'Yes, why not? He'd have to pick some room, why not yours? He assumed it was empty.'

'And why would he assume that at nine thirty p.m.?'

'Because what kind of person who's on a virtually unlimited expense account at a famous resort, with a party in her honor going on downstairs, would be all tucked up in bed at nine thirty?'

Lee had to laugh. It was the first time in a while and it felt good. 'I suppose that's a point too.'

'He probably looked under your door and saw there was no light and figured you had to be downstairs like everybody else.'

'Uh-uh, I don't buy it. Why wouldn't he have knocked first to see if anyone answered? If someone did he could just pretend it was a mistake and be on his way. No, it was me – me, specifically, that he wanted.'

Peg shook her head just a trifle impatiently, as if she were reasoning, not very successfully, with an obstinate six-year-old. 'He was in a hurry, that's why. Chances are, he was probably planning to rifle all the rooms while everybody was downstairs.' She frowned. 'Maybe he *did* rifle some of the other rooms. That'd be something to look into.'

Lee was equally impatient. 'And just how was he planning to get into all the rooms?'

'How would I know? How did he get into yours?'

Lee slowly drank some more of her chocolate, holding the mug in both hands. 'Could he have been a hotel employee?'

'Uh-huh. And do you want to tell me why a hotel employee would be sabotaging Roger's game?'

'Forget that part of it for a minute. Don't they have master keys? That's the only thing I can . . . uh-oh.' She put down the mug and sank back against the sofa.

'Uh-oh, what?'

'Uh-oh, I know how he got in. When we were in the lounge? With Burt? I got so excited when Roger came by and said I had five minutes to change, that I left my key card on the bar. Then when I came back down to get it, it wasn't there. So I figured I must have left it in the room earlier after all, and they made me another one, but I bet that's when he took it.' She banged her fist against her palm.

'Burt Fischer? You think Burton Fischer broke into your room?' Peg stared at her, astonished.

'No, of course not. I mean "he", "him", whoever it was.' She thumped the ice pack on her thigh. 'I *thought* I'd put it on the bar, but I figured I just wasn't remembering right.'

'Well, why would you have put it on the bar?'

'I always put my key card out. We all do. That shows the staff not to charge us.'

'But Burt invited us for juleps. Did you think he was going to try to get away without paying?'

'No, it was just automatic. Look, Peg, the important

113

question is: who would have had a chance to take it? How long did you stay after I left?'

'I didn't. I left when you did. With Burt.'

'And I was back looking for it inside of two minutes, so we're talking about a two-minute space of time. Who would have been able . . . ?'

They looked mutely at each other for a few seconds. It was Lee who put into words what both of them were thinking. 'The team,' she murmured. 'The whole team. They were all there, hanging right over our shoulders when Roger told me to get going for the photo shoot.'

Peg nodded slowly, apparently picturing the scene in her mind and counting off the people. 'Every . . . cotton-pickin' . . . one.'

There was a quiet knock on the door, followed immediately by Graham's voice, sounding a little tired. 'It's me.'

Lee threw down the ice pack, ran to the door, and flung it open. Graham dropped the shoulder bag he was carrying and gingerly embraced her. 'You OK?'

'I am now,' she said, hugging him back so hard he laughed. 'Ouch. Have pity on my ribs. Peg, thanks a lot for staying with her.'

'No problem,' Peg said. 'Actually, we've made quite a bit of progress on the case.'

He smiled. 'Why am I not surprised?'

He *does* look weary, Lee thought. 'Come on and sit down. And you look like you could use some hot chocolate.'

'I could. It smells great.'

When Graham was on the sofa beside her, Lee poured some chocolate into her mug and handed it to him. He drank gratefully. 'Mm, good,' he said with a sigh. 'That's better.' He put the mug down. 'OK, let's hear your theory.'

'We think it was one of the team members,' Peg said and explained.

Lee and Peg had come up with theories to 'help' Graham before, and he was generally somewhat skeptical, to say the least. But this time there were no counter-arguments. 'Good thinking,' he said thoughtfully.

Peg was shocked. 'You're not going to argue?'

'No, it makes perfect sense, why would I argue? All right, let's take it a little further. Lee, you said before that the person who attacked you was a "he".'

She nodded.

'So if it *was* one of the team members, we're talking about one of four people.' He ticked them slowly off on his fingers. 'The captain, Roger Finley; the young guy with the big mouth, Jordie Webster; the one with the Scottish accent, Dougal Sheppard; and . . . who am I missing?'

'Dave Hazelton,' Lee supplied.

'I see where you're going with this,' Peg said. 'The next question is: Why would any of those people want to attack Lee?'

He shook his head. 'Not exactly. One, we haven't established that the point of the break-in was to attack Lee. Second—'

'If you'd been there, you wouldn't say that,' Lee said petulantly. 'I'm telling you, he tried to kill me. I'd think at least one of *you* two would believe me. I'm not exactly given to flights of fancy.'

'Of course you're not,' Graham said soothingly. 'Far from it. But let me ask you this. I didn't want to press you while the police were going at you with all those questions, but . . . how sure are you that it was a man in your room?'

'I'm sure.'

'Why are you sure? You couldn't see him, could you?'

'No, it was too dark. And I think he may have had something over his face – a knit cap or something like that – because I couldn't make out any features. But then I hardly had a chance to look at him.'

'Then how can you be that sure?'

For the first time, Lee felt a flicker of doubt. How *could* she be that sure? 'Well – I just assumed . . . I mean, he just *seemed* like a man . . . he was too strong for a woman—'

Peg emitted a snort of laughter. 'Are you kidding? Tell me, who would you put your money on in a wrestling match between Ginger Rolley and Roger? Or anybody else on the

115

men's team? You know that short seventeenth hole? I bet Ginger could *throw* Roger to the green. So could Dinny, probably.'

The flicker became a wide swath. 'I may have been a little hasty,' Lee admitted. 'I was barely awake, I hardly knew what was going on until it was all over, I—'

'OK, then we're talking about eight people, not four,' said Graham.

'Nine, actually. Roger's wife was with them in the lounge too,' Peg said. 'But I repeat: What possible reason could any of those people have to break into Lee's room?'

'And *I* repeat,' Lee said. 'Somebody might have wanted to keep me from talking about what I knew about the cause of Roger's problems—'

'About which you knew nothing.'

'About which I knew nothing,' Lee agreed, 'but whoever it was might have thought that I . . . that I . . .' But the more she came back to the thought, the less water it seemed to hold, and she let the sentence die of its own accord. She was thoroughly worn out. Her mind felt threadbare.

Graham was tired too. He leaned back and rocked his head in half-circles. 'Ladies, I'm bushed. We all are. And Lee needs to be in shape for tomorrow. How about continuing this in the morning?'

Peg, looking at the two of them sitting side by side, with Lee's fingertips lightly resting on the back of Graham's neck, suddenly jumped up with a smile. 'You know what? I think it's time for me to go. You want to meet for breakfast in the Carolina Room, then?'

'Could we do it somewhere more private?' Lee asked. 'Everybody's going to be talking about this tomorrow morning, and I'd rather put off the attention until after I play.'

'Why don't we get something in the village? There's bound to be a breakfast place. We could meet at, say, eight o'clock, and walk over.'

'That sounds good, but better make it seven forty-five. I need to be at the practice range at nine.'

'Roger's instructions?'

'Yes, but I'd be doing it anyway. Play begins at ten.'

'Fine.' She slipped into her shoes and stood up. 'And now,' she said, with a little flourish of skirts, 'I'm out of here. Good night, you two.'

As soon as the door closed behind her, Lee slid over to work her way under Graham's arm and nestle there. 'Does the bag you brought mean what I think it means?'

'Definitely. Given what's happened, I think this floor can use my personal protection. And there aren't any vacant rooms.' He leaned his head down to nuzzle her hair.

'What about the room I just left?'

'Under police seal. No, I'm afraid you're stuck with me.'

'Uh-huh, and what happened to those work ethics I've been hearing about?'

'Sometimes you just have to bite the bullet and make an exception, as unpleasant as it might be.' He untangled himself, stood up and held out his hands to help her up. 'And now I think we both ought to get some sleep.' He gestured with his chin at the two queen-sized beds. 'Which one's mine?'

'That better be a joke, Graham.'

He tipped up her chin to kiss her. 'Now, really, am I the sort of person who would joke about a thing like that?'

She snuggled into him again. 'Because I think you're just the ticket I need to keep the nightmares away.'

Seventeen

In travel guides, the phrase 'village of Pinehurst' is not to be found unless preceded by the word 'quaint', and there is usually a 'charming' hovering in the vicinity as well. And quaint and charming it is, a tiny hub of local commerce that, except for the automobiles and the modern dress of its strollers, might pass for a nineteenth-century New England village, complete with curving, cobblestoned streets, brick-faced, white-columned buildings, a white-steepled church, and a tree-shaded village square.

'More like a nineteenth-century New England village theme park,' Peg responded when Graham had said something along these lines. 'Too clean for a real nineteenth-century New England village. And too polite. Everybody's so nice.'

'And I bet it wasn't that easy to get *café au lait* back then either,' Lee said, raising her cup.

They were in the center of the little town, in Market Square, at Grounds and Pounds, an appropriately charming, old-fashioned coffee shop – marble-topped counters, antique red coffee grinder, oval hooked rugs on the wooden floors – halfway through their breakfast of sausage-and-egg biscuits. Peg finished the first of her two biscuits, picked up the other one, and paused.

'Did either of you ever hear of Goldstein's Law of Interconnected Monkey Business?'

Lee shook her head, as did Graham.

'He was an old professor of mine a million years ago, and what he meant was that when too many seemingly unrelated incidents occur to the same set of people in a shared

context, the probability that they are in actuality uncon-
nected diminishes in proportion—'

'Careful, you're losing me,' Lee said.

Peg put down her biscuit. 'What I'm saying is that I'm
starting to think that everything that's been happening must
be related. I think there has to be some kind of connection
between Roger's golf game, Dylan's murder, and what
happened to you last night. There *has* to be.'

'*Are you serious?* When I said something like that to you
yesterday, you flat-out said it was a lousy idea.'

'No,' Peg said, smiling, '*you* said it was a lousy idea.'

'Well, I don't remember you arguing with me.'

'That's because I agreed with you. At the time. But now,
I'm not so sure. Only I can't come up with any kind of
rationale for it. What was your reasoning again?'

'It was something Lou said. He told me Dylan claimed
he knew what was wrong with Roger's game but he was
keeping it to himself.'

Peg peeked inside her second biscuit, appeared satisfied,
and started in on it. 'But how does that make any sense? The
less money Roger made, the less Dylan was going to get.'

'Exactly, but then maybe he was ticked off at Roger about
something – people do dumb things to get back at someone
else – or maybe . . . maybe . . . I don't know, maybe . . .'

Graham, quiet until now, came to her rescue. 'I don't
know either, but I think Peg is right. And I've come around
to thinking you're right too, Lee. I believe whoever was in
your room last night wasn't any souvenir hunter. I think he
was looking specifically for you.'

She looked at him gratefully. 'You *do* think he was trying
to kill me?'

'I don't know about "kill" – hurt, maybe, or frighten, or
warn—'

'Warn about what?' Peg asked.

'I don't know, but I guess I subscribe to Professor
Goldstein's Law too. The way I look at it, everything has
to revolve around Roger. First his game goes. Then his
caddie, who claims to know something about it—'

119

'Also goes,' Peg said dryly.

Graham nodded. 'And then his Stewart Cup partner is attacked and *almost* goes.' He slid his empty plate to one side, brought over his coffee, and drank deeply. 'Got to be related. But as to how – I don't have a clue.'

They finished their *cafés au lait*, and Graham went to the counter to get two more big cups, one for him and one for Peg. (With restroom breaks during the matches awkward, to say the least, Lee typically restricted her pre-game liquid intake.) As he set them on the table, Peg was musing aloud.

'If Dylan claimed he'd spotted what was wrong with Roger but wouldn't tell him what it was, doesn't that imply that if he *had* told him, Roger could have fixed it? And doesn't *that* imply that it was some simple, small thing, maybe some kind of hitch in his swing that could easily be repaired, or else some kind of problem with his clubs – I don't know, some misalignment of the loft, or the lie angle, or the shaft flex, or maybe the swing weight – something that could also be easily fixed once he knew about it?'

'Yes, exactly,' Lee said eagerly. 'That's what I was trying to tell you last night. That's what I tried to tell Roger – that there might be something wrong with his equipment. But—'

'You told him that?' Peg said, surprised. 'What did he say?'

'He very politely told me to worry about my own game, not his.' Recollecting their uncomfortable conversation on the twelfth hole, she grimaced. 'Or maybe not so politely.'

'OK, let's think this through a little more,' Peg said, absently stirring her coffee. 'Assume for the sake of argument that Roger's problem did stem from a problem with his clubs. Assume for the sake of argument that Dylan really did know what it was. Seems to me it would follow from that that it was Dylan himself who altered the clubs, or adjusted them, or—'

'Sabotaged them?' Lee said.

'Yes, sabotaged them.'

'Could be something to that,' Graham said with a markedly mild show of interest.

'Well, if so, does that suggest . . . don't jump all over me, you two, I'm only thinking out loud here . . . that Roger found out about it and Roger *himself* might have killed him?' She held her breath waiting for their response.

'Why?' Graham asked, unimpressed.

'Why? Because . . . because . . . Oh, I see your point. What he'd want to do is fire him or expose him, not kill him. I mean, it's conceivable he would have killed him in an uncontrollable rage, but can you imagine Roger Finley in an uncontrollable rage?' She went back to her coffee. 'Oh, well, I tried.'

'But let's take your idea and run in a different direction with it,' Lee said. 'Remember what I suggested last night? What if somebody *else* was sabotaging the clubs and Dylan somehow found out about it, and was going to expose him—?'

'Or blackmail him!' Peg put in excitedly. 'And *that* person killed Dylan!'

Graham nodded his approval. He was starting to go with the flow now, Lee thought. 'Blackmail's an interesting idea, Peg. That would explain why Dylan wouldn't tell Roger. There wasn't any money in telling Roger.'

But as involved as Lee was in the conversation, it was increasingly hard to keep her mind from turning toward the day's events. In not much more than one hour from now, Stewart Cup XXIII would begin on Pinehurst's legendary Number Two Course . . . and first off the tee for the United States, and for the tournament, was none other than Lee Ofsted of Portland, Oregon. At the thought, she felt her stomach contract and her throat go dry.

She licked her lips. Also dry. 'Can I have just one sip of your *café au lait*?' she asked Graham. 'And then I'd better get going. Things to do today.'

'Don't look so nervous,' Peg said, draining her own coffee. 'There is one good side to all this.'

'There is?'

'Sure,' Peg said in her cheerful foghorn of a voice. 'Now,

121

if you shank that opening tee-shot everyone will blame it on the attack.'

Lee smiled weakly. 'Thank the Lord for small favors.'

They were on the Sand Path, the pedestrian shortcut that led from the village back to the hotel, walking in the dense shade of the trees and holly bushes that bordered it, before Lee was able to pluck out the thought that she'd felt nibbling away at the edges of her mind all through breakfast. She stopped walking so abruptly that Peg and Graham kept going a couple of paces before they realized she wasn't there.

'What?' Peg said, turning.

'It *was* sabotage!' Lee exclaimed. 'That's just what it was – sabotage! Lou told me – well, just as good as told me.'

They came back to her. 'Told you what?' Graham asked.

'How could I forget?' She smacked her forehead. 'When I was talking to him yesterday, he said that one of the things Dylan was saying in the bar was that not only did he know what was wrong with Roger's game, he knew who was responsible! He even knew what it was *about*. Doesn't that—'

'He said *what*?' Graham cried. 'Why didn't you say so before this?'

'I'm telling you, I just plain forgot. I didn't really pick up on it at the time. I had other things on my mind.'

'Well, why the hell didn't Lou tell *us* when Nate and I were talking to him? I mean, we've got a homicide on our hands here, somebody's been murdered, and this little . . . turkey of yours doesn't tell us something like that, something obviously important, that the guy said at Duffer's a few hours before he was killed? I swear . . .' He turned a menacing scowl on her. 'Is something funny?'

'I'm sorry,' she said, laughing. 'It's just that you're so darned cute when you get mad. Your upper lip kind of bristles, and your eyes get this glinty, steely sparkle. I'm sure I'd be petrified if I was a criminal, but—'

'Lee, dammit—'

'Graham, Dylan didn't say that at Duffer's the other night, he said it three weeks ago, in Scottsdale.'

Graham was only marginally mollified. 'So why didn't he tell us that?'

She put a placating hand on his forearm. 'Come on, Graham, we all know Lou Sapio pretty well by now. He's a funny guy. If he didn't tell you about it, it was because—'

'—we didn't ask him about it,' Graham said, nodding, and then he cracked a smile too. 'And it's true. We didn't.'

They were standing so still that a mother quail, trailed by a smoothly weaving line of tiny offspring, came leisurely out of the underbrush, practically right up to them. But then Graham shifted his position a little and Mama Quail, with what Lee would have sworn was a startled expression, scooted back into the brush, followed by her brood, their matchstick legs moving so fast they looked as if they were on wheels.

That started the three of them moving as well. 'So are you going to talk to Lou again?' Peg asked Graham. 'He might remember something else if he's prodded a little.'

'I'll ask Nate to,' Graham said. 'It's his baby, this is his turf. But if he'll let me, I'd like to sit in.'

'Can I make a suggestion?' Lee asked. 'Why don't you let me talk to him first? Lou gets his back up when people he doesn't know start "prodding" him. Especially the police.'

'Yeah, I've noticed. Why is that, anyway? Does he have something to hide?'

Lee shrugged. 'It's just his way. He doesn't intrude on other people's lives, and he doesn't like it when other people intrude on his.'

Not long before, Lee had posed the same questions to Peg, who had used her formidable research skills to find out everything there was to know about Lou Sapio. The result had been: not much. He wasn't wanted for anything, he'd never been convicted of anything (although he'd been arrested once for drunk driving, once in connection with a brawl, and once for refusal to pay alimony; but these were

123

all many years ago). He was a high-school drop-out, he'd been married once, for three years, he had a grown daughter somewhere (hard to imagine!), and, other than caddying, he'd never stuck at a job for more than a year or two.

'Lou is Lou,' Peg declared now, for Graham's benefit. 'What you see is what you get.'

'So, what do you say, Graham?' Lee asked. 'Will you give me a shot at him first? I could talk to him this morning, at practice.'

She expected at least a show of argument, but he surprised her. 'OK, do. You'd do better at it than Nate would. And let me know what you find out.'

'I will.'

Lee didn't know whether she was more pleased or more disconcerted that he'd gone along with her idea. Pleased, yes, because she liked it that he had confidence in her. Disconcerted because now she had one more thing on her mind when she knew all her mental energies should be focused on golf.

They had reached the resort villas, which were located at the edge of the property, and Graham left her with a few more unwelcome things to occupy her mental energies before he peeled off for his morning staff briefing.

'Look, people,' he said pensively. 'You realize what all this adds up to, don't you? If it really is sabotage, and if all these events really are connected, then that narrows things down quite a bit. The person we're looking for has to be someone who's had access to Roger, or at least to his equipment, for the last couple of months; who had access to Dylan a couple of nights ago; and who was able to get through the lobby and upstairs to the reserved floor of the hotel last night without attracting my guys' attention as an uninvited guest. As I see it, that means it *does* have to be somebody on the team – the American team, eight people – or one of the caddies. Sixteen altogether. Fourteen if we don't count you and Roger. Thirteen if we don't count Lou.'

'Twelve,' Peg said. 'Roger's caddie is brand-new. He's

a local, he's not with the tour. He wouldn't have been able to get at Roger's clubs before.'

'Neither would most of the other caddies,' Lee said. 'Except for Lou and Too-Tall Jack – he carries for Dave Hazelton – all of the others are family or friends, not professionals who'd have had access in the past. So if we eliminate them, that leaves . . .'

'A total of seven,' Peg said. 'Three of the women team members and three of the men. Plus Too-Tall Jack.'

'Not Too-Tall Jack,' Graham said. 'The professional caddies weren't on the list of invitees. And Too-Tall Jack isn't exactly the kind of guy who could slip in unnoticed.'

'Six,' Peg said. 'We're doing great.'

Graham smiled. 'Let's keep going. See if we can get it down to one. That'd save a lot of work for Nate.'

Lee doubted just how serious he was, but in her opinion they were getting somewhere, and she had something more to contribute. 'Make that three. The women play on the WPGL tour, not the men's. They wouldn't have been able to get at Roger's clubs either. So that leaves exactly three people.'

'Dave Hazelton,' said Peg soberly. 'Jordie Webster. Dougal Sheppard.'

'May as well throw in Roger Finley too,' Graham said.

They stared at him. '*Roger*?'

'Well, we're talking about the people who had access to his clubs and who are also here at Pinehurst. That includes Roger, doesn't it?'

'But sabotage himself?' Lee said. 'Why would anyone do something daffy like that?'

'I have no idea. We're not up to "motive" yet, are we? We're still talking "opportunity".'

'But it's crazy,' insisted Lee. 'There's no possible benefit to him. He'd just be hurting himself. Nobody goes out of his way to—'

'I wouldn't take him terribly seriously,' Peg said. 'I believe the gentleman is having some sport with us. Am I right, Graham?'

125

He smiled. 'Well, maybe a little. Not, of course, that you aren't making perfectly good sense. It's just that it's all a little too neat for me. I don't know that I'm quite ready to agree we've whittled the suspects down to three. Not yet, anyway.'

'OK,' Peg said with a nod, 'let me make it a little messier for you. What about Burt Fischer?'

'And why would Burt Fischer—?'

'Aren't you the one who just said we're not talking about "why", we're only talking about who had a chance to do everything? And Fischer would have. He's at a lot of the tournaments, so he could have easily gotten hold of Roger's clubs, and he's here at Pinehurst, so he could have killed Dylan, and he could have been the one in your room last night.' She looked at them. 'Well, couldn't he?'

Lee was as doubtful as Graham looked. 'Peg, getting into the bag rooms at a professional tournament isn't as easy as that. There's security. For anybody but one of the players or the caddies, it's a tough proposition.'

'Yes, but for somebody like Fischer? Wouldn't—?'

Graham was shaking his head. 'No, Peg, that couldn't have been him in Lee's room last night. He wasn't on the attendee list, and nobody got into the party without his name on the list and a picture ID to match.'

'Graham, there must have been two hundred people there last night,' Peg said. 'Are you saying you remember every single name that was on that list?'

'A hundred and eighty-one, to be exact. And, yes, I probably do.'

'Oh, come on, be serious. You can't—'

'He is serious,' Lee said, smiling at Graham. 'Mind like a steel trap.'

'Fischer was on the original list of invitees,' Graham said, 'but he RSVP'd his regrets, so he wasn't on the final list. Besides, no one got to go up to the fourth floor unless he or she had a room up there, and Fischer's staying—'

'In one of the villas, near us,' Peg said, visibly impressed. Lee noted that there were no suggestions this morning of

126

careless bathroom breaks by his people or of cunning distractions. 'OK, you win, scratch Burt.'

Lee was suddenly aware of the time. 'I have to go,' she said. 'Roger's jumpy enough as it is. He'll have a fit if I'm not at the range when he shows up.'

'Yes, go ahead, let us worry about this.' Peg embraced her lightly. 'Good luck, Lee. I'll be in your gallery, rooting for you all day.'

Graham did not embrace her but put a hand on each arm and looked into her eyes. He was serious enough now. 'Lee, be careful out there. Either I or one of my people will be close to you all day, but we don't *really* know what's going on or who we're looking for. Whoever attacked you last night, whoever did kill Dylan – he's still out there, and God knows what he has in mind next.'

Eighteen

'Will you just look at that goddam bruise,' Lou muttered to himself, his face dark, as he dropped Lee's bag into the holder beside one of the perfect pyramids of immaculate golf balls faultlessly spaced – as if someone had measured the intervals with a yardstick – along the driving-range slots. 'If I ever find out who . . .'

Lee glanced at her shoulder. It really wasn't as bad as all that. Dr Matthews had warned her that there might be some discoloration as a result of torn blood vessels under the skin, and, indeed, a few streaky, purplish blotches had shown up on her upper arm this morning. As a result, she had considered ignoring the manual's dress code for the day and switching to a golf shirt with sleeves instead of the sleeveless one. However, a moment's thought convinced her that she'd be better off sporting a little discoloration than she'd be if she disregarded Mr Micro-Manage's meticulously worked-out clothing schedule. Roger might not be subject to uncontrollable rages, but she knew enough about him by now to know that he could get extremely persnickety if his directions weren't followed to the letter.

'Oh, it's not as bad as it looks,' she said, slipping on her golf glove. 'I'm fine, really.'

'That's not the point,' she heard him mumble, apparently to the bag.

'In fact, the more I think about it, I'm better than fine. I'm mad. I'm angry that someone picked yesterday to attack me – the night before the most important day of my life. And if they think they can ruin my life like that, they have another think coming.'

She realized that she was doing the same thing Lou was: speaking more for her own benefit than for his, and she corrected that now. 'Remember what Ben Hogan used to say about playing "cool-mad"? Well, I've played that way before and played one of my best days ever, and that's the way I'll be playing today.'

Lou turned his scowl from the bag to her. 'Snead,' he said.

'What?'

'Sam Snead, not Ben Hogan.' The scowl held on for a few seconds, and then gave way to his toothy, twisty grin. 'Right you are, we'll do fine. We'll do *great*.' He reached into the bag to get the wedge she liked to start her warm-ups with, but she stayed his hand with hers.

'Lou, before we get started – before the others show up – I need to ask you something about what you told me before.'

Goodbye, grin. She could practically read his mind. *For once in my life I blab about something somebody said to me, and now I'm gonna get in trouble for it. It serves me right.*

'This is important, Lou. I know how crazy this sounds, but I think what happened to me last night – and Dylan's murder, for that matter – has something to do with Roger's problems and with what Dylan said about them.'

Lou rolled his eyes. 'Are we on that again? I told you, and I told your boyfriend, and I told the local sheriff or whatever he is: he was just blowing smoke. A lot of the guys do that kind of stuff. You can tell.'

'You're probably right, but, after all, he'd said the same thing before, hadn't he? Didn't you tell me he talked about it in Scottsdale too, and that he'd said even more – that he'd said he knew who was responsible for Roger's problems?'

Lee saw his eyes swivel toward her arm. He was at war with his natural tendency to say as little as possible about anybody to anybody – especially under questioning – and his smoldering anger at someone who'd had the nerve to hurt his player. It didn't take long for him to come to a decision.

'Yeah, something like that,' he said with a sigh.

'Can you remember *exactly* what he said? And how he said it?'

'What does that mean, how he said it?'

'Well, for example, did it sound as if he was joking?'

'Who knows? I told you, I wasn't paying a lot of attention.'

'OK, thanks anyway, Lou,' she said, disappointed. 'I guess I'll take that wedge now.'

He slid it out of the bag and handed it to her. With his head down, still holding on to the club head, he mumbled with obvious reluctance: 'Maybe the other guys would remember.'

'Other guys? There were other people there?'

'Couple of other guys I know, yeah. Caddies. You know.' He released the club head.

She surprised herself by laughing aloud. *Why didn't you tell me that before?* she might have demanded, but she already knew the answer: *Because she hadn't asked him, of course.*

'Well, tell me, who were they?'

'You probably don't know them. Pokey and Bear. Mostly do the men's tour, but they're like me, they don't work regular bags.'

'What are their last names?'

As she expected, he shrugged. 'Pokey carries for Bob Lampert sometimes, and Bear works a lot for Romano. They'd probably know.'

'He carries for Jim Romano?' Lee said, beginning her side-to-side stretching with the club across her shoulders. 'Is that Bear? A big, slow, shambling, hairy guy, sort of like a . . . like a . . .'

'Bear,' Lou supplied. 'Yeah, that's him. Hey, here comes everybody,' he said with palpable relief. They could finally get back to golf. 'I just hope Finley packed a compass in his bag this time.'

130

But Lee wasn't quite ready to let him off the hook. 'Lou, I need you to do one more thing for me. I'd do it myself, but I don't see how I could squeeze it in. When I'm not playing, there are ceremonies.'

He looked doubtfully at her. 'What do you want me to do?'

'I want you to get hold of Graham at some point before the day's done and tell him exactly what you told me. He needs to know what Dylan said. And he needs to know about Pokey and Bear.'

'Ah, Lee, for Christ's sake, he'll get ticked off at me—'

'He won't get ticked off at you. He's *already* ticked off at you. This will help smooth things over, believe me. Lou, I really need you to do this, it's—'

'All right, already, I'll do it. OK?'

She smiled. 'OK.'

'Fine. Good. Great. Now say good morning to your team-mates and let's whack a few golf balls.'

Lee steeled herself to meet the rest of the team. She'd called Roger first thing in the morning to beg off joining them for the scheduled team breakfast, and, although he'd agreed, he'd sounded a little miffed, probably because he wanted to make sure for himself that she was up to playing. But it had been a wise decision on her part. She'd slept blissfully, nestled against Graham, and the breakfast brainstorming with him and Peg had both refreshed her and reinforced her determination not to let some creep ruin her tournament. It had certainly helped steel her nerves when she thought of what was facing her that day. The crowds around the resort had grown huge, and seeing the gorgeous, red-white-and-blue-bannered pavilion and the rows of reserved seating that had been set up near the clubhouse for the opening ceremonies – less than an hour from now! – had given her goosebumps.

To her relief, she hadn't needed to worry about whether the team would see her as damaged goods on account of the attack; as even more of a weak link than she already

131

was. Roger was the first to reach her, and when he did he gave her a hearty, avuncular hug, something that was much appreciated, especially because it seemed wildly out of character for him.

'There's my partner,' he said warmly. 'Nothing daunts her.'

The others responded similarly: hugs, and encouragement, and jokes about all the free publicity she had brought them in the media. Apparently the Internet was already abuzz with wildly inaccurate details and laughable suppositions about what had happened. Her teammates, once beyond their initial concern and supportiveness, treated the whole affair with a lightness that was very welcome. Perhaps it was an act they'd decided on to make her feel relaxed, but if so they were doing a good job of it and it was working.

Even Dave Hazelton had a grin pasted on that long undertaker's face of his, the unnaturalness of which brought her up short with a chilling and disagreeable thought that she'd somehow shoved to the back of her mind: if she, Peg, and Graham had been right in their suppositions, one of these people – Dougal, Jordie Webster, or Dave Hazelton – was not only putting on an act this morning, he had been in her darkened room less than twelve hours ago, crushing her in an entirely different kind of hug. If he had been trying—

She shook her head abruptly. No. Stop that right now. Graham was concerned that she might be in some danger, and that was as it should be. That was his job. But she had a different job, and it would be impossible to perform if she were looking over her shoulder at every strange noise and unexpected movement. Let Graham and his security detail do the worrying. She had more than enough on her plate to give it any further thought.

All the same, it was comforting to notice one of his men standing in the cheerful crowd that had begun to gather behind the ropes, inconspicuous but alert, his eyes on her.

'That's enough nice-nice, everyone,' Roger said. 'Time for us to get to work.' He nodded toward the far end of the range, where the British team was already hitting, looking very smooth and competent. 'Our esteemed colleagues have gotten the jump on us.'

Lee, who had already taken a few practice swings, treated her first swipe at a ball very gingerly; a three-quarter-strength effort with the pitching wedge. Then she held her finish, not moving a muscle, not even breathing, trying to sense any pain, any hitch, anything different at all. Nothing. She was fine, as good as new. Her typical fluid swing was working for her, and the ball had flown in its typical, beautiful, high arc, bounced twice, and rolled to a stop at its typical three-quarter-swing distance of ninety yards.

'Lookin' good,' Lou grunted.

Relieved, she let out her breath and got down to serious work. Even practice at Pinehurst had its own particular thrill. 'Maniac Hill', as they'd long ago dubbed the range, was every bit as much a legend as the early courses themselves were; the oldest, most venerated practice range in the United States, consecrated by just about every great golfer who had ever lived.

But she was good at locking out such distractions and focusing strictly on her own game. As usual, the time went quickly, so that before she knew it they were at the opening-ceremony pavilion and Roger was leading them toward the decorated dais, with the British team approaching from the other side. She knew Peg and Graham were out there watching but she was too excited to pick them out. As soon as the teams were seated and ready to be introduced, the Stars and Stripes and the Union Jack were simultaneously run up on flagpoles at either side of the pavilion, to unfurl and fluff out in the breeze. The anthems were played by a small band, with Lee savoring every second, trying her hardest to imprint it on her memory – how she felt, how blue the sky was, how burstingly proud she was to be there – so that no matter what happened, no matter how well she played or didn't play, this glorious moment would be with her forever.

Nineteen

Graham, who considered himself something of a cynic, or at least a skeptic, or at least anything but a sentimentalist, found himself unexpectedly moved by the scene: flags flying, distinguished guests, the players – including his own Lee – up there on the dais looking so proud and happy, the large, well-behaved audience singing along with both national anthems as well as they could.

It was perhaps the first time that he'd been at the always-ostentatious start of a golf tournament without one or two of the wealth of witticisms about the sport springing automatically to mind. ('In the old days, when men beat the earth with sticks and cursed, it was called witchcraft. Now it's called golf.' 'Golf is like sex: you never score as well as you think you should.')

It wasn't that he had no respect for what Lee did and at which she worked so hard, but that he couldn't honestly think of golf as a 'sport'. Graham, a diehard Oakland A's fan, saw all sports through the prism of his beloved baseball. A true sport required a team, a blending of athletic ability and coordinated group effort to defeat another team. It required competition, and where was the competition in golf? Sure, players were always talking about competitive spirit, but when it came down to it, who did they compete against? The ball, standing there nice and white and motionless, patiently waiting for you to take your time and hit it. Most of the time, golfers didn't even know how well their closest 'competition' was doing, because they were playing their own games, in front of a different gallery, 500 yards away and more.

What kind of sport was that? And in what other sport did a walloping 300-yard drive and a dinky two-inch putt count exactly the same: one stroke?

Game? Sure. Sport? No.

Still, he had to admit that the Stewart Cup kick-off had set his blood tingling. As the ceremony wound down, he spoke into his collar-microphone, making sure that his people were all set. There would be two of his best men, Coulter and Mahnerd, sticking with Finley and Lee all day, and one each with the three foursomes to follow. The five affirmative responses came in over his earpiece. Graham reminded them that he expected them to check in every half-hour, then moved to the first tee, along with Peg and the herd of people behind them.

'Is this thrilling, or what?' Peg said.

'I have to admit—' he began before he realized that Peg had been speaking to the man on her other side.

'Thrilling, thrilling, one of the truly great moments in sport, and how privileged we all are to be part of it.' The man, wearing a classy Harris tweed sport coat and with well-cut, crinkly, gray hair, was dapper, hearty, and jovial. Coming from somebody else, the grandiloquence would have rung false. Coming from him, they seemed right.

'Graham Sheldon,' Peg said, 'I want you to meet Burt Fischer. Burt is Mr Comet Golf. He knows everything there is to know about golf clubs.'

Fischer spread his hands helplessly. 'What can I say? It's true, every word of it.'

'And Graham is in charge of security at the tournament. He's also Lee's fiancé.'

Fischer's ruddy face lit up. 'Well, now, there's a lucky man for you! That little gal of yours has everything! Brains, beauty, talent, one heck of a personality. That little gal's got everything it takes to be a star. Maybe you can help me convince her that she couldn't take a better career step . . . ?'

It took the course marshals' holding up their Quiet signs

135

to turn off the flood of words, and even then he managed to finish his sentence and tack on another one. '. . . than to endorse a really superior product. Modesty forbids my mentioning which one.'

'First up . . .' The starter's monotone came through the public-address system. 'For the United States . . . Lee Ofsted.'

A surprised Graham looked at Peg. 'Lee's the first one to tee off?' he shouted through the ripple of applause. 'In the whole tournament?'

Peg nodded. 'Yes, sir.'

'Why didn't she tell me?' he shouted, but the applause stopped just as he started and he was peremptorily shushed by the nearest marshal.

'It's nerve-wracking, isn't it?' Peg whispered. 'There are *millions* of people watching her right now. If that was me, I'd freeze up solid over the ball and they'd have to come up there, tip me into a wheelbarrow, and cart me away.'

Graham watched as Lee bent over to place the wooden tee in the turf, set the ball on it, straighten up, and rotate her neck from side to side as if working out a kink. She sucked in a deep breath through her mouth, held it momentarily before letting it out with a 'whooo' that seemed almost audible, closed her eyes for a fraction of a second, and took her stance over the ball. Another deep breath as she settled into the stance. And an absolute silence fell over the crowd. Every pair of eyes in the giant gallery was fixed on her. A lot of other people were holding their breath too.

To a casual observer, nothing about Lee would have seemed out of the ordinary, but to someone close to her, like Graham – and no doubt, Peg – her tension and anxiety were practically screaming out loud. That turning of her neck, the closed eyes (a prayer?), those deep, shuddering breaths; none of them were anything like the Lee he knew. Even Lou Sapio, surely one of the world's great stoics, looked as if he were in pain, as if the air was being pressed out of him as he stood with her bag a few yards to the side.

Graham too closed his eyes as guilt pressed in on his

heart. He knew why she hadn't told him, all right; why she hadn't shared this supreme, terrifying moment with him. It was because she'd thought that he wouldn't understand, that he'd make light of it. And she was right; he would have joked it away with a flippant sentence or two and asked what she wanted to do for dinner. But now, all at once, realizing the terrific pressures involved, he did understand. If he had been up there in her place in front of all those staring eyes, all those cameras, trying to properly hit that tiny ball with that ridiculous instrument, they'd have had to bring in a second wheelbarrow for him.

Unlike baseball, he understood now, golf was a game that had to be played cold. There was pressure, worry, tension, sure; but not the energizing, focusing rush of adrenaline that comes from live competition, from a pitcher standing sixty feet away and throwing a ball toward you at ninety-five miles an hour. And that – how had he failed to grasp this before? – made golf harder, not easier, in a hundred ways.

He opened his eyes as she pressed her knees forward to kick-start her backswing, and now the old Lee took over. The club went back smoothly and whipped forward with a movement both athletic and graceful. The ball jumped off the tee with hardly any sound of impact, only a soft click, as if a couple of billiard balls had come together, and soared high and straight. The crowd let out its breath and broke into applause.

Lee had a huge smile on her face – something else she didn't usually do in the tee box – and quickly sought him out in the crowd. When their eyes met he pumped his hand in the air and threw her a kiss. She blew him an unostentatious kiss in return, then laughingly accepted congratulations from Roger.

Graham's mind was running in unaccustomed channels. He was thinking about how difficult golf was, and how important the clubs were, and in particular about this morning's exchange between Lee and Peg on how a player's game – specifically, Roger's game – might be sabotaged by small adjustments in 'loft angle' or . . . or whatever else they'd said. He wished now that he'd been paying more attention, but help was fortunately at hand. When Dianna Gentry, the British female player, stepped up to the tee, Graham turned to Fischer.

'Burt, can I ask you a couple of golf-club questions?'

Fischer's square, friendly face lit up. 'Sure!'

They moved off to the side so as not to bring any further wrath from the marshals. 'OK, what are loft angle, and . . . and swing flex, and, um, shaft weight?'

Fischer laughed delightedly. 'I think you mean lie angle, shaft flex, and swing weight. And loft. Does that sound right?'

'I think so, yes.'

There was a smattering of applause as the woman from the UK got off a decent first shot too.

Fischer stroked his chin. 'Are you a golfer, Graham?'

'No, not really.'

'Then may I ask what prompts your interest in things like this?'

'Well, I was just thinking about clubs, and how important they are, and how much even a small, uh, misalignment might negatively affect a player's game, and whether—'

Fischer laughed again. Obviously, laughter, and hearty laughter at that, came easily to him. 'I thought that's what this was all about. Roger Finley's incredibly shrinking game, am I right? Well, it's a nice theory, but I have to tell you that what I said to him in the lounge yesterday – about needing a good club-fitting? – was just my little joke. Not serious at all. Roger is one of the most serious students of the physics of golf that we have on tour today. Neither I nor anyone else needs to tell him about swing weight or anything else that has to do with a golf club.'

Graham hadn't meant to tell Fischer what was on his mind, and he was unfamiliar with the incident the older man was referring to, but obviously, the cat was out of the bag. So be it; no real harm done.

'All the same,' he said, 'I'd like to know.'

'Certainly. The—'

The crowd cheered again, then went abruptly silent.

'That's got to be Roger's tee shot,' Fischer said. He listened intently. 'Brief applause followed by silence. No groan, at any rate, which is a good sign. I'd interpret it to mean the ball started off well, but ended up not so well – but not too very terribly either. Probably in the short grass to the left, if he's hooking it again today, would be my guess. Now, what was I saying?'

'Loft, lie angle—'

'Oh, yes. Loft is simply the sole-to-crown slope of the club face as measured by its angle in relation to the surface on which the sole of the club rests.' He demonstrated something with his hands, but it was lost on Graham. 'Naturally, therefore, loft is the primary determinant of the upward trajectory of the ball. Lie angle, on the other hand, is the back-to-front angle between the shaft and the surface of the ground when the club is placed in the proper address position. Now, swing weight – there we have to get a little more complex, because what we're really dealing with is inertial resistance, based on the length of the shaft and the mass of the club head. What you do is balance the club head on a fulcrum . . .'

He waved a hand in front of Graham's slowly glazing eyes. 'Am I starting to lose you?'

'You lost me a long time ago,' Graham said. 'I think it was just after the word "simply".'

'Graham, let me ask you something. You said you weren't really a golfer. About how often have you played, would you say?'

'Well . . . never would be a pretty good guess.' He was obscurely embarrassed.

'Have you ever even swung a golf club?'

Graham had to think. 'No, I guess I haven't.'

The answer surprised him more than it did Fischer. How could it be that, aware as he was of how important – how critical – the game was in Lee's life, he had never once been interested enough to pick up a club and swing it, just to see what it was like?

'How'd you like to try it now?' Fischer said. 'There won't be anybody on the range.'

Graham considered. His staff had things in hand for the time being, and he hadn't assigned any specific duties to himself. If he was needed, there was always the two-way. He could certainly be away from things for half an hour or so. 'I'd like to very much,' he said, 'but it can wait. I'm sure you'd rather watch the action.'

'Not a bit. When it comes to a choice between talking about the physics of golf clubs and merely watching people swing them, it's no contest.' He clapped Graham on the shoulder. 'Come on, let's go by my tent, pick up a few clubs, and start your education. Golf One–Oh–One.'

Half an hour later, Graham was indeed a wiser man, but also much chastened. He had never been as bad at anything as he was at hitting a golf ball, even after some basic instruction from Fischer. For at least a hundred swings he'd struggled to hit it a) generally in the right direction; b) more or less in a straight line; c) at least a little up in the air; and d) over fifty yards. By the end of that time he'd managed to achieve each of those goals – but never more than one with any one shot. And he'd worked up a sweat and damn near thrown his back out trying. Those effortless, graceful, seemingly casual swings of people like Finley (until recently) and Lee that sent the ball rocketing well over 200 yards down the center of the fairway – they were smoke and mirrors, some kind of magic act that masked tremendous power and an athletic, uncanny coordination of eye, hand, and body. And it wasn't something you could learn in half an hour. That he could vouch for.

So maybe it *was* a sport, at that. It was no joke, that was for sure. Maybe – and this was the real surprise – watching a professional golf match wasn't the most boring thing in the world, if you knew what you were looking at. He had, he now acknowledged to himself, a few apologies to make to Lee.

But that was for later. For now, what had his attention was what he'd learned from Fischer's ongoing lectures on the way out to the range, on the range itself, and on the way back; namely, that very small maladjustments in the club could throw off a golfer's game in a major way, and the better and more consistent the golfer the greater the effect would be.

Did Graham know, Fischer had asked, that with an absolutely perfect golf swing – the kind of swing that could only be made by a club hooked up to a mechanical ball-hitter – a deviation of only four degrees in the lie angle would cause a pitching wedge, an absolutely perfectly swung pitching wedge, to be twenty-six feet off target at 120 yards? Or that on a mechanical putting machine, a putter whose face was two-fifths of *one* degree out of kilter would miss a ten-foot putt, no matter how faultlessly the ball was struck?

There was more of the same, all of which added weight to Lee and Peg's conjecture that the root of Roger's difficulties might be in his clubs. And when you took Dylan Blanchard's strange remarks and his subsequent death into account, it was even starting to seem that their 'sabotage' theory might have something going for it.

While they were in Graham's car, on the short drive back to the Number Two Course, Graham got his check-in calls from his people. All was well; no problems at all with any of the four groups of players, and nothing of significance with the crowds. Lee and Finley had just finished up the sixth hole and were getting ready to tee off at the seventh. How were they doing? Graham asked, but neither Coulter nor Mahnerd had any idea of how the scoring was going. That was good. They were doing their jobs, paying attention to what they were supposed to be paying attention to.

'Thanks a lot, Burt,' he said as they climbed out of the car in the restricted lot beside the clubhouse. 'That was very interesting.'

141

'You're more than welcome. I enjoyed it. So, are you going to tell me what this was really about?'

'What I said. I was just wondering if Finley's problems might have something to do with his clubs.'

From under bristling gray eyebrows, Fischer peered skeptically at him. 'One of the most important events in golf is underway. A caddie is murdered. A golfer – your fiancée, no less – is attacked . . . and the chief of security has nothing better to do than to devote his time to helping Roger improve his score? Come now, give me a little more credit than that.'

'I'm not a cop, Burt, I'm a consultant. Those things are the responsibility of the Pinehurst chief of police, and I can assure you that he's taking every—'

Fischer waved his remarks away. 'You think someone is undermining Roger's game, don't you? You think someone has been doing cunning, dastardly things to his clubs, and his caddie found out about it, and that's what got him killed. Am I right?'

Graham hesitated. Fischer was sharper than he'd given him credit for. 'Well—'

Fischer leaned forward, grinning wolfishly up at him. 'Am I right?'

Graham smiled. 'That's about it, yes. Is it possible, do you think?'

Fischer thought about it as they walked toward the third tee. 'In theory, certainly. In practice, unlikely. Roger's been having problems for a month, perhaps more. And Roger, as I told you, is quite learned in matters of club design and mechanics. His clubs are made for him by Sovereign, but the specifications are almost entirely his own. And he has his own measurement and evaluation equipment at home. Don't you think that a thorough examination of his clubs would be just about the first thing he'd see to when his game fell apart? Wouldn't it be the first thing you'd do?'

'I suppose so. Still . . .'

'Still, you need to check it out. If nothing else, to exclude it as a possibility.'

'That's about it. How would I do that?'

'Well, Sovereign does have an equipment trailer here – every maker with players in the event does, in case a club has to be repaired or replaced, and Sovereign has a couple of people playing; Roger and one of the British girls. Their man, Carter Rowen, is good. He'd have Roger's specs, naturally, and he'd be able to compare them against the clubs that Roger is using.'

'So, what I need to do is have Roger bring his clubs over to the trailer?'

'Well, you have to understand. Roger thinks he knows more about club design and physics than Carter does – even more than I do, difficult as that may be to comprehend. And, just between us, he may very well be right. So, the first thing you have to do is to get him to agree there might possibly be a problem with his clubs, and then you have to get him to agree that Carter might be able to spot it when he couldn't, and then you have to get him to actually bring them over to the trailer to be examined.'

'Is that going to be hard?'

Fischer tilted his head to one side. 'Not going to be easy.'

Twenty

The final putt of Lee's match was sunk by Dianna Gentry of Britain to bring them to a tie: one half point for the Americans, one half point for the British. An inconclusive beginning to the tournament. The gallery, a little disappointed not to have a more definitive outcome, applauded good-humoredly and began to disperse to catch up with the following foursomes. Roger and Lee shook hands, quite cordially, with their British counterparts, and then watching family members were permitted inside the ropes to hug and congratulate their player relatives.

Lee jumped when someone touched her shoulder, but when she saw it was Graham she beamed as he wrapped her in his arms.

'Were you watching?' she said. 'I didn't know you'd be here when we finished.'

'It's a good thing I was,' he said. 'Otherwise you'd be hugless, wouldn't you?'

'Mm,' she said as he squeezed a little tighter, then pulled back to look up into his face. 'That hat is definitely *not* you, she said. 'Has to go. You need one of those classy Panamas. Or maybe just a visor. You'd look good in a visor.'

He was wearing a neon-orange baseball cap with *CMI* – for Countermeasure Inc. – in big, bold white letters on the front. 'I'm not wearing it for sartorial purposes,' he said. 'We all have them. Makes it easier to spot each other in a crowd if we have to.'

'Oh. Well, couldn't you at least come up with a different color? I mean . . . *orange*?'

'Never mind my cap. How're you holding up?'

'Well, I survived. I got through one whole day without disgracing myself.'

'Survive?' he said with a sudden burst of earnestness. 'You did a lot more than survive! You were terrific, you were great. That shot out of that sand trap with that big ledge on whatever hole that was? Tremendous, my heart was in my mouth! I watched you every chance I got. I can't tell you how proud I am of you.'

She just stared at him with her mouth open. 'Uh . . . what?'

'Can't stay,' he said. 'Have to talk to Roger. See you later. Great game!' One more squeeze, a prim, noisy buss on the cheek, and she was standing there mutely looking at his retreating back.

'Problem?' With the marshals gone, Peg had ducked under the rope to join her.

Lee looked at her friend, laughing. 'Far from it. I'm just wondering at this sudden conversion on Graham's part. He seems to have finally figured out that golf has something going for it.'

'Took him long enough,' Peg said stoutly. 'You were magnificent. Hey, don't let me hold you up. I just wanted to congratulate you. I know you need to go and join the galleries and root for the rest of the team.'

'Don't you want to come too?'

'I'd love to,' Peg said, already heading off, 'but I have to go check my e-mail.'

Lee found herself confusedly watching another retreating back. *Check her e-mail?*

Standing just inside the ropes, Graham waited politely while Roger provided his caddie with detailed instructions on precisely how his clubs were to be cleaned and stored. Roger's manner, his very posture, made it obvious that he was far from pleased with himself or with anything else. A few feet away, a heavy-set woman, whose eyes never left Roger, also waited, clutching her purse with both hands: his wife Marie.

145

'Mr Finley?' Graham finally said, when Roger showed no signs of coming to a conclusion with his caddie any time soon. 'Do you have a moment, please?'

'Yes?' Roger turned to him with the wary look of a man whose day had not gone well so far, and who had no reason to expect anything other than more of the same. But the baleful gaze moderated slightly when he recognized Graham. 'Oh, you're Lee's, er, friend . . .'

'That's right, Graham Sheldon. I'm also the tournament's security consultant, as you might remember, and I'm working with Chief Oates—'

'Chief Oates, yes,' Roger echoed vaguely, his mind a million miles away.

'—on Dylan Blanchard's murder and on the attack on Lee last night. I was talking to Burt Fischer a few hours ago and the possibility came up that your clubs—'

'My clubs, yes.' Roger was looking somewhat longingly over Graham's shoulder toward the seventeenth hole. Clearly, he was eager to go and cheer on the rest of his team, and he had no idea what Graham was talking about.

Graham decided it was time to cut to the chase. 'Sir, I'd like your permission to have your clubs looked at by the Sovereign technician to make sure that they're not out of whack in some way. All of them, if possible, but at least the driver, the putter, a wedge, and one of the middle irons.' That was what Burt had told him to ask for.

Roger shook himself like a man coming out of a trance. 'My *clubs*?'

Well, at least I finally have his attention, Graham thought. 'Yes, the thing is—'

'I know what the thing is,' Roger said, suddenly irritated. 'Your fiancée—' A brief, poisonous glare after Lee, of which she was fortunately unaware. '—has kindly shared with me – in addition to obviously sharing them with you, and with Fischer, and with anyone else who cared to listen – her theories on the source of my difficulties. Questions of their dubious accuracy aside, Mr Graham—'

Graham thought it best not to correct him.

146

'—I fail to see how this is any of your concern.'

'I can certainly understand how you—'

But Roger was in a talking mood, not a listening mood. 'It's not that I don't appreciate the interest of everyone and his dog, but my golf game, deplorable as it may be, hardly qualifies as a police matter. And now I'm sure you'll excuse me—'

'I'm afraid it *is* a police matter because it's possible that your caddie may have been murdered over it.'

'Oh, come now, don't you think that's a little—?'

'We think your clubs may have been tampered with, and that Dylan may have found out who was responsible and may have been killed on account of it.' He didn't bother to say that, other than himself, the 'we' consisted of Peg Fiske and Lee Ofsted.

'Tampered with?' Roger stared at him with a mixture of annoyance and incredulity. 'Are you telling me someone has purposely altered my clubs without my knowing it? To throw off my game? Is that what you're telling me?'

'Sir, I'm not trying to tell you anything,' Graham said evenly. 'I'm trying, as politely as you'll let me, to ask for your cooperation in examining your clubs.'

'And what you don't seem to understand is that it's ridiculous. Aside from the fact that I regularly check them myself, why in God's name would anyone be interested in ruining my game? How would they possibly *get* at my clubs to do it? Who would want to ruin my game enough to—?'

But Graham, whose fuse was not especially long, had had enough. 'Mr Finley, let's get something straight. We're not talking about your golf game. I hate to be the one to tell you this, but your golf game is not the most important thing in the world. Between us, I don't give a damn about your golf game. We're talking about a young man whose life has been cut off in its prime, and a young woman who's been attacked, and if those two events had anything to do with the condition of your clubs I damn well want to know.'

'I—'

'I would also like to know it if they didn't, so we can move on to other things.'

'I—'

'And my name is Graham Sheldon, not Sheldon Graham.'

Finley blinked. 'I'm sorry,' he said stiffly. 'I wasn't thinking. Yes, of course Carter can look over my clubs. He won't find anything, but he's welcome to try.' He spoke to his waiting, dreaming caddie. 'Gabe, will you take them over to the Sovereign trailer, please? And don't just leave them. See that they go directly into Carter Rowen's hands. Also, you might as well show him that place on the lob wedge where the grip is coming loose. Maybe he can do something about that while he has them.'

'Clean 'em after he finishes?'

'Yes, it won't take that long. You stay with them while he has them. And then they go directly into locked storage. I don't want them out of your sight.'

He turned back to Graham. 'I really am sorry. I apologize for the way I acted.' He seemed a different man, no longer the put-upon celebrity but a normal, everyday human being, contrite into the bargain. He looked like somebody you might meet at a barber's convention. 'Sometimes in this business, with all these media people, and the crowds and all, it takes a shock to remind you that you're not really the center of the universe.'

'That's OK, Mr Finley, I understand the kind of stress you're under. I appreciate the cooperation.'

Finley's wife was pointing to her watch and edging closer in a proprietary kind of way, and he lifted a finger in a be-with-you-in-a-minute wave. 'You know, now that I think about it,' he said to Graham, 'it would be lovely if Carter did find that my clubs were all "out of whack".' He sighed. 'At least that would be fixable.'

148

Twenty-One

Peg leaned back and rubbed her hands together like an expert pastry chef surveying the assembled ingredients of a complex and magnificent soufflé she was about to begin constructing. In her case, however, the ingredients were not butter, eggs, flour, and cream, but tidbits of information that were at this moment scrolling upward over the screen of her humming laptop.

After yesterday's late-night session with Lee and Graham, she had come back to her villa and, worn to a frazzle though she was, she had booted up the laptop and sent an SOS pleading for information to Hetty's Hackers, her golf chat group. In the morning, having slept through the radio-alarm, she'd been too rushed to check the returns, but now at last, sitting at her patio table in the pleasant afternoon sunshine, with a pot of room-service coffee beside her, she was reaping the rewards of her industry.

The note she'd sent was a request for information about enemies that Roger Finley might have made over the years, particularly among those present at this year's Stewart Cup. She had given no explanation for her request, but in this group, no reason was required: golf gossip was its own reward and its own reason for being. She had headed the message 'Who's Got It in For Roger?' and she was pleased but hardly surprised to find that the thread under that title already consisted of thirty-two entries, some with sub-threads.

As usual, the majority of them were, to put it mildly, somewhat speculative, but several consisted of forwarded newspaper or Web-magazine articles, and these she regarded as at least marginally more reliable. Within twenty minutes she had printed up three of them, along with their follow-up articles and the sub-threads they'd generated.

'Oh, Lordie, Jordie.'

'Deadpan Dave Hides Secret Pain.'

'"What, Me Angry?" Snarls Sheppard.'

She'd gone through the entire set one more time, sat back sipping the last of her coffee, and, on consideration, had added one more sub-thread. This one had no media articles to support it, but the heading was captivating enough to include it.

'Hey, Roger, Who's That Hottie I Saw You With?'

Then, satisfied with a job well done, she gathered up the printouts and went to find Lee.

Twenty-Two

'I wouldn't be too worried at this point,' said a worried-looking Roger, opening the post-play strategy session. 'We still have two days to go, and we're not that far behind. We'll get it together tomorrow, never fear.'

'We'd better,' Dougal Sheppard growled. 'From where I sit, those Brits are looking very capable and confident indeed.'

'I remember something Tom Watson was supposed to have said when he was captaining the Ryder Cup team,' a pensive Ginger Rolley put in. 'He said the British have a feel for the game that no one else has. Over there, even people who don't play have a natural understanding of it. It's almost genetic. That gives them a big psychological advantage, a lot of confidence.'

'Does it ever,' Toni Blake-Kelly said. Toni, stick-thin and petite, was three or four years older than Lee, but looked even younger. She sounded younger too, with a breathless little-girl voice that might have been modeled on Marilyn Monroe's. Or Betty Boop's. 'Gosh, playing against Evan today was like playing against a machine. On four he sank a thirty-four-foot downhill putt and didn't even have the decency to look surprised!'

'Let alone apologize,' Dave Hazelton said, cracking open the cap on one of the plastic Perrier bottles that had been set out for them, along with coffee, on the Centennial Board Room's gleaming, oval table.

'Well, Toni,' said Roger, 'let me finish Ginger's quotation for you. Tom also said: "Everything they invented, we perfected."' He offered a genial smile. Toni seemed to bring out the fatherly in him. 'You might want to keep that in mind.'

'Thank you, Roger, but all I need to keep in mind is the super thought that today's over, and Jordie and I won't have to compete against SuperGolfer again.'

'Speak for yourself,' growled Jordie, tossing his handsome, golden head to get a lock of hair off his forehead. 'I'd love another crack at that guy. He had more lucky breaks today—'

'Save the bravado for tomorrow,' Roger snapped, 'when you're up against George Gatchet and Alicia Daly. Maybe *you'll* have more luck.'

The thin-skinned Jordie's eyelids came halfway down. He lowered his chin, but not enough to hide the pink flush that flooded into his throat and cheeks. Sitting directly across from him, Lee couldn't say she blamed him. After all, Roger wasn't in the strongest position in the world to talk. His play had been erratic at best, and if she hadn't scrambled, chipped, and putted their way out of the trouble he'd put them in, they too would have lost their match instead of tying. Of their four teams, only Dinny Goulapoulos and Dave had won. Ginger and Dougal had lost, as had Jordie and Toni. The result was that the Americans stood one point behind after the first day's play – not an insurmountable lead, as Roger said, but not as nice as being a point ahead would have been.

Roger, taken aback by Jordie's reaction, apologized at once. 'I shouldn't have said that, Jordie. *I'm* the one in need of a little luck.' He smiled. 'A little skill would be appreciated even more.'

'No problem,' Jordie muttered, not lifting his gaze from the table.

Given what she'd heard from Peg an hour earlier, the exchange was particularly interesting to Lee. After Peg had left to check her e-mail, Lee had continued to watch her teammates play their last few holes. Then, just as Ginger had sunk her final putt to finish up the last foursome, Peg, her eyes sparkling, had briefly caught up with her. 'Got some things that are going to knock your socks off, Lee. Tea, my room, after your press conference. Bye.'

She hadn't exaggerated, either, having come up with several people who had plausible motives for sabotaging Roger. The most credible was Jordie's. One of Peg's contacts had e-mailed her a copy of the members' newsletter from the Pelican Island Golf and Country Club in Florida, which happened to be Roger's home course. A front-page article described an incident that had occurred a year earlier, during Jordie's self-inflicted hiatus from the tour. Before he'd gotten himself straightened out, he'd taken to supporting himself by playing high-stakes golf with amateurs, which was a distasteful but not unknown practice of some pro golfers. In Jordie's case, the stakes had been very high indeed. His specialty, according to the article, had been $10,000 'Nassaus', a betting game in which three separate bets are placed: on the front nine, on the back nine, and on the entire eighteen. That would have been bad enough, but Jordie had been a hustler in the true sense of the term, not merely playing other gamblers and would-be hustlers, but enticing 'square Johns' – ordinary weekend-golfing busi-nessmen – into playing a round with him by offering them seemingly failure-proof handicaps.

Not only had one of his severely stung victims been a fellow-member of Roger's at Pelican Island, but the infa-mous round itself had been played right there – right outside Roger's sixteenth-fairway window, so to speak. When Roger had learned about it, he'd not only had Jordie banned from Pelican Island, but he'd put the word out to a dozen or so sister clubs. He'd done it right up front too, sending Jordie a letter informing him of the fact. He'd also told him that he was considering reporting him to the PGL Board, some-thing on which he'd apparently never followed through.

But what he *had* done was more than enough to make himself an enemy for life, especially when you took Jordie's hair-trigger temper, impulsiveness, and all-around reck-lessness into account. Did Jordie hate Roger enough to take the enormous risk of somehow stealing his clubs from a

153

locked room somewhere, throwing off their calibrations, and then sneaking them back? Enough to kill Dylan to keep him from telling? Could that actually have been Jordie in her room last night?

Lee studied him: the flush, dull and streaky now, but still visible; the hurt, brooding cast of his eyes and mouth; the stolidly lowered eyes.

Could be, she thought.

She was startled when the lights went out, but then a schematic, colored drawing of the third hole popped up on the brightly lit screen, waggled around a bit, and then settled. Lee had been so preoccupied she'd never even seen Roger put the transparency projector on the table. *Pay attention*, she told herself. *Your job is golf.*

'All right now,' Roger said, 'I'd like to start with three. We didn't have a lot of trouble there today, but then the pin was placed at the front, nice and easy. Tomorrow may be another story. My guess is it'll be at the back, so let's assume that that's the case. Now, er, the weather's supposed to be even drier and warmer, so the greens are going to be firm. That means that if you fly at the flag and overshoot, you're a goner. If the pin's on the left, you'll roll off toward the fifth green. If it's on the right, you'll wind up heading for the fourth fairway. My advice would be to, er, stay away from the driver altogether and settle . . .'

Roger was not the world's most sparkling lecturer, and Lee found her eyes and attention wandering in Dave Hazelton's direction. Dave, long-faced and gaunt, was watching Roger attentively, but there was something about the set of his back, and the way both bony hands grasped the arms of his swivel chair, and the way he was rocking with quick little motions, that strongly suggested impatience with the way Roger was going about it; as if he, Dave, and not Roger, should by rights be the one who was up front telling the rest what to do and how to do it.

Or was she imagining things, constructing a scenario to fit one of the notions that she and Peg had hatched? The theory, and not a bad one, it seemed to her, stemmed from

154

some common golf tittle-tattle of which Lee had been typically unaware. Dave and Roger, it was generally known, had been the top contenders for the captaincy of the Stewart Cup team. When it had been given to Roger, Dave, while not getting nasty about it, had not been as gracious as he might have been. And then, when Roger's game began falling apart, there were reports that he had expressed the opinion that Roger, in the interests of the team's welfare, should have voluntarily stepped down and left it to the next in line. But these were private opinions, privately expressed, and understandable – perhaps even sensible – under the circumstances. Never had Dave griped to the press or shown anything like anger or open resentment.

So they had thought. But one of Peg's e-mails, an article from a Wellington, New Zealand newspaper, said differently. 'Deadpan Dave Hides Secret Pain' was the headline, and the piece described his press-tent interview after winning the Cook Strait Classic, a non-PGL tour event, by a phenomenal eleven strokes a few weeks earlier. He had been asked the question point-blank: 'Considering Roger Finley's recent poor showings and how brilliantly you've been playing, do you think Mr Finley should resign as Stewart Cup captain and that the committee should appoint you in his place?'

Dave's initial response had indeed been deadpan, and the purest PR fluff: 'The committee made the right choice. Roger Finley is one of the finest golfers of our generation. It's an honor to be on the same team with him.'

But when the questioners had continued in this vein for some considerable time, Hazelton had finally let his hair down. 'Look,' he'd griped, 'do I really have to explain to you that the team captain is the sentimental favorite, period, end of story? It has nothing to do with performance.'

The delighted media representatives had naturally jumped on that, and the sweaty, tired, increasingly touchy Dave had obliged. 'What, were you under the impression that it was supposed to have anything to do with merit?' and, 'For Christ's sake, will you people drop it? Finley could shoot

155

a goddamn eighty-five in Scottsdale next week, and he'd *still* be captain,' were two of his more choice remarks.

Luckily for his sake and for the team's, neither the Associated Press nor any of the other services had picked it up, but then the infinitely resourceful Peg had contacts that AP could only dream about.

Lee studied Dave's skeletal profile, seen now in semi-darkness, so that the tip of his long nose seemed to be reaching out to touch his chin. Was he the one? Over tea, she and Peg had speculated thusly: Dave had been Roger's chief competitor for the captaincy. Popular opinion had it that they'd been running neck-and-neck earlier in the year. Then Roger's game had suddenly gone south. Wasn't it at least possible, they reasoned, that Dave, trying to tip the scales in his own favor, had doctored Roger's clubs to throw off his game?

If so, the effort had backfired. There had been an outpouring of sympathy and support for Roger from the entire golfing community – including the Stewart committee. But that, as Peg said, wouldn't have negated his original motivation. He had guessed wrong, that was all.

Lee had had reservations. Yes, it was a conceivable motive for club-tampering, especially in Dave's case. Like Roger, he was getting a little long in the tooth; they were both forty-eight. That meant he'd be eligible for the senior tour the year after next. If he followed the usual pattern, he'd quit the regular PGL on his birthday to join the seniors while he was still hale enough to outclass the rest of the old guys. Since the Stewart was a biennial event, that meant that this was his last chance to be captain. So, sure, maybe he'd be tempted to do a little sabotage. But *murder*? Surely not.

Peg had agreed, but had pointed out that murder wouldn't have been in the cards until Dylan found out about it. At that point it had become a matter, not of jealousy or competitiveness, but of self-preservation. Still, Lee thought—

She jumped in her seat as Dave very suddenly jerked his head around to glare straight into her eyes. She had the

156

unpleasant sensation that he had not only sensed her continued staring at him, but had read what was in her mind. Quickly, she swung her attention to the screen, accidentally knocking over a (thankfully) capped bottle of Perrier with her elbow. That brought another glare, this time from Roger. She smiled apologetically and did her best to look utterly engrossed in the projected image, but even in school she hadn't been very good at manufacturing absorption. Roger sighed his displeasure and went back to his presentation.

'Now, as I was saying, several of us, myself prominently included, had trouble with the second shot on number eight. The trick there is to avoid that up-slope left of the green. If you use a long iron in hopes of . . .'

And Lee went back to her personality studies. What about the sober, scholarly Dougal Sheppard, sitting there chewing on the corners of that great, sandy mustache? A possible murderer? Peg had so far dug up nothing on him, which pleased Lee. She didn't *want* it to be Dougal. She didn't think it *was* Dougal. At the same time, she knew only too well that at the core of every great athlete, no matter how sober, or scholarly, or kind, or just plain nice, there was a mean streak; a killer instinct. It didn't matter whether you were a prizefighter or a golfer. The margin between winning and losing at the exalted level at which the people around this table played was so razor-thin that you couldn't worry about stepping on another athlete's hopes, or feelings, or career. The tiniest kernel of concern for your competitor could turn you from winner to loser. And Dougal had a whole lot of wins under his belt.

So put him down as another *maybe* . . . but an unlikely one.

The most intriguing theory – the 'juiciest' one, in Peg's terminology – concerned someone who wasn't even in the room, someone to whom they hadn't given a thought until Peg had received her 'Hey, Roger, Who's That Hottie I Saw You With?' e-mail. One of her correspondents, an inveterate tournament-goer, had reported that she'd several times spotted a gorgeous, leggy young blonde following

157

Roger around in the gallery – nobody with her – and had gotten the distinct impression that there'd been a lot of eye-contact and secret little gestures between them: a wink, a smile, a waggle of the fingers, a lift of the eyebrows.

'You know,' Peg had said casually, 'the kind of thing you and Graham are always doing.'

Lee had said nothing, but she was taken aback. Were they really that obvious? Was it that easy to spot from the gallery? How embarrassing!

At any rate, others had responded with similar stories. One said that during a tournament she'd seen Roger having drinks with a knockout blonde – movie-star-quality – in a dark little bar in a town fifteen miles away from the course. And another even came up with a name: Eileen Westerbrook, a twenty-four-year-old model with Hollywood aspirations.

There was more: rumors that Roger was planning to dump his wife to take up a life with Eileen; rumors that Roger's wife Marie had found out about their trysts and had even hired a private detective to stay on Roger's trail on those rare instances when she wasn't with him on tour. If there was a divorce, she wanted it on her terms.

So the rumors said, and *there*, Peg had happily pointed out, was a heck of a motive. Some people called Marie the Velcro Wife for the way she stuck to her husband, like an eagle guarding its offspring from predators. Wasn't it possible that the bulky, ageing Marie had ruined Roger's career to get back at him? And didn't Lee think she was capable of braining Dylan?

But what would be the point of it? Lee had asked. Wouldn't she have found some other way to pay him back? Her own welfare, her style of living, depended on Roger's income from his golfing career. That'd be true even if she divorced him. Why would she torpedo it?

'To *hurt* him,' Peg had said sagely. 'Never underestimate the ferocity – and the resourcefulness – of the faithful wife scorned.'

So, OK, that was one more possible—

Roger's voice, at its briskest, cut through her thoughts.

'Lee, if you have something more important to think about, feel free to leave at any time.'

'I'm sorry, Roger. I was . . . I was still thinking about what you said about the eighth.'

'I'm still *on* the eighth.' He gestured over his shoulder at the screen behind him. 'Here, before your very eyes, is the eighth itself, in all its glory. If you would like to tell us how *you* think it ought to be played . . .'

'Sorry, Roger,' she mumbled again.

Roger loosed another theatrical sigh and went back to his lecture.

He had been cool toward her right from the start of the session and sometimes, as now, downright nasty. She thought she knew what it was about, too. Peg had run into Graham near the villas, where he'd mentioned to her that Roger had reluctantly agreed to have his clubs examined by the Sovereign technician. But it had been like pulling teeth, Graham had said.

No doubt, Roger had assumed – correctly – that she'd been the one who'd put that particular bug in Graham's ear and he was upset with her about it. Well, if it came to that, she was upset with him too. She was only trying to help, after all. More than that, she'd saved his bacon on no less than four holes today, and it seemed to her he owed her something more than a prissy cold shoulder on that account.

All the same, she was pleased that Graham had talked him into it. If nothing else, it would resolve the basic issue of whether or not Roger's clubs had really been tampered with. If yes, they were at least heading in the right direction in their speculations.

If no, it was back to square one.

Tweny-Three

If you had to pick a single image to capture the feel of the Carolina Hotel, it would surely be the columned, wraparound porch with its long row of spotless, white wicker rocking chairs that look out over the smooth lawns. The scene, especially when a few people are rocking slowly back and forth, bespeaks elegance, comfort, and Southern-style leisure.

On the west porch, looking out over an old but perfectly maintained putting green, the straw-hatted man in one of the two occupied chairs looked anything but leisurely. His chair was in motion; jiggling, or perhaps wiggling, but hardly what anybody would call rocking. On his face was an expression of extreme consternation and disbelief, and in his slack left hand was a single sheet of paper filled with printed figures and hand-drawn diagrams.

He waggled the sheet – a small, defeated gesture – and looked helplessly at Graham.

'I still can't believe it. I just can't believe it.'

Graham sighed, trying to make it sound sympathetic. He'd been sitting on the porch hearing that Roger couldn't believe it for twenty minutes now. And that was after a similar half-hour spent in Sovereign's equipment trailer, where Carter Rowen had concisely presented his findings ('Ten of your fourteen clubs have been seriously tampered with.')

The stunned, incredulous Roger had responded with a remarkable and entertaining rendition of the five classical stages of grief, progressing from first to last in the space of ten minutes: from *denial* ('Impossible, I don't believe it. Your machines are calibrated wrong. Your figures are

160

screwed up. And anyway, it wouldn't make that much difference in my game.'), to anger ('Damn it, Carter, this is stupid, just plain stupid! If something was wrong with my clubs, don't you think I'd know it'), to *bargaining* ('Well, couldn't it be that they're a little bit off from usage?'), to depression ('Oh, God, it's my fault . . . all that rotten play that I could have . . . why didn't I check them before the tournament? We could have won today.'), to not quite wholehearted *acceptance* ('OK, Carter, I guess the measurements don't lie. I can live with this. I mean, if that's really all that's wrong with my game, I should be happy. . . . but I still don't believe it.')

'I mean,' Roger went on now, '*sabotage*? It's bizarre. Who ever heard of anything like that? Who would hate me enough to do that? What would they get out of it?'

'Roger, let's forget about why for the moment. Tell me who you think *could* have done it? That is, who might have gotten at your clubs over the last month or so – and is also here in Pinehurst now?'

'Nobody, only me, that's the thing!' He was still jiggling away. 'Well, my caddie, of course, Dylan, but he . . .' The jiggling stopped, much to Graham's relief. Roger put a hand over his eyes. 'Oh, dear.'

'Are you sure? Wouldn't other golfers have access to the club rooms? Don't the clubs sit there for a while sometimes before they go into the lockers?'

'Well . . . I suppose so . . . plenty of times there aren't lockers for them, they just sit out on the rails in the club storage room, but the storage room's always well secured when there's a PGL tournament on, so there's no way for—'

'How about these people?' Graham went through the list that he, Lee, and Peg had come up with: Dougal, Dave, and Jordie.

An unreadable expression – interest? Doubt? Second thoughts? – flitted over his face at the mention of Dave, but in the end he shook his head. 'No. I can't believe that of any of them. Anyway, if access to my clubs is your criterion, why not include my wife in there too? She could get at my clubs.'

'We did. Couldn't come up with a credible motive.' He decided not to mention the 'hottie' who an excited Peg had briefly told him about when she'd caught him in passing earlier.

Roger stared at him with his mouth open. 'You're serious! Graham, Marie knows less about golf than you do. She wouldn't know how to begin altering a club.'

No, Graham thought, *but, being your wife, she'd know plenty of people who would.* 'OK, let it pass. No motives at all that you can think of? For anybody?'

Roger began to say something, but changed his mind and shook his head again. 'No. Sorry.'

'Did you know that Dylan told several people he knew what your problem was—?'

Roger waved his hand. 'Oh, Dylan always thought he knew—'

'And that he knew who was responsible?'

Roger frowned. '*Who* was responsible? He said that?'

Graham nodded. 'And why.'

The jiggling started again. 'Graham, forgive me, no offense, but that simply cannot be true. If Dylan knew, or even thought he knew, something like that, don't you think he'd have come to me with it? Who is he supposed to have told?'

'A couple of other caddies. That was all they could get out of him, though. No details.'

'No, no, no, I don't believe it. Think about it. Dylan's income was completely dependent on mine. The more I made, the more he made. The less I made, the less he made. Wouldn't he have told me, if he thought he could help me play better?'

'Well, the story is, he was planning to make more by *not* telling you.'

'Now I'm completely lost.'

'We think he was planning to blackmail whoever was doing it.'

162

'Sorry, but this is getting a little Byzantine for me. It sounds like a James Bond movie.' He tried a smile. 'In fact, I think I may have seen it.'

Graham didn't smile in return. 'Roger, listen to me. Dylan is dead. Someone murdered him. There's a reason for it, and I think it's tied up with this sabotage business.'

The jiggling stopped. 'Of course. You're absolutely right to pursue it. Only—' He hunched his shoulders. '—Jordie? Dougal? It's just so, so—'

'When was the last time you checked your clubs to see that the calibrations were all correct?'

Roger pondered. The afternoon sun had dipped lower now, and his chair had him looking directly into it. He tipped his straw boater down to keep it out of his eyes, giving him an incongruously jaunty, Maurice Chevalier kind of look, as if he were about to jump up and do a buck-and-wing. Graham had some time ago pulled the bill of his cap down about as far as it would go.

'Well, let me see now,' Roger said. 'It would have been about three months ago. I always check them when I get them from the factory, which would have been four months ago, and then re-check a month later to make sure they're holding up. I guess that was the last time.'

'And your difficulties started when?'

'At the Waimea Pro-Am,' was the prompt response, accompanied by a shudder. 'That would have been, oh, a little over a month ago; five weeks.'

'Well, then, I guess there's something I don't quite understand,' Graham said, leaning forward. The rocking chair creaked under him. 'I would have thought you'd have re-checked them the minute your game, uh—'

'Went south,' Roger supplied equably. 'Well, yes, I understand why you'd think that, and I would've done so if I'd been having problems with my putter, or my driver, or my fairway woods. But I was having trouble with *every-thing*. I just couldn't hit anything at all. And it was simply out of the realm of possibility that *all* my clubs had gone out of whack.' He shook his head slowly back and forth.

'Of course, the idea of sabotage wasn't in the picture then.'

He began rocking again, more moderately now, and for a few meditative moments he was silent. 'You know, I really haven't given much thought to the upside of this.'

Graham joined him in the rocking. It was very restful. He felt like an old Southern gentleman. 'Which is?'

'That if those clubs really are the source of my problems – and I'm beginning to think they are – then my problems would be over, wouldn't they? Carter has promised to work on them all night, if necessary, so that I can have them tomorrow. In fact—' He jumped to his feet, a different man from the one who had sat down a short time ago. '—if it's all right with you, I'm going to go join him now. I can't wait to see how things are going with the refitting, and I have some ideas of my own, and I might even have a chance to try out one or two—'

Graham got up too. 'Roger, I'd appreciate it if you'd go talk to Chief Oates in the village instead. I'll give you a lift, if you like.'

Roger's face fell. 'But why? What can I tell him that I haven't told you?'

'Maybe nothing, but remember, I'm not a cop, it's not my case. Nate is the one who's heading up the investigation, and he'll need to hear this from you. And he'll probably have some other questions.'

'Well, but surely they can wait till after the matches tomorrow. It's late now, and I only have an hour before another one of those endless dinners—'

'Roger—'

With a rueful smile, Roger held up his hand to stop him. 'I know. You don't have to say it. My golf game is not the most important thing in the world.' He clapped Graham gingerly on the shoulder. 'All right, let's go and see the chief. Can you stay with me, though? The man scares me a little.'

'Glad to,' Graham said, happy to have an excuse to do just that.

164

Twenty-Four

After the second day's matches, the mood displayed by the American team during the press conference was one of mild optimism and warm, sportsmanlike praise for the other side. In private, it was rampant jubilation, full of chuckling, back-slapping, and high-fiving. It had been a terrific day, an amazing day. They had won all four of their matches, thereby erasing the British one-point advantage and replacing it with a huge three-point lead for the Americans, with only one day's matches to go. More important, the momentum was overwhelmingly with them, and to a professional golfer, momentum was better than luck, better than skill.

And most important, Roger Finley, the old Roger Finley, was back. Shot after perfect shot: from the tees, from the fairways, from around and on the green, from everywhere. He was alive with joy over his rediscovered brilliance, almost hysterical, laughing and joshing with his caddie, with Lee, with the British pair, with the gallery, with the marshals, with anybody who'd let him. It was as if a hundred pounds that he'd been lugging around on his shoulders had at last been lifted.

Lee was both exhausted and exhilarated. The reasons for the exhilaration were obvious enough, but she wasn't quite sure where the exhaustion was coming from. The day's play had been high-pressure from beginning to end, and the din had been a strain. With all four matches going on at once, and each one just a hole or two behind the next, unexpected roars, shouts, and groans seemed to be erupting from every direction, usually just when she was lined up over a difficult putt.

But she was used to pressure (admittedly, not at this level) and noise, and it usually didn't drain her quite like this. She wondered if the unaccustomed adulation and respect she was getting from Roger and Graham, so extremely pleasant at first, wasn't what was wearing her down. Roger, she could understand. He was a new man. His career, his income, his very life, had been rejuvenated because he'd finally given in and allowed his clubs to be examined – a suggestion for which he'd not very graciously rebuffed her yesterday. So he was feeling guilty and trying to make it up to her.

But by the sixth hole, his delighted exclamations ('Did you see that one?' 'Did you see *that* one?') and his endless expressions of gratitude to her had started to interfere with her concentration, wearing the edge off the keen focus she required to play at her best. This time, it was Roger who had to carry her, and that, thank goodness, he was now well able to do.

Graham was something else altogether. It had started the night before when he joined her at the evening's cocktail reception and dinner, this one at the house of an ex-senator who lived in Southern Pines, a few miles from Pinehurst. (The hotel had provided vans for the team; Lee had yet to find a reason to call for her complimentary white Cadillac – something she still planned to do, just for the heck of it, if she ever found time to squeeze it in, which was now becoming unlikely.) Clearly, Graham's interlude with Burt Fischer had transformed his view of golf as a sport. He had Lee and Peg – and before long, a few of the others: Jordie, Ginger, and Toni – doubled over with laughter describing his adventures on the driving range with club and ball. ('It's *hard*,' he informed them.)

By morning she could have used a little less admiration, cosseting, and – especially – appreciation of how extremely difficult the game was. At breakfast, she'd had to tell him, as gently as she could, to knock it off. She *knew* how extremely difficult it was; she really didn't need reminding, certainly not right then, so could they please talk about something else? For instance, she'd been thinking about this sabotage thing—

But now she'd gotten him so worried about interfering with her concentration on golf that he'd clammed up. 'Don't you give all that a thought, you have plenty on your plate as it is. Nate's handling things just fine, and I'm pitching in where needed. You just worry about your game.'

Well, he probably had a point there, and throughout the day's match she'd followed his advice as well as she could. But now the match was over, the press conference was winding up (inasmuch as Roger handled just about all the questions, she was beginning to wonder why the rest of them had to be there at all), and she wanted to know what was going on. They'd talked about the case at the reception the previous night, and both Peg and Lee had been gratified, and a little surprised, to see that he actually took their speculations on motives seriously. After his brief, 'drive-by' exchange with Peg that afternoon, he'd kept an eye out for the 'hottie', and he'd found her: a truly spectacular, leggy blonde in short shorts and strapless heels, always alone, hovering about at the edge of Roger's field of vision but always well beyond the eagle-eyed Marie Finley's.

'So that's what you do all afternoon,' Lee had said. 'It's a wonder they pay you.'

'Just doing my job, ma'am,' he replied.

'Uh-huh. Strapless heels, huh?'

'A good three inches. Stilettos. It's a wonder she could walk in them.' He cleared his throat. 'It's the kind of thing I'm paid to notice.'

'I see. And what kind of shoes – no, don't look down – am I wearing right now?'

'Right now,' he'd said coolly, before laughter got the better of him, 'I'm not on duty.'

Beyond that, there had been little for him to add: only that the police were still trying to get hold of Pokey or Bear, and that they were chasing a couple of other leads, but nothing solid as of yet.

167

But that was then. Another day had passed now, and she was eager for an update. If for no other reason, she needed something to take her mind off tomorrow, the third and final day of the tournament. The Americans' three-point lead came about as close as possible to putting the tournament on ice – they'd just about have to come apart at the seams to lose now – but the format was going to be eight singles matches, not the four team matches of the first two days, so she'd be out there on her own against one of the Brits, and that was what was worrying her.

The fact that she'd never played any way but on her own before the Stewart Cup came along didn't seem to give her any comfort. She was nervous. While an American victory was almost guaranteed – the way the scoring worked, the British would need a miracle to win – there was no guarantee that Lee herself wouldn't make some gut-wrenching, disastrous blunder that would haunt her for the rest of her life. And haunt her it would; Lee's match with her English Rocky-slot counterpart would be the final one of the tournament. Every golf fan in the world would be watching.

Leaving the press tent with the rest of the team, she nabbed her security detail, the stolid, ever-present Coulter and Mahnerd, and asked them if they knew where Graham was.

'Sorry, ma'am,' Coulter (she thought he was Coulter) said, the first words she'd heard from either of them, 'he's busy right now.'

Twenty-Five

'Say again?' Graham pressed the earpiece into his ear to hear better over the sounds of the crowd and the crackle of the two-way itself.

'I said we got a small problem, Graham. Nothing too bad, but you said to let you know anything that concerns the players.'

He ducked his chin and spoke into his collar. 'What's up, Howard?'

'It's just a little scuffle down here at the entrance to the club-storage room – you know, under the clubhouse, that driveway? Me and Nan are here. One of the caddies was beating up on this guy and raising a hell of a ruckus besides. The guy's talking about pressing charges.'

'OK, I'm on my way. What's it about?'

'I'm not clear on that yet. The guy claims he's some kind of reporter. What's funny about it is he's a big, hulking dude . . . six-three or four, maybe two hundred and sixty pounds, and the caddie's this little, dried-up, old guy, but I guess the big guy was getting the crap beat out of him. I'm afraid the caddie works for—'

'Don't tell me,' Graham said with a sigh. 'He works for Lee. It's Lou Sapio, right?'

'Hey, how'd you know that?'

Graham smiled. 'Lucky guess?'

The reporter's name was Michael Foura, and he was sitting on a folding chair that Howard had set up for him on the Astroturf carpeting between the club-storage room and the cart-storage area. The place smelled of grease, oil, and

169

cleaners. Foura was big, all right, and fat, overflowing the sides of the chair, and he had a kind of stuffed, over-inflated look, as if, were you to stick a pin in him, there'd be a *POP* and then a *f-s-s-s-t*, and off he'd go, scootling around the place, ricocheting off the walls.

And he was very upset. 'Are you in charge?' he demanded when Graham came in. 'I want this man arrested.'

He pushed his slightly bent wire-rim glasses up on his nose and pointed at Lou, standing a few yards away in Nan's care. Lou was disheveled, bouncing on his toes like a fighter that had been in a tough scuffle so far but was more than ready to go another few rounds.

'Well, suppose you tell me what happened first,' Graham said. 'Your name's Michael Foura, and you're a reporter?'

'That's right. I—'

'Ask him what paper,' Lou said.

Graham leveled a finger at him without looking at him. 'You keep out of this. I'll get to you.'

'I work for *Buzz*,' Foura said, staring challengingly up at him. He had a fringe beard – no mustache – short and meager, and straggling down his neck.

Graham nodded. He'd seen it on the checkstands, a mix of patent nonsense and nasty gossip. 'Two-headed Baby Born Speaking Ancient Assyrian', 'Did Bisexual Priest Hire Hit Man to Kill Ex-Lover Nun?'

'Ho,' said Lou. 'Some paper.'

Graham swung his head around. 'OK, that's it. Take him somewhere else. I'll talk to him in a few minutes.'

'Hey, wait a minute,' Lou said, offended. 'I didn't do—'

But Nan was already hustling him down the corridor, one hand at the back of his collar. She loomed over him by a good four inches.

Graham looked for the card hanging on a lanyard from Foura's neck. 'I don't see a press pass.'

'I don't have one; I'm not covering the cup. I don't need one to be in here.'

Graham nodded. That was so. 'OK, what happened?'

'Like I told these other officers, I just innocently walked

up to the guy and explained that one of his buddies, Dylan Blanchard, had been doing some data-gathering for us, and would he like to take his place? For a fee, of course. Very polite, very businesslike. All he had to do was say no. Instead, he goes nuts and jumps me. Pulls off my glasses, starts whaling away. You people need to put him away somewhere.'

'What kind of data-gathering?'

Foura pursed his lips. 'I don't see how that's relevant.'

'Why'd you pick Lou?'

'Somebody told me he was Lee Ofsted's caddie.'

Graham's interest jumped markedly. 'And why is that important to *Buzz*?'

'I'm afraid that's all I'm at liberty to say.' He folded his arms, dipped his head, and looked at his toes, or at where his toes would be if he could see them. Obviously, he'd decided he'd said too much already.

'He told me he'd heard about the attack on her,' Howard said casually, from where he leaned against the wall. 'Got here pretty fast, didn't he? They're headquartered in San Diego.'

'Look, Mr Foura,' Graham said. 'We've had some pretty serious trouble here. I need to know what you're doing here. I need to know what your association with Dylan Blanchard was.'

'I'm afraid that's impossible.' With his arms still folded he looked up to meet Graham's eyes. 'We in the media have an obligation to protect the welfare and privacy of our sources, as well as to ensure that we cause no harm of any kind to innocent persons. Living or dead.'

Graham barely kept himself from laughing. Did these guys carry little 'we in the media' cards with them, the way cops carried Miranda warnings?

'Mr Foura, I want to know—'

Foura surprised him by erupting angrily from the chair. He loomed over Graham by as much as Nan did over Lou. 'And I want to know why you're making it sound as if I've committed some kind of crime or something. *I'm* the one who was attacked!'

171

'I understand. No one's accusing you of anything.'

'As I told the other officers—'

'We're not officers, we're security personnel.'

'Well, then, why am I talking to you at all? I want a real officer. I want to press charges. I was physically assaulted.'

'I'll have you at the police station in fifteen minutes to do just that. But Chief Oates is going to want to know about Dylan too.'

Foura lifted his scraggly chin. 'I have an obligation to my profession.'

Graham sighed. 'Howard, have somebody bring a car around, will you? Mr Foura and I are going to the police station in a few minutes. And I'm going to want Lou there too.'

'It's about time,' Foura said. 'Jesus, what an operation. I should have known you weren't real cops the minute I saw those stupid orange hats.'

'Better put the two gentlemen in two separate cars,' Howard said, 'if you want my advice.'

'Absolutely,' Foura said. 'No way I'm getting in the same car with that fruitcake.'

Lou and Nan were at the end of the corridor, about fifty feet away. Graham looked pointedly from Foura, to Lou, and back again. 'I have to say, it's pretty hard to imagine *him* attacking *you*. How'd he even *reach* your glasses?'

'I'll tell you how. He *climbed* me, like he was some goddamn monkey and I was a goddamn tree!'

Graham smiled. 'That's a heck of an image. If you want to go into a court and tell that in public, I guess that's your affair. Howard, will you stay with Mr Foura for a little while? I want to talk to Lou and hear the other side of this.'

'What other side?' Foura muttered, settling down again. 'There is no other side.'

And there wasn't, at least not as far as Foura's story went. Everything he'd said was frankly, even enthusiastically, verified by Lou. Foura had been waiting for him in the driveway. He'd approached him as Lou had come out of the storage area after cleaning and storing Lee's clubs. He'd

172

asked him if he'd be interested in gathering some information for *Buzz* . . . and Lou had attacked him. That was the way it had happened.

'Lou,' Graham said, 'you can't just go around doing this kind of thing, you know.' Nan had gone off for a car in which to drive Lou to the police station.

Lou shrugged. 'He provoked me.'

'Even so, you may be in some trouble here.'

Shrug. 'I been in trouble before.'

'Well, what did he say that provoked you so much? What did he want?'

'He wanted dirt on Lee.'

Graham's eyebrows shot up. 'On *Lee*? What kind of dirt would there be on Lee?'

'Anything. It didn't matter. They'd look at it, and if they could use it, they'd pay me.'

'And that's why you hit him?'

Lou responded with one of his rare, straight, eye-contact looks. 'Yeah, that's why I hit him. What kind of thing is that to ask me? I'm supposed to rat on Lee to *him*? I mean, like there was anything on her to rat on? She's the straightest, best damn bag I ever carried. If they were all like her, this'd be . . .' For him, it was a long, emotional speech, and he ground to an awkward halt. 'Ah, what the hell.'

Graham looked at him with a more kindly eye. *I could actually get to like this little guy*, he thought. 'Well, what made him think there *was* anything?' he asked.

'What happened to her. You know, last night. He figured there had to be something juicy there and she's a big shot now, so anything would be good.' He looked beyond Graham to where Foura still sat beside Howard and made a growling noise. 'Dirtbag.'

'And you think they sent someone all the way from San Diego just on the off-chance there was something? Seems kind of funny, don't you think?'

'Well, that's not where it started. See, first he started talking about Dylan, pussyfooting all around him.'

'About the murder, you mean.'

173

'No, not about the murder. See, if I got it straight . . . how about if we go outside? Stuffy in here – all them bags. I got delicate sinuses.'

They walked up the driveway from the basement and out on to the shaded lawn beside the old, porticoed clubhouse.

'That's better,' Lou said, sucking in air. 'So where was I?'

'What about Dylan?'

'Oh, yeah, well, Dirt Bag was being real careful about it, but here's what I got: Dylan was doing this article for them about how he knew all about what Finley's problem was and all. And Dirt Bag was trying to find out if maybe I could take over for him. See, Dylan went around bragging—'

'I remember, Lou. He said he knew what was wrong, and why, and who was causing it.'

'Right. So the way I figure it now, maybe the kid really did know something about who was screwing up Finley's game and was giving it to *Buzz*, and they were going to paste it all over the newsstands – and then the TV and everywhere else, you know?'

Lou lit up a cigarette, which presumably didn't bother his delicate sinuses. He did it one-handed, striking the match, cupping it against the breeze, and applying it to the Marlboro in a single motion. 'I mean, why would someone bother to croak him if he didn't really know anything?'

Graham nodded. This certainly added a new wrinkle. Could it be that Dylan hadn't been up to blackmail at all? That he'd planned to cash in on what he knew by selling it to *Buzz*? Or perhaps he was using the threat of exposure via *Buzz* to extort more from his intended victim? Or that he was somehow planning to do both?

'If they already had the information on what was going on from Dylan,' he said pensively, 'why would they need you?'

This, he thought, was certainly getting weird. If someone had told him yesterday that he'd be seriously asking Lou Sapio for his opinion on the case, he'd have laughed.

'Who knows?' Lou said. 'Maybe they needed proof. Pictures, like, or maybe they wanted me to wear a wire or something. You know.'

Not bad. Highly possible. He was beginning to see what it was that Lee saw in Lou. Now he, or more likely Nate Oates, would have some pretty good questions for Michael Foura too.

'Thanks, Lou, that makes a lot of sense.'

Nan pulled up in the car a few yards away and waited. 'Now, listen to me, Lou,' Graham said. 'I'm going to get Foura and drive him to the police station. Nan is going to drive you—'

'What, the guy's afraid to get in the same car with me?'

'Yes, and I don't blame him. You can't go around climbing people, you know.'

'I told you, I was provoked.'

'Well, don't get provoked when we're talking to Oates. If Foura really wants to push it, you'll certainly be charged, you understand? Or if you make Oates mad enough—'

'Oo, I'm really scared.'

'—you could be charged anyway. You could do jail time.'

Lou gave one of his shrugs and flipped away the cigarette butt. 'It was worth it.'

'Was it? And what if you aren't there tomorrow for Lee? If you're sitting in a cell? How's she going to get along without you?'

'Hadn't thought about that,' he admitted, scowling.

'You'll be good, then?'

'I'll be good.'

'If he asks you a question, you'll answer it?'

'I'll answer it.'

'The whole question, the entire implied question, not just the part of it you feel like answering?'

'Yeah, sure.'

'Even if it gets personal, into areas you're not in the mood to go into?'

Graham got the first smile he'd ever received from Lou. 'Hey, don't push me.'

175

Twenty-Six

To Lee's surprise, the final day of the tournament turned out to be anything but gut-wrenching. Instead, it was the most relaxing and enjoyable day of golf she'd had in months. Her opponent, Diana Anderson, was a pleasure to play with, and the big three-point lead the Americans enjoyed to start the day provided a huge cushion of comfort.

And playing last was fine too. By the time her match came up, the tournament was sure to have been wrapped up – the odds of a British comeback from that far behind were infinitesimal – so the pressure was off. They were just playing through for form's sake. As soon as they came off the final green, there'd be the ceremony, and the Stewart Cup would go into American hands for the first time in four years.

Even playing by herself, instead of with one of the others, was appealing, because she'd become conscious of a certain irritation toward her by the rest of the team, with the exception of Ginger, who remained her friendly self, and of Roger. In some way, she realized, they found her to blame for the tremendous disruption they were suffering right in the middle of this most important of golf events. Everybody, including Lee herself, had had to be interrogated about their own whereabouts and their memories of the others' whereabouts during the previous two evenings, when Dylan had been killed and she had been attacked. And it all had to be fitted in between the usual commitments and festivities, making everybody just a wee bit testy.

Putting the blame on her made no sense at all, of course, but all the same she understood how they might feel. She wondered if they might also be annoyed because they assumed that her coziness with Graham meant that she was privy to all kinds of information that was being kept from them. In point of fact, she didn't know much more than they did. Last night, all she'd been able to get from Graham had been that the reporter from *Buzz* was sticking to his guns, refusing to tell them anything, and that Pokey, one of the two caddies that Chief Oates was trying to get hold of, had been tracked down to a Connecticut address but not yet interviewed.

Whether that was really all he knew, or his new-found appreciation for golf had made him decide not to burden her mind with details, she wasn't sure.

After seventeen challenging, enjoyable holes, she and Diana were tied at eight-and-a-half each. The final hole would decide the winner. Being the competitor that she was, Lee dearly wanted to take it, but if they tied the eighteenth ('halved it', in golfing parlance) and the match itself therefore ended in a tie, there was no shame in that either. But to win her one and only Stewart singles match! – that would really be something.

Roger, who had just concluded his own match one hole ahead of her, was waiting for her as she left the seventeenth green. And he was worried. 'Remember, we really need this,' he said quietly as they walked to the eighteenth tee. 'Don't let it get away.'

She was so astonished she stopped too suddenly, stumbling over her own feet. '*What*?'

The way golf is structured, with people playing simultaneously at several holes, an individual golfer rarely has any idea how the tournament as a whole is going. Lee could have casually asked a marshal, or someone in the gallery, if they knew what was happening on the big board, but she hadn't given it a thought. Not with a three-point lead and Roger Finley, Ginger Rolley, and Dave Hazelton playing in the matches before her. How could . . .

'They caught up,' he said miserably. 'We've only won one match so far – mine. They've won four, and we've

177

halved three. We're all tied for the cup, eight to eight. Everything depends on you. I'm sorry it all has to come down to this, but ...' She'd never seen him look so despairing, even when he'd been hitting balls every which way but on to the fairway.

Now she understood the strange, inscrutable eye and hand signals she'd been getting from the other team members as they joined the gallery one by one after concluding their own matches. They'd been trying to tell her that, against all odds, the Brits had turned things around, but according to the rules, they weren't allowed to coach her or talk to her during play. Only the team captain could do that, and he could do it only between holes, when the ball wasn't in play.

'Don't you worry, Rog,' she told him confidently, 'the eighteenth is made for me, it's my favorite hole here. I know it backwards and forwards. I'll take it, all right.'

She chucked him reassuringly on the shoulder while her stomach sank to somewhere around her ankles. *This isn't fair*, she wanted to scream to the watching TV cameras. *Why me?*

'Lee.' He grabbed her forearm. 'Play it safe, play it smart. Just good, solid golf, the way you've been playing the last two days. Don't ... take ... chances. I know you want to win – we all do – but the big thing is, don't *lose* it for us on some shot you *hope* you can make. A tie is better than a loss.'

He peered into her eyes, as if willing his own skills into her. 'We're all counting on you, remember that.'

She nodded, too terrified to speak.

'And Lee – try not to be too nervous.'

Pinehurst's par-four, 432-yard eighteenth hole is known as one of golf's finest finishing holes, but it was a long way from Lee's favorite. In truth, she feared it with a passion, never more so than today. Big fairway bunker on the right that acted like a magnet on tee shots, and then another one of Donald Ross's damned domed greens, made even trickier by an unusual ditch – everybody called it 'the swale', but it was a grass-covered ditch – that started in the middle of the green and drained steeply to the right. And then there were the trees and the sandy patches of wire grass that crowded the fairway more closely than they had any right to.

And she was up second. She didn't like that either.

When she realized she was muttering aloud she made herself stop. Then, out of nowhere, she surprised herself by laughing. Here she was, little nobody Lee Ofsted, in fifty-first place in the WPGL and winless in two years on the tour, standing in the eighteenth tee box at Pinehurst's legendary Number Two Course, with the outcome of the Stewart Cup resting squarely on her shoulders, cussing out the great Donald Ross.

Who would have thought?

The laughter seemed to loosen the fist that had been squeezing her insides. And her stomach moved up to somewhere above her knees. What the heck, all she could do was the best she could do.

She held out her hand. 'Let's have that three-wood, Lou.'

Her first shot successfully avoided the bunker, as had Diana's. Diana then hit a workmanlike second shot, laying up to about 15 yards short of the green and perhaps thirty yards to the hole, which was in a back-right position today. A good chip from there, and she might be able to one-putt for four strokes total: par. But it also left open the possibility that she might do it in one – sink a chip from there, or even a putt – for a one-under-par birdie. It wouldn't be easy – that nasty swale lay between her ball and the hole – but it was certainly makeable.

And if she did make it, then the only way Lee could beat her was by holing the ball right from where she was, more than two hundred yards from the pin. But the odds on that occurring were laughable. Sure, shots like that had occasionally been seen, but they were freak accidents, like holes-in-one. You couldn't do something like that on purpose, so there was no point in thinking about it.

That left the other likely possibility – that Diana would par the hole. In that case, Lee would shoot for doing the same thing Diana had. It was the safest route to take, but the outcome would be a tie in the match and in the tournament. The cup would stay with the team that had won it last, and that meant it would be on its way back to London. But coming out of this with a tie would be no badge of shame.

Still, there was another possible route: to shoot not merely for the fringe, but for the right side of the green itself, as close to the hole as she could come. From there – assuming she were lucky enough to make it – she might be able to one-putt and thereby bring home the cup. It was risky, though. If she landed her ball full on the green and didn't do it just right, the infamous dome would do what it did best; roll the ball off the green altogether, and into the rough. Or she could land in the swale and roll off. Either way, it would all be over. The Americans would lose.

On the other hand (was there another hand left?), if she didn't try it, the very best she could hope for was a tie – and that would happen only if Diana *didn't* make her first putt. If the putt fell in, the Americans would lose. So that was risky too.

She turned to Lou. 'What do you think, Lou?' she asked, knowing that he would understand exactly what she was talking about.

'You know what I think,' he said. 'Same as you.'

That bucked her up. 'I'll take the two-iron this time.'

'Good choice,' he said, handing it to her.

But it wasn't a good choice. She overshot and the ball did what she most feared it would; it hit the down slope on the far side of the green and caromed out of sight and into the rough. Her stomach promptly dropped to ankle level again. The rough there was notoriously difficult, blocked by pine trees and scrub oaks. Unless she was able to overcome those formidable obstacles by chipping out to within a few yards of the hole, and then one-putting, she was finished.

She didn't think things could be any worse, but when she got there she saw that she was wrong. Her ball had come to rest on the far side of a scrub oak, only two inches from the gnarled base and overhung by low branches. The big problem, and it was a heck of a problem, was that the bush sat exactly – not approximately, but exactly – where she needed to stand to get at it. It was impossible for her, or for any right-hander, to swing at it. She would have to declare an 'unplayable lie', which would allow her to pick up the ball and drop it within two club lengths of where it lay (but no closer to the hole). Since there was some open space to the right of the oak, she was fairly sure that if she dropped it there, she'd be able to put it up on the green in one.

But unplayable-lie declarations came at the cost of a one-stroke penalty. Thus, assuming she did get the ball on to the green, she would have taken a total of four strokes to get there, with the putting yet to come. Par would be impossible. A win would be out of the question. It would have to be either a tie or a loss, and a tie would require Diana to three-putt from the fringe and Lee to one-putt, neither of which was likely.

'Bad,' she said.

'Not good,' Lou agreed. 'Too bad you're not a leftie.' He was doing his best to look as if there were still some hope, but he wasn't having any success. He looked like a whipped dog on a leash.

'Cheer up, Lou,' she said, slowly moving around and around the bush to see the situation from every angle. 'I'm getting an idea.'

'Me too. I'm thinking about committing suicide.' It was perhaps the first time she'd ever seen him at a loss for positive ideas. It didn't last long, though. The old, familiar, twisty grin made its reappearance. 'Hey, wait a minute, I bet I know what your idea is—'

An abrupt hush from the crowd made them look up. Although Lee was in a far poorer position, Diana was farther from the hole. That meant that Diana went first. Lee stopped her reconnaissance to watch. Diana chose what looked like a lob wedge and struck the ball with a half-swing. She hit slightly behind it, however, and the ball flew short, landing thirty feet in front of the pin, on the back rim of the swale, where it seemed to hesitate and try to hold on, and then rolled down into it . . . and all the way down the slope to the very edge of the green, five yards farther away than it had been when she struck it.

Lee did her best to hide the jolt of guilty relief that surged through her. From there, it would surely take Diana two putts to hole out – a *five*. Even if she did it in one, which was unlikely, she'd have no better than par. That meant that, one-stroke penalty notwithstanding, Lee still had a good chance, a better than even chance to tie.

'Tie don't bring home the bacon,' Lou said, reading her mind as easily as if she'd spoken. Or maybe she had spoken.

'Or the cup.' She grinned at him. 'I think a three-iron would be best, Lou, don't you?'

'Maybe a two,' he said.

To please him, she agreed – he was probably right anyway, but who really knew about such things? – and he handed it to her.

'You ever done this before?'

'In a tournament? No, but I saw Scott Hoch do it once, and I tried it on the range a few times. Sometimes I even *did* it.'

One of the rules people was hovering nearby, hands clasped behind his back, patiently waiting for her to declare the lie unplayable.

'I'm going to play it as it lies,' she said.

He stared at her as if she'd told him she was going to eat it as it lay, and backed off.

Lee circled around to the far side of the bush and tried a couple of soft practice swings. This was going to require precision, not strength. The gallery, which had become more and more enormous as the earlier matches finished up, began to buzz as a few aficionados grasped what it was she was going to attempt and passed the word along. You could almost see the excitement sputter like an electric spark through the gallery around the green, and then from person to person down the lines bordering the near fairway.

She was going to hit it left-handed. With the back of her club.

But when she set up to take her stance, she saw that even that wouldn't do the trick. The low-hanging branches of the oak, only six or seven inches off the ground, obstructed both her vision and her swing path. She took in a breath and adjusted her stance accordingly. This time full-blown gasps – of astonishment, of disbelief – came from the gallery. Even the jaded cameraman a few yards away from her couldn't contain his excitement.

'Whoa!' he exclaimed.

She was going to hit it left-handed with the back of her club. From her knees.

'In for a dime, in for a dollar,' she said to Lou.

'You can do it,' Lou said as if he believed it.

She didn't understand how she could be so calm. She'd heard other athletes talk about crashing through the terror ceiling during a clutch moment and entering a zone of tranquility and clarity, when your trembling stopped and your heartbeat seemed to slow way, way down, and a wall went up around you that sealed you off from everything and everyone else in the world. She had always privately thought that it was so much baloney, but now she wasn't so sure. But whatever it was, wherever it came from, she hoped it didn't go away, at least not for another five seconds.

Still, she longed for some touch of reassurance from someone, somebody besides Lou, and she glanced momentarily up at the gallery, looking for a neon-orange cap, hoping for a glimpse of Graham's strong, comforting face. Unfortunately, she looked straight into Roger's instead. He looked stricken, like a man who had just taken a pie in the face and was expecting another momentarily.

That had been a mistake. She looked quickly away from him and down at the ball again. She was playing it back in her stance, opposite her left knee, so as to de-loft the club

183

and keep the shot low. She made her mind go blank, gripped the unfamiliar-feeling club halfway down the shaft, took it back a scant foot, and swung: a punch shot, short, choppy, and precise, with no follow-through.

The ball jumped out from under the branches in a low, flat trajectory, bounced once on the fringe, twice on the green itself, and rolled to a halt ten feet from the pin.

The zone of tranquility abruptly evaporated. Lee's heart jumped, not down to her ankles, but up to her mouth. Had she really done it? What had made her take such an insane chance? With the heel of the club where the toe should have been, and with an irregular, cavity-back surface serving as the face, and with her on her knees, the ball could have gone anywhere . . . right, left, up, down . . .

She was floating somewhere high above the green, over-flowing with triumph, elation, and incredulity. 'Lou . . . Lou . . .'

The wildest acclamation she'd ever heard from a golf audience drowned her out so that he didn't hear her.

'Told you you could do it,' he said easily, reaching out a strong, knobby hand to help her up.

Without it, she wasn't sure she could have made it.

Playing the remainder of the hole was like walking through a dream. Later on, she would have no memory of it. Diana took one stroke to get back on to the green and then two-putted, giving her a bogey five. Lee one-putted for her par.

The cup was coming back to America.

Twenty-Seven

Her happy daze continued through the awards ceremony, which was held on the clubhouse veranda, and when the media descended on her she was tongue-tied and bashful, hardly able to follow their questions. Then the crash that naturally followed the adrenaline rush hit, and the press conference went into slow motion, dragging on, and on, and on, until she was on the edge of sleep. But the coffee they brought her helped, and by the time it was finally over, she felt as if she were in her own body again.

Next on the official schedule, two hours from now, was the closing reception and banquet at the Carolina. But, for the moment, for the precious, once-in-a-lifetime moment, Roger had arranged a private, informal champagne reception for them right there in the clubhouse.

This was a party strictly for the American team; no Brits, no press, no sponsors, no VIPs, nobody but the eight team members and their friends and families, thirty or so altogether. Later on, for the evening affair, they'd all be on exhibit and thus on their best behavior, so this was meant to be their chance to let their hair down without anyone watching, to congratulate themselves and each other, to decompress, and to decorously whoop it up. Roger had thoughtfully booked the Donald Ross Grill for them, the famous clubhouse restaurant with its pillars, its golfing memories and memorabilia, its balustraded balcony, and its high, white, barrel-vaulted ceiling.

He had also provided the Dom Perignon out of his own pocket (privately instructing the waiters to keep a watchful eye on Jordie) and had led the first toast. 'To my team, the greatest, pluckiest bunch of sportsmen and women it's ever been my privilege to be associated with.'

They'd all sipped, and then he'd lifted his trademark straw boater, which he was wearing indoors for the occasion, tipped it toward Lee, and said: 'And in particular to my wonderful partner, Lee Ofsted, who made what may well be the most spectacular shot in Stewart history ... even though I *still* think she shouldn't have tried it! If I didn't get a heart attack then, I never will.'

Lee herself was by now in a strange state, tremendously happy and excited, but somehow removed from it all, even from Graham and Peg. It was as if it were all happening to someone else, as if she were an observer up there on the balcony, and not a participant. The extraordinariness of her being there at all, let alone of making the shot that had clinched it for them – what an insane stunt that had been! – struck her almost like a physical blow, so that a sheen of sweat had popped out on her forehead and her fingers had begun to tremble again. Her stomach wasn't feeling all that steady either. My God, had she been out of her mind? Had she even stopped to think about the odds of making that shot? What if she'd missed! What if they'd lost the cup because of her recklessness?

But you didn't miss, did you? a happy, self-satisfied little voice sang out from somewhere inside her. *You saved the day!*

All the same, she was shaky and disoriented enough to want to get away from the unbridled euphoria for a few minutes, if only to be alone for a little and to splash some water on her face, and she was slinking unobtrusively toward the hallway when Roger called for attention again. He'd had mementos made for everyone, friends and families as well as team members, and was having the waiters hand them out: gold-veined white onyx paperweights about the size of a deck of cards. Fixed in the center of each was a pewter medallion with a low-relief image of the urn-like cup and the etched words *Stewart Cup 2004, Pinehurst, North Carolina* encircling it. They were handsome little things, they were unexpected, and they brought expressions of appreciation from the recipients, Lee included.

After which she continued her discreet movement toward the exit and went gratefully down the corridor toward the women's restroom and lockers. Here at Pinehurst even the ladies' john had historical significance, being the very first women's room installed in any golf club in the United States, and very likely the world.

And it was a nice one. She washed her hands, rinsed her face, used the mouthwash, combed her hair, and sat down on the comfortable *chaise longue* to collect her thoughts and pull herself together. *Whew. Some day.*

After five minutes, not much more composed than she was before, but feeling that she ought to be with the others – Peg and Graham were there too, as her guests – – she headed back. The corridor, she realized now, was more museum than passageway, lined as it was with photographs and gleaming, golden tournament plaques. Jack Nicklaus, Arnold Palmer, Peggy Kirk Bell, Babe Zaharias, Ben Hogan, Walter Hagen – all the names from the Glory Years were here. And hers, she thought, with a shiver of mixed delight and disbelief, was going to be right up there with them as a member of the 2004 Stewart Cup team.

The *winning* 2004 Stewart Cup team. Unbelievable.

Calmer now, she wandered tranquilly among the ghosts. The walls weren't only for the famous. There was a Caddie Hall of Fame plaque too, for the Pinehurst caddies. She paused in front of it. They sounded like the kind of people Lou would have known in the old days, with names like Hardrock, Ratman . . .

Roger, coming from the men's restroom, stopped beside her. 'Hardrock Robinson,' he said reflectively. 'Prince of caddies. Carried for Hagen and Snead. A fabulous tap-dancer too, they say. They sure don't make them like that any more.'

'Oh, I don't know about that,' Lee said. 'Lou's a bit of a throwback, wouldn't you say?'

'Absolutely. I don't see him tap-dancing, though.'

'No, maybe not tap-dancing,' she said, laughing.

187

He fidgeted a little. 'Lee, I just want to apologize again for coming down on you like a load of bricks when you suggested that my clubs—'

'Roger, you've apologized on every chance you've gotten for the last two days. *Please* . . . consider your apology accepted. I'm just so glad I could help. If I don't accomplish anything else in my life, I'll always be able to tell myself that I actually helped Roger Finley in some small way.'

'It was anything but small,' Roger said as they began to walk back to the grill. 'And you'll accomplish plenty more in your life. That amazing shot on eighteen, my goodness, the steady nerves that took . . .' He shook his head and came to a stop as his sight fixed on a photo of Johnny Miller's celebrated three-wood shot on the sixteenth hole at the 1974 Pinehurst US Open. But his thoughts were elsewhere.

'Lee,' he said softly, 'I just can't make myself stop wondering . . . one of the people in that room, one of the men on the team – Jordie, Dave, Dougal – hates me enough to have tried to ruin my life, to kill Dylan, to try to kill you. I just can't—'

'I know, I keep wondering too. I don't know, maybe we have it wrong, maybe it's somebody else entirely. I hope so.'

'I hope so too. I *believe* so,' he added earnestly. 'I mean, I recognize that there might be some hard feelings between Dave and me, but murder? Sabotage? No, no, it couldn't be. And Jordie, well, sure, he has a few problems, but he's not a *murderer*, for God's sake. And how could it be Dougal? Can you see Dougal . . . ? No, it's ridiculous.'

'Well, that leaves you,' Lee said lightly. As important as it was, she wanted to get him off the subject. She didn't want to talk about treachery and murder, she wanted, for at least a while longer, to bask in the glow of the wonderful, terrifying, unforgettable day she'd had. 'You wouldn't be sabotaging your own clubs, by any chance?' she said with an easy laugh as she started them walking again.

Only Roger didn't start walking again. He stood frozen, as still and rigid as one of the restaurant pillars.

Surprised, she turned to look at him.

And recoiled.

His face . . . !

What at first she took to be an expression of inexplicable despair, she quickly realized was horror-stricken rage. It lasted only a second, a withering blaze of fury and madness that distorted his features, flashing over them like a roving searchlight, then moving on.

Only a second, but in that second everything fell into place. She saw it with sudden, needle-sharp clarity. They had gotten it all wrong. They had gotten it backwards. It *was* Roger. He *had* sabotaged himself. How could they have failed to see that he *did* have something to gain from it? It all turned on the blonde, Eileen Westerbrook. The rumors had it right. He *was* going to divorce Marie for her. And so he'd . . . he'd . . .

The details – what he'd done, why he'd done it, how he'd done it – flashed through her mind not serially but all at once, in a kind of numbing explosion. For an instant she was petrified, mentally and physically. Then her rational thought processes, or at least her instinct for self-preservation, kicked in.

'Only joking, of course,' she said casually, as if she'd never seen his expression. She started walking again. In the Grill was sanctuary. People. Graham.

But just as she had read his face, he had read hers. Before she'd taken her second step, he had leaped forward to bull her into the side corridor that led to the now-closed pro shop. He shoved her hard against the wall, pinning her arms against her body. The corner of a plaque dug painfully into her shoulder blade.

She felt herself lose heart. *He's stronger than I am*, she thought desperately. *Despite that mild, prissy appearance, he's as much a conditioned athlete as I am. Only he's a male. And he outweighs me by twenty pounds.*

'I'll scream,' she said, knowing that screaming was hopeless. The Grill was too far away, and with all the noise that was going on in there, they'd never hear her.

Roger didn't hear her either. 'I should have killed you when

189

I had the chance,' he said in a strangled mutter. His hands went to her throat. Closed on it. His thumbs pressed in.

With her hands freed, she clawed and hammered at his arms, but without result. She hit him in the face with her clenched fist, but he only squeezed harder, panting with the strain of it. Strangling, terrified, she jabbed at his eyes, kicked at his crotch, but he somehow writhed out of the way, never losing his hold on her throat. Her hands, fluttering uselessly at her sides, brushed something in her pocket: square-cornered, solid, heavy.

The onyx paperweight.

She grasped it in her right hand, closed her fingers around it. Made a fist with it in the center of her palm. She hit him again, aiming for his nose, but striking him high on the forehead instead when his head jerked. With a thrill of hope she felt the added weight and force that the onyx added.

Roger felt it too. An 'Ai!' escaped from his throat. His head went back. The straw hat fell to the floor and rolled tipsily around on its rim. His grip loosened ever so slightly, but enough for Lee to be able to push him a little further away. She thrust herself back against the wall for leverage and, throwing the full heft and torque of her body into it as if it were the tee shot of her life, she hurled another onyx-laden punch at him, aiming for the center of his face.

When Roger flinched and threw back his head, she missed her aim again. This time her weighted fist caught him on the very point of his upturned jaw. She felt his head wobble loosely on his neck. His hands came loose from around her throat. He blinked, uttered a soft, quizzical 'Oh!' and collapsed, going straight down to his knees with a thump, and then toppling face-forward on to the carpet at her feet. She heard a long, long sigh, as if he were settling down to a much-needed nap.

Her mind was peculiarly empty and unfocused, skittering around the edges of what had just happened, and her body was utterly drained. Whatever dregs of adrenaline had been left in her system after the match, they were more than used up now. She stepped over Roger on watery legs and tottered back out into the main corridor, knowing only that she needed to put distance between herself and Roger. And she needed Graham.

Once she was around the corner and beyond the sight of the inert Roger, she stood with her eyes closed, steadying herself against the wall, kneading the sore places on her neck and trying to slow down her breathing before going back to the Grill to get Graham.

When she opened her eyes she saw Police Chief Oates and a blue-uniformed officer striding down the hallway toward her with considerable speed and deliberation. 'Chief—' she began.

'Howdy, Ms Ofsted,' he said amiably. 'We're looking for Mr Finley. Have you seen him?'

'Have I—?' She gestured them vaguely toward the side corridor. 'In there.'

'What the hell!' she heard Oates exclaim as the two men rounded the corner. A moment later there were some confused sentence fragments from Roger: 'Where was—? How did—? What am I—?'

'He's coming to, Fred,' Oates said. 'When he's all the way back with us, stand him up, cuff him, and read him his rights.'

Oates then came back out to see Lee, who had yet to find the strength to move. 'What happened to him?'

'Well, I—I hit him,' Lee said.

'With what, a sledgehammer?'

'With this.' She weakly held up her hand and opened it so he could see the paperweight.

He took it from her and hefted it appraisingly. 'Heavy little bugger. What is it?'

From around the corner she heard a low monotone: 'You are under arrest for the murder of Dylan Blanchard. You have the right to remain silent. Anything you say . . .'

'It's a souvenir,' she told Oates. 'From Roger.'

Oates tipped back his Stetson. 'I'll be danged,' he said, and Lee had the distinct impression she heard him chuckle.

Twenty-Eight

The drive to the police station did her good. It took only a few minutes to get there, but it served to block out the unreal, overwhelming world of international tournaments and world-class resorts, and even the hurly-burly of the frozen-in-time little village center. To get to the station, Graham drove them through an unpretentious, unself-conscious neighborhood of quiet, pine-tree-shaded, curving streets and clean, middle-class homes that had old-fashioned porches with rockers and swings. The 'lawns' were basically weeds and pine needles, but they seemed right, giving the place a sleepy, unhurried, Southern feel. And everywhere was the dusty, pungent fragrance of pine. It all served to remind her that there really did exist a more mundane, relaxed, everyday world in which life today was pretty much like life yesterday, and murders happened only to people you didn't know.

The police station itself was a modern, unassuming, one-story building on McCaskill Road, directly across from Bill Clark Chevrolet. Even that seemed right.

Lee spent half an hour in a stark interview room, gulping down three cups of sweetened coffee and giving a deposition on her struggle with Roger to a sergeant and a stenographer. When she came out, Graham was waiting for her in the lobby.

'If you're up to it, Nate wants to talk to us. But if you'd rather go to the dinner, tomorrow's OK too. Unfortunately, the reception's over by now.'

'Good,' she said. 'I've had enough receptions to last me a while. And as for the big dinner, I think I'd rather skip that too, now that I have an excuse. It's going to be a pretty uncomfortable affair anyway, with the winning captain in the hoosegow.'

'Are you kidding? People love that kind of thing. It'll probably be the liveliest Stewart banquet in history. With the press hovering outside to get at everyone – you, especially.'

'Then I'd definitely rather give it a skip. Do you think – I know that this is a pretty extravagant request, but – do you think you and I could actually have dinner together? Alone? Where nobody can see us?'

'Alone? You mean, without Peg? Not that I don't dearly love Peg.'

'Without Peg,' she said, laughing. She put a hand on her chest. 'Oh, that feels good – laughing.'

'The answer is yes,' Graham said. 'I can definitely arrange that. I know just the place. Our room – catered by room service. Now let's go see what the chief has to say.'

The chief was in an expansive, talkative mood. It took only one question from Graham – 'How did you come up with Finley as the perp?' – to get him started. Leaning far back in his creaky chair, with his big, booted feet propped on a lower desk drawer and his hands clasped behind his neck, he took them step-by-step through his investigation and his reasoning.

He had started with the reporter, Michael Foura, trying to get out of him what kind of information Dylan had been gathering for *Buzz*, but Foura had stuck to his ethics-of-the-profession guns. A phone call placed to editorial headquarters in San Diego, however, had elicited the information from the publisher with no trouble at all ('As long as you agree to publicly credit *Buzz* as the source of this information. Oh, and my name is spelled "D-u-t-t-l-e-y". That's two *t*'s and one *l*, and an *e* before the *y*.')

Dylan, it seemed, had contacted the paper a month earlier, saying that he could hand them a sensational scandal involving a famous golfer, and were they interested, and how much would they be willing to pay? After hearing his story, they had dickered for a while and settled on $30,000, provided that Dylan could provide proof. If the proof were in the form of clear, incontrovertible photographs the paper could use, the fee would increase by $5,000 for each photo, and if more than three were used—

'What was it that Dylan was selling them, Nate?' Graham gently interrupted.

'Ah, what was he selling?' Oates said, uncrossing his feet and putting them on the floor. 'Mind if I light up a cigar, Ms Ofsted? I don't get the urge that often.'

Lee shook her head. He was more than entitled to his celebratory cigar. Besides, he could have lit up a bale of alfalfa and not disturbed her concentration.

Oates pulled a pack out of his middle desk drawer, took his time taking off the cellophane wrapper, extracted one of those crooked, black, Italian stogies, and lit up with a sigh. Then his feet went back up on the drawer. 'Ah. Now, then.'

Dylan, it seemed, had somehow found out that his employer, Roger Finley, had been tinkering with his clubs with the aim of sabotaging his own game—

'I knew it!' Lee said triumphantly.

'I sure didn't,' a rueful Graham said. 'What was the point?'

'Well, we don't know that for sure, but apparently Finley was planning to dump his wife for this other lady—'

'I knew it!' Lee said.

Graham turned to her. 'You might have mentioned it,' he said wryly.

'I would have, but I didn't figure it out until two seconds before he had his hands around my neck.'

'And I guess,' Oates went on, 'that the whole thing had something to do with the divorce settlement he was trying to set up. I'm not clear on that part of it yet—'

'I think I can help you there,' Lee piped up. 'Once they split their property – houses, whatever – the rest of the settlement would be based on his future earnings, wouldn't it?'

'Guess so,' Oates said uncertainly.

'Well, if his game suddenly went south and showed no signs of ever coming back, then his projected future earnings would be way down and his wife would get a lot less, right?'

'Yeah, guess so,' Oates agreed.

'But *he* would be making a lot less too,' Graham pointed out. 'He makes more, she gets more. He makes less, she gets less. So it amounts to the same thing, really. Why would he fool around doing something stupid like tinkering with his own clubs if the result is the same?'

'But it doesn't amount to the same thing. If he wanted to, he could just drop out of competitive golf for a year, trying to "find himself" again. You see, he's forty-eight right now. Say he gets his divorce taken care of and sits out next year. Then, the year after, when he's fifty, he "suddenly" recovers his game and joins the senior tour, for which he's now eligible.'

'And clobbers them all,' Oates said slowly, 'bringing in more money than he knows what to do with, and his wife's not entitled to any of it. A foolproof plan – except Dylan found out about it. That's good. When did you figure that out, Ms Ofsted?'

'I don't know,' she said honestly. 'It sort of came to me right there in the corridor, but I'm not sure how clear it was.' She shrugged. 'Could be, I didn't really put it together – not specifically – until just now, until I said it out loud.'

'Well, you know, it makes one hell of a lot of sense,' Oates said. He was looking at her as if surprised to discover that golfers, and in particular female golfers, actually had useable brains. He looked for an ashtray on his desk, didn't find one, and tipped the ash from his cigar into a paper-clip niche in the center drawer.

'I think it does, too,' Graham said. 'One question, though, Lee. Why mess around with his clubs? Couldn't a pro like him – or like you, for that matter – just change his swing a little and play lousier golf?'

'Yeah, come over the top, or swing out to in, or come off the shot once in a while?' said Oates, who obviously knew quite a bit more about golf than Graham did. 'Wouldn't that be a whole lot simpler than physically changing the clubs?'

'No, I don't believe it would,' Lee said, thinking about it. 'If he artificially changed his swing, he'd have to change it back again, and that's not anywhere near as easy as it sounds, because a change, even in some tiny part of your swing mechanics, is going to throw off something else, something you're not even aware of – your balance, your tempo, your shoulder-hip coordination, something. Really, altering your own clubs would be the smartest way to do it, especially for someone who knows as much about them as Roger does. With his clubs adjusted just right – or rather, wrong – he's awful. When he changes them back, he's fine. All without taking a chance on fooling with that priceless swing of his.'

Oates pondered this and turned his gaze from Lee to Graham. 'She's pretty smart.'

Graham laughed. 'Tell me about it.'

The rest of Oates's story was simply good, solid police work. They'd located Pokey at home in New London, Connecticut, and Oates had interviewed him by telephone that morning. Among the things he'd learned was that Pokey had been caddying at a two-day charity pro-am in Tenafly, New Jersey the previous Monday and Tuesday. Roger had also been there, along with Dylan, who had hurried off after the last hole to spend a couple of nights at his parents' house in East Brunswick, but Roger had stayed on in Tenafly, and Pokey, still stewing over Dylan's remarks in the bar back in Scottsdale, had sought him out.

Pokey, in a state of righteous indignation (caddies weren't supposed to keep important secrets from their golfers) and fervent patriotism (the Stewart Cup was coming up and the slumping Roger was at the helm of the American team) had told Roger exactly what Dylan had drunkenly claimed: that he, Dylan, knew exactly what was wrong with Roger and who was responsible, but he was keeping it to himself – and expecting to make a profit from it.

'You see what that tells us,' Oates said, looking wise.

'Yes,' said Lee. 'That Roger knew Dylan was on to him.'

196

'Correct. Also that he only found out about it a couple of days before Pinehurst. Wednesday was the first chance he had to take any action. That explains why he killed him when he did, and not before.'

'And it tells us something else,' Graham said. 'When this whole business of sabotage came up, and then when we found out that the clubs *had* been altered, Roger acted as if it was the first time he'd ever thought of such a thing, as if it was the most surprising thing in the world. I told him what Dylan had been saying, and that was supposedly a big-time surprise too. Never, not once, did he mention the talk with Pokey.' That may not exactly be evidence against him, but it's a pretty damning error of omission.

'That's right. And he had plenty of chances to do it with me too – and didn't. So, anyway, once I put all that together, naturally I decided to check out Finley's car.'

'Wait a minute,' Lee said. 'What does his car have to do with it? Why "naturally"?'

'Because,' Graham explained, 'the ME told us that Dylan's body had been moved. So if Roger had been the one to move him, there might be some evidence in the car. Am I right, Nate?'

'On the button. Well, an hour later, when we looked in the trunk—'

'An *hour*? Boy, you get warrants a lot faster here than we ever did in Oakland.'

'Didn't need a warrant,' Oates said, brandishing the cigar with the air of a magician who'd just pulled a rabbit out of a hat. 'The car's a loaner from Larsen Motors. It's their property, not Finley's, and I knew D. J. Larsen wasn't going to have any problem with it.'

'That's right,' Graham said. 'Good thinking.'

Oates took a last drag, made a face, tamped the cigar out on the top of a metal filing cabinet, stuffed it in the drawer, and slammed the drawer shut. 'Ugh, terrible stuff. I can't understand why people smoke these things. So, what was I saying?'

'When you looked in the trunk . . .' Lee said.

'When we looked in the trunk we found fabric fibers, hair, even a couple of traces of blood; all kinds of stuff. It'll take the lab a while to sort everything out, but they've already given us a match on the blood type – Dylan's – and a tentative match between the shirt he was wearing, and one of the fiber specimens. That was enough to make us come calling on old Roger at the clubhouse, and there we are.'

He smiled; a lopsided country boy's grin. 'And this little lady had him all neatly laid out for us.'

'Think nothing of it,' Lee said with a smile, although the truth was that her heart rate jogged when she thought of the struggle in the corridor. 'Always glad to help.'

'Where's Roger now?' Graham asked. 'Do you have a holding facility here?'

Oates shook his head. 'Not much call for it. We use the County Jail in Carthage. That's where he's spending the night.'

'Has he said anything?'

'Yeah. "I want my lawyer." So some big-shot Miami Beach shyster's already on the way.' He stretched. 'Well . . .'

The conversation was over and they both stood up. Oates did too, warmly shaking hands with each of them.

'Thanks, Graham.'

'My pleasure, Nate.'

'And you, young lady, you did good. If this golf thing doesn't turn out to be what you want, and you're looking for an exciting new career, you just give me a call.'

'I'll keep it in mind, Chief,' Lee said. 'But to tell you the truth, golf has been more than exciting enough for me so far.'

He walked them to the door of his office. 'Oh, and one more thing I want to say to you, Ms Ofsted.'

'Chief?'

'That was one hell of a shot today,' he said soberly. 'I saw it on the highlights and practically fell out of my chair. On the *eighteenth*, yet!'

Lee laughed. 'I almost forgot about it,' she said. And meant it.

Twenty-Nine

Lee had slept, and slept, and slept; on the flight from Charlotte to Dallas, and Dallas to San Francisco, and San Francisco to the Monterey Peninsula. And when they'd gotten to Graham's house in Pacific Grove she'd gone straight to bed and slept for nine more hours.

Now she was wide awake. And so hungry that she was practically salivating at the sight of the food that was being placed before them. On Graham's recommendation they had ordered 'San Francisco Joes', and the plates of spinach, ground beef, and cheese folded into puffy scrambled eggs, along with sides of hash-browns, fruit, and warm croissants, looked like an invitation to heaven and smelled like heaven itself.

Graham was feeling similarly empty, and for a while they both tucked in with little other than sighs of heartfelt appreciation.

'It's wonderful to be anonymous again,' Lee said, looking around at other people similarly engaged, none of whom was paying any attention to her. 'I don't have to worry about people saying, "Isn't that Lee Ofsted over there, stuffing herself like a pig?"'

'I'm afraid you're never going to be anonymous again,' Graham said. 'Not He shook his head. 'What a shot. I couldn't have come close to doing that with the club turned around the right way, and standing on my feet. Or my head.'

'I wonder, though,' Lee mused. 'Things sure have a way of turning out funny, don't they?'

When she'd first been picked for the Rocky slot, she'd

realized that a wonderful shot at fame and fortune had fallen into her lap. And she'd certainly gotten her measure of both, although she was realistic enough to know that it would take more than one freakish shot to sustain either the boost her playing career had gotten or the lovely new endorsement offer she had for Lady Sweetspots.

There had been another, unexpected benefit too. Graham seemed finally to have grasped that golf was something more than a subject for jokes. He'd always been supportive, of course, but he hadn't really *understood*. Now it was clear that he'd come to a real appreciation of the game, of her talent, and of her dedication.

And that meant the world to her.

She polished off the last of her croissant, resisting the temptation to mop up the drippings with it, then slid her plate away and went back to looking out at the gorgeous, wave-flecked Pacific, pearly-blue under a bright noon sun.

They were at the Tinnery, a window-walled restaurant that overlooked Pacific Grove's Lovers Point with its park-like lawns and its rocky, surf-battered shore. There was a wedding in progress on the lawn with the couple getting married in full regalia: tuxedo for the man, satiny, voluminous white dress for the woman – a girl, really, no more than eighteen. Twenty feet away, along the roadside, scuba divers stood at the backs of vans and pick-ups, squeezing into their gear for a swim among the fishes.

'It's a nice place to get married, don't you think?' she asked.

'I suppose.'

'I envy them, in a way . . . Getting married, I mean.'

'Mm. You want some more coffee?'

He certainly wasn't taking the bait, Lee thought. If anything, he was being a bit thick-headed. 'Lovers Point,' she said. 'Even the name makes me feel romantic.'

'The original name was Lovers of Jesus Point, from the days when Pacific Grove was a church camp, not a town. "Lovers Point" is just a shortening.'

'Graham, I'm trying to—'

But their waiter came to clear away their plates and check their coffee pitcher. When he'd gone she tried another tack.

'You know that call I got as we were going out the door?'

'Uh-huh. What was all the mystery?'

She smiled. 'Well, it was from the golf pro who first taught me how to play when I was stationed in Germany. He has a great new job as head pro at this posh country club, and they're having a big seventieth-year anniversary bash in a couple of months. They're going to have a celebrity skins game, and I guess I must be a celebrity now, because he's invited me to play in it.'

'Skins game? What is this place, a nudist colony?'

'Come on, don't be difficult. It's a sort of exhibition-type golf game where the prize money gets distributed hole-by-hole. It's fun. Anyway, I said I'd get back to him after talking to you.'

'Me? Why? I mean, I'm flattered, but who am I to give you advice on when or where to play golf?'

'Well, it's not the golf I'm thinking about,' she said.

'Uh-huh. And are you planning to tell me what it is you *are* thinking about?' he asked.

'The club is in Hawaii, you see, on Maui, and I can't think of a better – or a more romantic – place for two people to have a . . . to have a small . . .' She was suddenly shy.

'A small what?' he asked blankly.

'A *wedding*, dopey!' she shouted, bringing turned heads from other diners. She flinched and lowered her voice. 'I want us to get married! Why are you being so obtuse?'

And now his face slowly creased into that big, wonderful smile of his. 'Because I wanted to hear you say it, that's why. I waited long enough.'

She laughed and relaxed. 'Well, I said it.'

'And how do you feel, now that you've said it?'

She considered the question for a moment. 'Pretty good, actually. So – do you want to come? Or should I get some-body else?'

He leaned in toward her and put his hand over hers. 'You just try it. I'll be there with bells on.'

Lee sighed. 'Well, I'm certainly glad that's settled. And now if you could call our waiter over and order us some of that cherry cobbler, my day will be complete.'